Mrs. Morgen John O'Connell

Charles Bianconi

A biography, 1786-1875

Mrs. Morgen John O'Connell

Charles Bianconi
A biography, 1786-1875

ISBN/EAN: 9783337013158

Printed in Europe, USA, Canada, Australia, Japan

Cover: Foto ©Raphael Reischuk / pixelio.de

More available books at **www.hansebooks.com**

CHARLES BIANCONI

CHARLES BIANCONI

A BIOGRAPHY

1786—1875

BY HIS DAUGHTER

MRS. MORGAN JOHN O'CONNELL

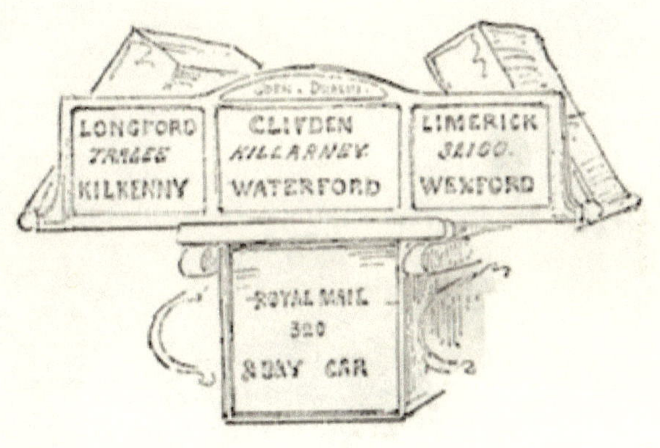

LONDON

CHAPMAN AND HALL, 193, PICCADILLY

1878

LONDON :
PRINTED BY VIRTUE AND CO., LIMITED,
CITY ROAD.

LONDON :
PRINTED BY VIRTUE AND CO., LIMITED,
CITY ROAD.

PREFACE.

THIS book was written at my father's bidding; but for his commands I should not have undertaken the task, for which I am hardly fitted. He was proud of his hard-won success in life; he was thankful to God for having blessed his endeavours. He was fond of the people among whom his lot was cast, and with whom he had become one in heart and in spirit. His name is a household word in Ireland, and I think it is enough known in England for some to feel curious as to what manner of man he was,—how he strove and prospered and grew rich in the country of his adoption. To show this truthfully has been my main endeavour. I have tried neither to hide his faults nor to exaggerate his virtues. If I have succeeded in giving a faithful picture of what my father was, my object will have been gained.

Save where the text will show the interposition of another hand, I have worked out and written all this book myself. I had, indeed, written very much more, but which my friend who revised my MS. has done well to cut out. But there are other shortcomings due to my sex and inexperience, which even his pruning-knife could not touch, and for these I would ask the reader's indulgence.

The drawings have been done by my old friend, Mr. M. Angelo Hayes, and Mr. Hayes has also written for me a long narrative which forms the whole of the fifth chapter. I hope he will allow me to express my thanks to him for the very kind way in which he has assisted me in bringing out this life of my father.

October, 1877.

CONTENTS.

CHARLES BIANCONI.

CHAPTER I.

AUTOBIOGRAPHY.

CHARLES BIANCONI, the second son of Pietro Bianconi and Maria Caterina Mazza, was born on the 24th September, 1786, at Tregolo, a village in the Lombard Highlands of Brianza, some eight or ten miles from Como. In the neighbouring village of Caglio there still stands the old family house, once known as the Casa Bianconi; but Pietro, who was himself a younger son, never lived there. He married early in life, and settled down on his own land at Tregolo, where he lived on the proceeds of a silk-mill, farming his own little property, and acting as land agent to the great Bonancina family, whose estates nearly surrounded the village. In those days small silk-mills were commonly to be found upon every Lombard farm; they have since been replaced by larger holdings, and by factories. It used to be my father's delight when he was a child to watch the working of the wheel of the silk-mill. The wheel was turned by a man walking round it inside the mill. Of course, in describing it to us at home, he imagined it to have been much larger than it really was, and this delusion he always affectionately cherished. The roof under which my father was born and passed his earliest years has since been pulled down, and two small houses with high narrow windows have been erected in its place. Many years afterwards, when he had become a rich man in Ireland, he was perplexed by being told that he had inherited a small patch of land at Tregolo,—the land having been equally divided among my grandfather's children. He left it afterwards to the orphan daughters of a younger brother.

My father had three brothers, who all lived to be old men. He corresponded with them occasionally, but he never knew them with brotherly friendship. He was very fond of his only sister, Barbara. When I saw her many years ago she was very like my father, though handsomer. She was a fresh-coloured, genial-looking old lady, with the same bright eyes as my father, and the same full and well-formed lips. Her grandson tells me that when she was young she was so fair and so winsome, that she was called " la bella bionda della Brianza."

My grandmother Mazza came of a prosperous family from Monza ; one of the Mazzas had endowed a hospital. My grandmother had brothers who rose to posts of honour in the Church, and of these, the Rev. Dr. Giosuè

Mazza, Provost of Asso—a place not far from Caglio—adopted my father, and my father remained under this good man's protection until he was sent off to make his own way in the world.

My great-uncle, Giosuè Mazza, was a man of considerable culture and great kindness of heart. I am sorry to say that, though my father shared his cheerful and sociable temperament, he had none of the worthy doctor's love of learning. Charles Bianconi was always fond of listening to the conversation of intelligent men. He liked well enough to have striking passages of biographies or of political works read to him, but he used to make it his boast that he never read anything but what was inserted upon a way-bill,—as the documents were called which were sent out daily with his cars.

Many years ago, at the request of Mr. Thomas Drummond, the Irish Secretary, my father began to write his biography. He never got on very far with it; indeed, it does not go beyond the days of his boyhood. He conceived the best plan for getting this autobiography written was that he should lie in bed and dictate it to an amanuensis. Accordingly he lay in bed for three days and dictated. I will give some extracts from it; but more than that the reader would hardly thank me for. My father regarded the work with mingled feelings of admiration and diffidence, and it will behove me best to adopt the side of caution.

After saying that he was brought up by his uncle, the Rev. Giosuè Mazza, Provost of Asso, and by his grandmother,—who was living with this son of hers in the Casa Bianconi at Caglio,—he goes on :—

"Soon after my removal to Asso I was sent to the "school of the Rev. Abbé Radicali. I cannot at present "remember the name of the town where it was situated, "but I know it was the school where my father and "uncle had been educated. The abbé was a great "favourite of theirs, and was reputed to have made "several good scholars. . . . . While I remained at "this school I was not merely the greatest dunce, but "the boldest boy in the place. It was the abbé's prac- "tice always to ring the dormitory bell from his bed- "room, and then proceed to church, where we joined "him for morning prayers as soon as we were dressed. "One of the ' good boys ' had once complained of me "seriously to him, and to be revenged I stole this good "boy's stockings, and stuffed the dormitory bell with "them, which naturally prevented its ringing as "usual. I anxiously waited the result of the discovery "of the stockings, and expected every moment to see "the tables turned on my antagonist ; but to my great "mortification, when the old gentleman saw whose "name was on the stockings, he turned on his heel, "and we never heard any more about it. I frequently "remonstrated about my situation at this school, but "no attention was paid to my complaints. I can now "honestly say that the advantages I got there were very "small. . . . .

"I was at this time, in 1802 about fifteen or sixteen "years old, a dunce, and a very wild boy; yet I am

" sure I had the credit for being much worse than I
" really was. I cannot say whether it was my ill-
" repute or the conscription that induced my father to
" send me abroad to sow my wild oats. I was, at any
" rate, bound to Andrea Faroni, who was to bring me
" to England. If I did not like to become a dealer in
" prints, barometers, and spy-glasses, at the expiration
" of eighteen months I was to be placed under the
" care of the late Mr. Paolo Colnaghi, who was to make
" new arrangements with my father. Faroni received
" a large sum for my maintenance, but he saved my
" father and Mr. Colnaghi all further trouble about
" me, for, instead of taking me to London, he brought
" me over to Ireland. This man had three other boys
" under his charge besides myself. One was Giuseppe
" Castelli, a son of the innkeeper in a town near Asso;
" the second was Girolamo Camagni, the son of a
" master tailor at Como: the third was Giuseppe
" Ribaldi, a plain, good lad, a year or two older than
" myself, and the son of a honest flax-dealer. My
" father had a great regard for old Ribaldi, and pre-
" vailed on him to bind his son to Faroni. This boy
" was to have been a kind of brains-carrier for me,
" being so much steadier than I was. As a reward for
" looking after me, he was to share all my advantages
" at the expiration of an eighteen months' apprentice-
" ship. . . . .

" On the eve of my departure, my uncle, the Rev.
" Dr. Mazza, gave an entertainment, not at his new
" living in the mountains, but at the inn in Como,

"where we boys were to meet our new taskmaster.
"Up to this time I had been much elated at the
"prospect of escaping from school and of seeing the
"world, but when I saw my poor mother faint at the
"festive board I began to realise that I was entering
"upon something very serious. During the few days
"that I had spent at my father's house she had tried
"to call my attention to my future life; but now,
"surrounded as I was by so many people, some whose
"faces were new to me, and others old friends of my
"father's, who stuffed my purse with louis d'or, I
"became so excited, that no sooner was I separated
"from my mother than I almost entirely forgot
"her."

Andrea Faroni and the four boys then started for
England, going on foot over the Alps into Switzerland.
My father has given in his autobiography some of his
recollections of the early part of this journey, but they
need not be recorded here. There was one point,
however, that interested him, which I will mention.
One Sunday morning they went to hear mass at the
parish church, and, much to his surprise, Lutherans
and Catholics officiated in turns on the same day.

"How very unlike," my father says, "to the state of
"things in Ireland, where my friend the Protestant rector
"of Clonmel threatened violence to my other friend,
"the Catholic pastor, if he attempted, unauthorised, to
"read the prayers of his Church over a friend's new-made
"grave in the churchyard common to both creeds, but
"in possession of the State Church. I regret exceed-

" ingly my inability to discern why men will make and
" enforce laws so contrary to the general interest, and
" as one would imagine so much at variance with the
" well-being of the children of our beloved and com-
" mon Father. . . . .

" We reached Dublin in the summer of 1802, and
" lodged in Temple Bar, near Essex Bridge. Our
" master at once set to work making small leaden
" frames cast from a stone mould by the aid of a huge
" fire." Faroni had brought with him from Italy a
great quantity of cheap pictures, the greater part of
which illustrated some sacred subject. His object was
to put these pictures into frames, and then sell them.
" In a few days he had made a great number of these
" frames. He mounted them in pairs, on sheets of
" paper which folded up like a book. Everything then
" was ready for what seemed to us to be a very singular
" operation. We were to sell the prints in a strange
" country, without knowing a word of the language.
" He further asked us to deposit our pocket-money in
" his hands, a request with which we dared not refuse
" to comply. He then turned us out into the streets,
" among people speaking an unknown language to us,
" to sell these little pictures. I shall never forget the
" ludicrous figure I cut in going into the street with
" a pair of these things in my hands, saying ' buy, buy,'
" to every person I met, and when questioned as to the
" price I was unable to reply except by counting on
" my fingers the number of pence I wanted.

" I soon learned a little English, and then I was sent

" off into the country every Monday morning with two
" pounds' worth of these pictures, and fourpence
" allowed me for pocket-money, on the understanding
" that I was expected home on the following Saturday
" evening. When we had quite beaten all the country
" round about Dublin, Camagni, the tailor's son, and
" I were ordered to Waterford and Wexford. This
" lad, who, as it seemed to me, was neither very moral
" nor very industrious, soon ran away, and Ribaldi was
" sent to replace him. At Waterford I found that
" the demand for my small prints was considerable.
" Besides the Scripture pieces, there were portraits of
" the Royal Family, of Bonaparte, and of his most
" distinguished generals. From Waterford I went to
" Passage, a village a few miles off, and there I was
" very much surprised at finding myself arrested, by
" the order of an over-loyal magistrate, for the treason-
" able act of selling Bonaparte's effigy. I was kept
" perishing all night in a guard-room, without fire or
" without bedclothes, but the next morning I was set
" at liberty.

" About this time my master began to make larger
" sized leaden frames for larger sized pictures, which
" we were to sell for a shilling the pair. This made us
" feel proud, and gave us a new interest in our work.
" As time went on, these pictures were succeeded by
" still better ones, with wooden frames, and this made
" me feel myself to be quite a person of consequence.
" Until then, ever since I had crossed the Alps, the spirit
" of my own existence seemed to have left me, and I

" thought of nothing but implicit obedience to a person
" whom I considered as holding my being in his hands,
" and that beyond him I had no alternative. Though
" his office as regarded me was not an enviable one, he
" always treated me with courtesy. At the expiration
" of eighteen months, which was to have been the
" period of my exile, if I had so willed it, he declared
" himself ready to fulfil his engagement with my
" father, and take me back to him. My pride was so
" mortified that I declined his offer. He therefore
" gave me back my purse with its entire contents, about
" a hundred louis d'or, which seemed to me then to
" be a very great sum.

" I at once got a box made to contain large framed
" prints. It was two feet long by one foot wide, and
" eighteen inches deep. This box I filled with an
" assortment of prints, from the largest to the smallest
" size. With this pack on my back, which weighed
" over a hundred pounds, I have frequently walked
" from twenty to thirty miles in the day. I was then
" seventeen years old, and I knew neither discourage-
" ment nor fatigue, for I felt that I had set to work to
" become a great man. It was not long before I came
" to perceive the great differences between the pedler
" doomed to tramp on foot as I was, and his more for-
" tunate fellow who could post, or ride on horseback.
" These thoughts were hovering about in my mind,
" along with the fixed idea that had become a ruling
" passion with me, how to become somebody; and
" this firm resolve enabled me to overcome the dis-

" couragement and discontent that had previously op-
" pressed me.

" In the course of my rambles through the country,
" I often met with great attention from many respect-
" able families. Up to this time I had made it a rule
" to decline all friendly overtures. But when I started
" in business on my own account, I began to think
" seriously that I was not in my right position in society,
" and that as I then was I was incapable of putting
" myself right. These ideas embarrassed me much, as
" did the kindness of many of my customers, who
" recommended the ' curly-headed Italian boy ' to their
" friends as having the cheapest pictures and the
" greatest quantity of them. Among these friends I
" must not forget William Cahill and Father Healy,
" afterwards the parish priest of Newport. Mr. Cahill
" at that time had a large trade as a brogue-maker,
" and he frequently bought his leather from Mr. Bald-
" win, a tanner at Cahir, in County Tipperary. On
" visiting Thurles, I found that Mr. Cahill had been
" making friends for me, which I was anxious to avoid,
" but on my next visit to Cahir I was obliged to yield
" to the hospitality of Mr. and Mrs. Baldwin, who
" afterwards became my very dear friends. I stayed
" with them frequently, and they treated me as one of
" their own children,—except that they allowed me
" greater privileges."

I have often heard my father speak of these excellent people, who were devout Catholics. There are no
Baldwins in Cahir now, but a close intimacy still exists

between our family and Mr. John Baldwin Murphy, Q.C., one of their descendants in the female line. He happened to mention, accidentally, that his mother-in-law, Mrs. Morrogh, of Kilworth, remembered that when she was a child she had bought little pictures out of my father's pack. I wrote to her at once, and received the following kind letter in reply:—

"I regret I am not able to give you much aid in
"your work relative to your respected father's early
"life in County Tipperary. I only recollect thinking
"him a handsome, interesting youth when I was a
"child staying with my grandmother, Mrs. Keating,
"in Cahir. She, poor old lady, had a great respect
"for the 'little genteel foreigner,' as she used to call
"him, and when he would come laden with prints and
"pictures for sale, it was always a great pleasure to
"her to see his store, and she was sure to make him as
"comfortable as she could. And if he were not dis-
"posed to eat she would make him sit by her side, and
"would coax him to take something. In those days
"all parties were more social, and they mixed more
"together than they do now. Numbers of people used
"to meet at her house on Sundays after prayers at
"church and chapel in the town of Cahir. Lord
"Glengall's band had orders to play at Mrs. Keating's
"door from two to four o'clock,—a great attraction for
"friends to meet. Then if 'the little foreigner' hap-
"pened to be in town, she would do her utmost to
"show off his stock, and to encourage buyers."

Another family at whose house Charles Bianconi

was made kindly welcome was that of Mr. Lamphier, of Parkstown, one of the sturdy old Protestant squires. My father has often told me that when he was first invited to dine there he refused, fearing that he might have been sent into the kitchen, but Mr. Lamphier dragged him into the dining-room, and set him down among his family.

"During these visits," he says, "treated as the " favoured guest of such amiable and hospitable people, " I frequently could have fancied myself at home in my " father's house until the thought of my real position,— " that of a better-class pedler,—would come before me. " These kind attentions only served to give me an " imperfect view of my solitary and forlorn state. " Then I would recollect my poor mother, and all my " dear friends from whom I was separated, and from " whom I had parted with so little concern. I would " sometimes resist the greatest luxury I could possibly " enjoy, and lock myself up in my bedroom, and there " cry bitterly. I could no longer submit to the picture " box, though it had not become heavier than before. " It was, indeed, nearly worn out, so I threw it away, " and got a portfolio of unframed prints in its place, " which, while its novelty lasted, did very well. How- " ever, as I formed fresh acquaintances, and became " more intimate in respectable houses, I felt more and " more galled by my unnatural position. So I boldly " resolved to throw away the portfolio, and retire again " into obscurity. I gave up all my friends and acquaint- " ances, and turned carver and gilder. I opened a

" shop in Carrick-on-Suir in 1806, and I endeavoured
" to become a proficient in the trade.

" During my former visits to Carrick, I had made
" the acquaintance of two very extraordinary characters,
" Patrick Lynch, a celebrated schoolmaster, father of
" the late Councillor Lynch, Keeper of the Record
" Tower in Dublin, and John Stacy, a printer.
" Through Stacy I made the acquaintance of Francis
" White, father to my kind friend, Dr. Francis White,
" who was one of the most learned and accomplished
" men of his day.

" I supplied my Carrick shop with gold leaf from
" Waterford, going down in Tom Morrissy's boat to
" buy it. Carrick-on-Suir is twelve or thirteen miles
" from Waterford by land, but the windings of the
" river make it twenty-four by water. This boat was
" then the only public conveyance. The time of its
" departure had to depend upon the tide, and it took
" from four to five hours to make the journey. In
" after years I had five four-wheeled cars and one
" mail-coach, capable of carrying one hundred per-
" sons, running daily between these two places.

" Once when I went down to Waterford by the
" boat, on a terribly wet day, and got my feet
" thoroughly soaked by walking about the muddy
" streets, I had to travel back at night without being
" able to change my clothes. The result was a severe
" cold, which turned into an attack of pleurisy, that
" laid me up for two months. During all this time I
" was attended by Dr. Francis White, and he visited

" me daily until I had recovered. I was more than
" willing to share my small means with my kind pre-
" server, but when I asked him for his account he
" positively refused to accept a penny."

Dr. White seems to have been more than a physician
to my father. He was his companion and his friend.
In his old age my father loved to dwell on this time,
which was a turning-point in his life. From things
he often said, I fancy the fact of finding that a young
man, who was a gentleman and a scholar, should seek
his company, gave him the moral courage to attempt
to raise himself. He says in his autobiography : " In
" this instructive and delightful mode of life I began
" to be myself again. Fresh ideas, sounder and more
" reasonable notions, entered my mind, and I became
" more rational and happy. As soon, therefore, as I
" was well and out of my kind doctor's hands, I
" removed to Waterford.

" At Waterford I took comfortable private lodgings,
" and I issued cards showing that I was a carver and
" gilder of the first class. I made up for the want of
" knowledge in the manual details of my business by
" incessant industry. I frequently worked from six
" o'clock in the morning until two hours after mid-
" night, with the exception of two hours for dinner
" and recreation. These precious hours I often spent
" in the pleasant society of the late Right Reverend
" Dr. O'Finan, afterwards Bishop of Killala, then a
" professor in the Waterford Catholic College. Another
" of my chosen associates was our common friend,

" Father Thomas Murphy. He was one of the kindest
" men I ever met. The poor never were in want
" of clothes or money while he had them to give.
" When he died of a fever in 1817, caught during his
" attendance on the sick people, he only left threepence
" behind him in money. Yet he had a large allowance
" from his sister, had good church preferment, and
" was the President of St. John's College."

Through Mr. Cahill, the brogue-maker at Thurles,
my father made the acquaintance of Edward Rice, the
founder of the "Christian Brothers" in Ireland. By
a graceful mistake the "Brothers of Christian Schools"
became shortened into "Christian Brothers," by which
name the fraternity is always known in Ireland.

Edward Rice was truly a benefactor to his country.
He devoted his life and means to these schools years
before the National Schools were established. My
father says of him: "This pure-minded man owes his
" elevation to considerable affluence and to his perse-
" vering industry. He must be happy in the reflection
" that he had the courage to invest the whole of his
" means in the foundation of this invaluable institution
" that contributes so much to the improvement of his
" country. Feeling as I do the want of education my-
" self, I know how great a blessing a man confers when
" he instructs the ignorant. . . . .

" At this time there lived in Waterford a bookseller
" and printer named John Bull, the most finished trades-
" man in his way that I ever met. He actually per-
" suaded me that books were not only the best things

" to buy, but that they were good also as an investment.*

" Among my purchases from him was Smith's ' Wealth
" of Nations.' I spent portions of six months in look-
" ing it over, and I only got half way through the first
" volume. I cannot now say whether it was my want
" of knowledge of the language or my ignorance of
" logic that hindered me from doing better. The
" things that struck me most were the division of
" labour and the value of time. . . . . When my dear
" old friend Doctor Francis White died, his rare library
" was removed from Carrick to Waterford to be sold.
" I bought some of his books, among others Doctor
" Fell's edition of Saint Cyprian's Works. I was
" greatly struck by the following admirable passage,
" which occurs in the treatise on the Lord's Prayer:
" 'The words of a Son so dear cannot but be acceptable
" to a Father so indulgent.' Nothing, I thought, was
" better calculated to arouse and cheer an isolated poor
" fellow so far removed from the fostering care of his
" parents. Another of Doctor White's books that I
" purchased was ' Sir Walter Raleigh's Remains.' The
" following passage struck me forcibly: ' Recollect,'
" he says to his son, ' in your will that your wife is the
" mother of your children and the partner of your life,
" —but should she marry again, her new lover ought
" not to lie on the feathers plucked from your bones.' "

While at Waterford my father received much kindness and hospitality from Mr. and Mrs. Fleming, and I

---

* Does not this remind us of Molière's " Vous êtes orfèvre, Monsieur
Josse " ?

have often heard him say how much he used to love to go to their house and play about with their children. Mr. Fleming was a goldsmith by trade, and he helped my father materially in his business, besides the pleasure that he afforded to him in his leisure hours.

"Having spent two years in Waterford, where I
"made myself more proficient in the mechanical part
"of my profession, and also improved my means, I
"went to Clonmel, and took a small shop in Dublin
"Street. From this I removed to the Corner House,
"opposite to the Main Guard, now No. 1, Johnson
"Street. I then wrote to my old friend Ribaldi, who
"was at that time a prosperous tradesman in London,
"and asked him to send me some mirrors. To enable
"me to pay the ten per cent. *ad valorem* duty on these
"goods, I got Messrs. Ryall Brothers, bankers in
"Clonmel, to accept my promissory note for £20; but
"as we had then no steamers, and the Liners were not
"so regular as they are now, my note became due
"before the goods arrived from London. I thought
"that the conduct of my bankers was most unkind in
"sending for the amount of my promissory note before
"I had made use of their money. When I went to
"remonstrate with them on the subject, they seemed as
"much astonished at my conduct as I had been at
"theirs. However, they held over my note, and
"allowed me to keep the cash; and, notwithstanding
"the strange irregularity of my first transaction with
"them, they subsequently acted towards me with
"fatherly kindness. In those days I used occasionally

" to go down to Waterford to see my old friends there,
" and at Clonmel I became acquainted with Parson
" Carey, the Head Master of the Clonmel Endowed
" Grammar School.   He was a man whose friendship I
" enjoyed for many years."

By this time my father's business was firmly established, and he felt himself quite at home in Clonmel.
He was elected one of a Society for visiting the Sick
Poor, and by an annual payment of three guineas he
made himself a member of the House of Industry.
His name, Charles Bianconi, became metamorphosed
into Bryan Coony,—Bryan of the Corner. It was
the fact of his shop being at the corner of the street
that gave rise to the play upon the words. The
Coonys were well-to-do farmers, and one old lady of the
family drove many miles to Clonmel and called on my
father to ascertain to what branch of the sept he belonged. She was rather disappointed that she could
not claim a relationship with so prosperous and well-
favoured a namesake.   Later on, when the "Corner
Shop" was a thing of the past, my father was always
called "Bian." So that in his youth he lost the first two
and in his old age the last two syllables of his name.

" About this time the Government began to sub-
" sidise the allied armies of the Continent, and the
" heavy and pressing demands for bullion at once set
" in.   My ' Corner Shop ' was an admirable site for
" buying the hoarded-up guineas of the peasantry, and
" I was commissioned by a highly respectable house in
" Dublin to buy up gold for them.   Thus I found

" myself engaged in a most responsible trade with
" inadequate means, and with a very limited know-
" ledge of the business. How shall I describe the
" conduct of my respected friends Messrs. Ryall, the
" bankers, who at this juncture enabled me to surmount
" the great money difficulty by giving me a most
" liberal accommodation ? Time and experience did the
" rest. Besides this new bullion traffic, which lasted
" for some years, and in which I was fortunately suc-
" cessful, I carried on the ordinary business of my
" shop. This was how I became so engrossed in my
" double business, that I neglected all my self-imposed
" charitable and municipal duties, leaving the sick poor
" at home and in the hospital to take care of them-
" selves. All my determinations and wishes to see my
" suffering fellow-pedestrians carried from town to town
" paled before this new and engrossing occupation."

In his autobiography Charles Bianconi has at different times expressed his sorrow at the fatigues that
the poor people had to undergo in performing their
journeys from one town to another on foot, and has
wondered whether some means could not be devised to
alleviate their sufferings. As has been said already, it
was doubtless the toils that he himself had borne that
made him think so much of the sorrows of others.

" During my former brief residence in Clonmel, some
" years before, I had become acquainted with John and
" James Corbet, two intelligent elderly men, and I now
" renewed my friendship with them. I felt a particular
" and almost a filial regard for them, and when I was a

" prosperous and well-to-do tradesman in Clonmel I
" loved to see them at my table. I derived extreme
" pleasure from hearing their reminiscences, extend-
" ing over the terrible times of the Rebellion of 1798
" and the atrocities that followed. One of their most
" stirring narratives was the execution of Father Sheely,
" judicially murdered in 1766 on the plea of having
" been accessory to the death of a man bribed to absent
" himself. The terrible doom that overtook Father
" Sheely's persecutors,—death in hideous forms, suicide,
" madness, loss of land and station,—was a favourite
" topic of conversation with the Corbets, and to me it
" was vividly interesting. All these narratives tended
" to increase my desire to see good and impartial laws
" duly administered among the people. This was the
" passion that animated Daniel O'Connell in his struggle,
" and was the mainspring of the great movement
" among the Catholics. One of the injustices of which
" the Corbets used to tell me was the unfair way in
" which the Catholics were taxed in Clonmel. Amongst
" others they related a practice then in existence. The
" Protestant shopkeepers, upon a certain day, used to
" go about the town levying a tax upon their Catholic
" neighbours who attempted to open shops within the
" town walls of Clonmel. They used to wring from
" each individual from two to four guineas, which
" they called 'Intrusion Money.' My informants
" specially praised an old Mrs. Ryan, dead now long
" since, who boldly refused to comply with their de-
" mands. The tax-makers therefore seized her goods.

" She afterwards recovered them at law, and her spirited
" conduct led to the abolition of this toll.   We Catholics
" had at one time to pay a tax upon all bought mer-
" chandise, while our more favoured Protestant and
" Dissenting fellow-townsmen were made free of the
" place, and saved not only from a needless expenditure
" but from the galling contact with such a class as the
" toll-gatherers.   Since these vexatious practices have
" been discontinued, it is hardly possible to describe
" the wonderful increase of business in the town, and
" the great extension of Clonmel itself.

" In the house numbered 112, Main Street was the
" Newsroom, which I joined.   I was greatly struck
" by the loud and consequential talk constantly going
" on between a Mr. Jephson and a Sir Richard Jones,
" and two more of their set, whereas I and my fellow-
" Papists were not allowed to speak above a whisper.
" This I resolved not to submit to, for I could see no
" reason why, when I had paid my money in a public
" place, I should not share all equal rights.   Others
" followed my example, and as we all, Protestants
" and Papists, indulged in equally noisy declamation,
" a stranger entering our newsroom would have been
" puzzled to say which party were the privileged
" administrators of the penal code."

Here Charles Bianconi tells at some length the well-
known story of the unjust flogging of a Protestant
gentleman, Mr. Barney Wright, for having on his person
a French letter which Mr. Barton, an ultra-loyal magistrate, was unable to translate.   It is consoling to know

that when milder times came Mr. Wright obtained heavy damages.

This is the end of my father's autobiography. But before going on further with the history of his life, it will be well to put in a short chapter giving some of the details of his early days, very kindly supplied to me by Miss Julia Bourke, of Breners, the only person now living who knew my father intimately seventy years ago.

CHAPTER II.

IN the early part of this century Miss Julia Bourke
and my father had been great friends. Her family had
once owned considerable estates, and since Cromwell's
time leased part of them from the ancestors of the
Earl of Bessborough. Miss Bourke lived to see the
old place of Breners pass totally away, but she never
lost the pluck, the pride, and the courtesy befitting
her long descent. My father used to tell us at home
that he had carried on a mild flirtation with her
for the last sixty years, and every Christmas he used
to make us all laugh by handing about at the break-
fast-table the cheery and sprightly letters he had
received from her. In July, 1875, I went to visit her
at Piltown, near Carrick-on-Suir, where she lived, with
the idea of learning from her some facts as to the early
days of my father's life in Ireland. Miss Bourke was
then eighty-five years old; she was poor and very
nearly blind, but she received me kindly and bade me
welcome. I thought I saw that in spite of the marks
that old age and misfortune had left upon her face, she

must, when young, have been pretty. She was small
in size, and had rather aquiline features. Her skin
was still clear and fresh-looking; her eyes were bright
blue in colour, and they could still laugh, though
they could no longer see. She said that her memory
was failing her, but I suspect that was in things of
every-day occurrence, for sometimes, when quoting what
my father said, she would use the same words and the
same quaint expressions that he had been wont to make
use of. When she was young she must have been a
great mimic, for she now unconsciously imitated the
tones of my father's voice, and the foreign accent that
somewhat thickened his Tipperary speech.

At first I told her some news concerning her own
relations, for I knew some of her connections who were
getting on well in the world. Then I listened to her
not unnatural expressions of feeling at the unbroken
friendship—lasting longer than many a lifetime—
that had subsisted between her and my father. Thus,
by degrees, I got her into the vein of speaking freely
of old times. All the old life and fun returned to
her, and from half crying she got to laughing. Then
she began :—

" I can see your father this very minute just as he
was when I first saw him at my Uncle Baldwin's house
in Cahir. He was so smart and full of life, and had
such bright brown eyes that looked through you, and
such thick black curls ! He came in with a portfolio
of prints under his arm, and we children all set at him
and rummaged his pretty things."

"How old was he then, Miss Bourke?" I asked.

"He was a grown boy, but not quite a man; he may have been about sixteen, or a little more. I was quite a little thing. He used to call me little Julia and 'leettle dheevil;' that was a pet name he had for me, my dear."

The old lady thus excused the indecorous phrase, which I knew quite as well as she did. My father used to call me, his daughter, "little dheevil," when he was in an extra good humour, even after I had been some years married.

"Did you think him handsome?"

"Well, he was very good-looking, but it was his eyes that were so bright. My aunt called his attention to me, but he looked at my cousin, and did not mind me. 'Why are you looking so hard at Bridget?' some one said. 'I am looking at her because I left a little sister at home that was fair too, and was like her, and would now be about her size.'"

Miss Bourke was speaking of the first time when she saw my father. She used often to stay with her aunt, Mrs. Baldwin, and he had strict orders from both Mr. and Mrs. Baldwin whenever he came to Cahir to make their house his home. Now, though a successful tradesman, my father honestly admitted that he was not a skilful craftsman. His hands were short and rather stumpy. He had no talent for driving in nails, or pruning trees, or playing upon any instrument. By sheer force of will and hard work he contrived to overcome this want so far as to do plain gilding fairly well, but as soon as he could afford it he employed skilled women to do the finer work. Before he had his regular shop, when it was possible, he would, in the most polite manner, show the young girls how to gild, and then coax them to help him. Miss Baldwin had been an early pupil of his, and when he got his great job,—the gilding of a dreadful pseudo-Gothic erection in Cahir Chapel, part tabernacle, part reredos, at which I have gazed in virtuous horror,—he availed himself of her slender fingers for the fine parts of the work. Her mother was too good a Christian to object to her daughter's helping to adorn the house of the Lord. So Charles Bianconi and Miss Baldwin worked together at the gilding, and the children ran in and out, watched and wondered, and did mischief after the manner of their kind and country.

"Did you help him too, Miss Bourke?" I asked.

"No, I did not, Mrs. O'Connell. I was too young and too giddy. I used to run in and out, and peep over his shoulder, and breathe on the gold, and he would call out, 'Run away, you little dheevil,' and hunt me out, and bolt the back door of the chapel. My aunt used to send me this back way through the garden and orchard to call them in to dinner, and Charles and I had a private signal of our own. I would snatch up a screeching hot potato, run down, and then present it to him."

"Did you sing in the choir? Were you one of the six young girls to whom he taught the Gregorian chant?"

"I was not; I was too young and too naughty. I know I have heard him sing, but I don't remember his voice, but I do remember how he used to say his prayers. Every night in the year my poor father used to have the rosary."

"What, ma'am! Is it out of Lent?" said I.

It is customary in most Catholic country-houses to have this family prayer said only in Lent and in Advent, and, if the people are very good, on Sunday nights also. The rosary, I may perhaps as well say, consists of short meditations on the principal events of our Lord's life, with repetitions of " Paters," " Aves," and " Glorias." These are counted by means of rosary beads, and the devotion takes its name from being offered "as a crown of roses " to the Mother of God.

"Yes, Mrs. O'Connell," said Miss Bourke. " Every night of the year, both in and out of Lent. Even when my mother was away my father would give it out himself. He said it in English, but the farm servants sometimes answered in Irish, and Charles would join in and pray very loud and very fast in Latin, or it may have been Italian. He prayed so hard and so fast that we small ones were hard set not to laugh out loud."

Miss Bourke went on :—

"My mother was very fond of your father, and he came to our house whenever he liked. He had his own seat at one particular corner of the dinner-table. Once he walked in after we were all seated. The table was quite full, and there was some little trouble in

putting in an additional chair. When we all sat down
he was put into my mother's usual place, and she sat
down among us children. She noticed that he was not
eating so heartily as usual, and asked him what ailed
him. 'Don't you see, Mrs. Bourke, you have taken
my seat?' he said. Then she laughed, got up, and
changed places with your father, and he afterwards ate
his dinner in peace."

I then made a remark about the very fine print of
the "Ecce Homo," that hung on the wall of Miss
Bourke's room. The frame, though much tarnished,
had been richly gilt, and it was deeper than one
usually sees round print pictures. It flashed across me
that it might have been a gift of my father's, and I
therefore asked Miss Bourke if he had gilt it.

"Yes, Mrs. O'Connell; your father gilded that frame.
We had a raffle long ago for the chapel, and he made
us a present of that print, framed and glazed, just as
you see it; and it was then considered a valuable prize.
The priest then gave him some tickets, and he, meeting
my little brother in the street, offered him one, which
won that picture."

We were then silent for a few moments,—she busy
with old memories, and I thinking over all that she
had been telling me,—when she turned the conversation, and began by speaking about my son.

"Your boy ought to be good," said she. "Two
good strains, O'Connell and Bianconi. But why did
you call him John instead of Dan?"

"He should be called John," I meekly answered,

alluding to the old Irish custom, as immutable as the law of the Medes and Persians. "He should be called John; it was his father's father's name."

"Ah! but Dan was the man of the people. We would have waded knee-deep in blood after him."

I ought, perhaps, here to explain that my late husband was Morgan John O'Connell, a nephew of Dan O'Connell, "the Liberator," as he was called in Ireland. Miss Bourke's reverence for the great man was so strong, that she would not hear any of my reasons for calling my boy John, after his grandfather.

As the principal object of my visit was to get some information about my father's shop in Clonmel, when I had exhausted her earlier and fresher recollections I turned my inquiries in that direction. Unfortunately Cahir and Carrick were the towns that Miss Bourke knew best, and she was only an occasional visitor at Clonmel.

"I do not remember the shop so well," she said. "I know it was a small shop, with a bow window, and behind the window there was always a beautiful mirror set in a rich frame."

But beyond that I perceived that I could get nothing from her. I then thanked Miss Bourke for her kindness, and bade her farewell.

CHAPTER III.

I HAVE had the greatest difficulty in finding details of this period of my father's life. Any chain of events, or any connecting links showing how things follow one another, I have been quite unable to trace. All that I can do is to put down truly such information as I have. Fidelity, indeed, is the only virtue that this book can have; to literary skill I make no pretensions; my object is to show my father as he was, and the events that his life brought forth. The Dick Whittington qualities will, I believe, prove as successful in Ireland as elsewhere, and the Irish people, if you treat them fairly, are as good neighbours to trade with, to live with, and grow rich with as any others. Such at any rate was my father's belief.

I have already said that my father took lodgings in Waterford, and there carried on business as a carver and gilder. I have been given a quaint advertisement, evidently detached from the back of a frame, showing where he lived in Waterford. Unfortunately it bears no date :—

" Charles Bianconi, Gilder and Print-seller, Looking-
" glass and Picture-frame Manufacturer, at Mr. Pren-
" dergast's, opposite the Royal Oak, George Street,
" Waterford, informs the Ladies and Gentlemen that
" he executes all kinds of Gilding in oil and burnished
" gold, equal to any other person in this country, and
" on as moderate terms. He frames and glazes Por-
" traits, Pictures, Prints, Drawings, and Looking-
" glasses, in the newest style, and on the shortest
" notice.

" N.B.—Country commands by a line (post-paid,
" directed as above) will be punctually attended to.

" Bought of Charles Bianconi."

An old lady assures me that he dealt in musical
instruments as well as pictures, but I am inclined to
think that she has confounded him with a Doctor
Briscoli, who was a professor of music and a dealer in
musical instruments.

When my father rented the house in Clonmel, which
he always called " The Corner Shop," his business must
have been prosperous. The house is still standing,
though considerable alterations have been made in it.
Its present occupant is Mr. King, a butcher. When I
went to Clonmel I was shown over the house, and was
told of the alterations that had been made in it. Mr.
King also showed me a copy of the lease by which, in
1815, my father had surrendered his interest in the
premises. For this house my father had to pay a
premium of £55, and an annual rent of £40; and to

enable him to meet these expenses he let some of the upper rooms to lodgers.

His first tenant was a Miss Mary Anne K——, a fashionable milliner. Miss K—— was well connected with some of the smaller Protestant gentry of that part of the country, and she not unnaturally thought herself a person of more consequence than her landlord, her junior in years, and who also was a tradesman, a foreigner, and a Roman Catholic. I have been told that she was a fine woman, and that she had the imposing look that a Roman nose will often give to a face. Miss K—— had an aunt then living in Clonmel, who used often to ask her niece to come and drink tea with her and her daughter. This daughter, who is now alive, is my authority for the story I am about to relate. After Miss K—— had been my father's tenant for a few weeks, he also was honoured with an invitation to tea, and he, nothing loth to spend a pleasant evening after he had done his day's work, sometimes went and drank his tea with the ladies, not imagining that anything could be required of him but to make himself agreeable.

Sixty years have now passed since the days of the pleasant little tea-parties, and my informant said to me not long ago: " Your father, my dear ma'am, was not the great man then that he became afterwards. He was just beginning to get on, but he was so steady, and such a nice, smart, clever-looking young man, that we thought he would do nicely for Mary Anne."

Mary Anne's aunt was certainly determined to provide a husband for her niece, if it were possible, for she said to my father in a most resolute tone, " What is the meaning of your attentions to my niece ?   Do you purpose seeking her in marriage ?"

" Bedad, ma'am," answered my father, " I have no time to get married, but I'll get a good husband for Miss Mary Anne."

Though the story was related to me so long after the event took place, I can quite believe it, and can fancy that I see it all, just as it took place.

A few days after my father had been so assailed, the substitute came forward, pressed his suit, and was accepted. The marriage turned out happily in every way. The gentleman's business prospered, and my father was enabled in after years to assist the sons of his old friend.

It was probably after this little adventure that my father began to hedge himself round with every precaution against lady lodgers, and to avoid the society of every unmarried woman.   His next lodgers were two artists,—a Mr. Alpenny and his apprentice, Edward Hayes. Mr. Hayes, in after years, became a member of the Royal Hibernian Academy, and was well known in Dublin as a water-colour portrait painter. He was the father of Mr. Michael Angelo Hayes, whose narrative of part of my father's life will form the subject of a later chapter. I may as well say here that this Hayes family was in no way connected with my mother's family. My father was always fond of art himself, and he received his new lodgers with a double degree of satisfaction. He was at any rate determined to have no more Mary Annes.

As it was, the three bachelors clubbed together in their household expenses, and though their fare was always of the simplest kind, they were none the less merry over it. Three-halfpenny worth of milk was their allowance for tea, and this, through some arrangement of their own, Mr. Hayes, the poor apprentice, always had to buy. It was also his duty to boil the kettle for tea; and when he and my father were both white-headed grandsires my father would sometimes playfully remind him of the evening when he was so engrossed in his book that he let the kettle boil over and got scalded, and laughed at into the bargain. Mr. Hayes was a man with some taste for letters. He used often to read aloud to my father, who much preferred this to reading himself.

My father soon began to employ assistants in his business. Before he left the " Corner Shop " in Clonmel he had in his employment three Germans, one of whom was a woman; and there was also Pat O'Neil, who afterwards came to be head clerk in the car-office. Pat O'Neil was the head gilder when my father gave up the business; and instead of carrying on the trade he preferred to follow his master's fortunes. He remained for a long while in my father's service, though before his death he had become a rich and prosperous grocer.

Early in life my father learned the value of good organization. As I have said, he was not a skilful craftsman himself; he therefore employed assistants to do much of the manual labour. And he did so, perhaps, to a greater extent than most other men would have dared on his limited income. While his workpeople were engaged in the shop, he would travel about the country, sometimes walking and sometimes driving. Occasionally he would deliver his goods himself, either travelling with a great case upon an outside car, or walking after the bearers, if the journey was short enough to admit of the merchandise being conveniently carried by men. And in a little time he started a yellow gig, which in after years came to be very well known in the country. On this gig he went about soliciting orders and buying goods, and was everywhere treated with kindness and hospitality.

I have had more difficulty in getting together trustworthy information for this period of my father's life than for any other; and yet it is one of the most important. It was at this time, when he was in his shop in Clonmel, that he became an Irishman in mind and in feeling. His thoughts were with the Irish people, not only during the natural hours of work in the daytime, but in the evening he used to assist in teaching in the Scripture and Catechism classes. I was told by Mr. Shaughnessy, of Clonmel, that he had been one of the scholars in my father's Catechism class, and that he used to find it very hard to understand my father's speech, especially his improved explanations of the Christian doctrine. Another gentleman of Clonmel has told me a peculiar story of the manner in which my father used to say his prayers in those days. I do

not scruple to repeat it, because I believe it to be a
true characteristic trait of the man. Every Saturday
evening about eight o'clock Charles Bianconi was seen
to rush into the small dark Friary chapel and fling himself down on his knees before a certain confessor. Any
fair devotee that happened to be before him would be
requested by the priest to give way to the busy foreigner.
While a lady would be saying her *Confiteor*, Charles
Bianconi would have prayed and confessed and gone off
again. My father was a man of much practical religion,
but doubts or fears never troubled him in either spiritual
or temporal matters. He was a pure-minded, honest,
hard-working man ; he gave a fair share of his time—
that with him was his money—to the service of God and
his neighbour. He never troubled his director with
anything but his actual sins, and this may account for
the celerity with which he got through his religious
duties. When he did consult his friends the clergy, as
he was often in the habit of doing, it was at his office
desk or across his own mahogany table that the con-
ferences used to take place.

I have come across two unimportant documents belonging to these days of the "Corner Shop." One is
a bill for £12 for a chimney-glass in the year 1819. It
is written on a narrow slip of paper, and a quill pen
was probably used for the purpose. The handwriting
is more Italian in its character, and is less illegible
than it grew to be in the latter part of his life. There
seems to be some little retouching about the spelling of
the word "chimney." The letters *e y* were always a

difficulty with him, and we had a standing joke against him of spelling even "money" incorrectly; he would write it "mony." I have also seen a bill paid by my father to a Jew for a large number of ungilt frames that he bought at the rate of 3*s.* a-piece. I have never been able to ascertain how, when he left his business, he got rid of all his stock; whether he had an auction and sold his prints, frames, glasses, &c., or whether, as he sold off his goods, he failed to replace them. There are still picture-frames and mirrors in the hotels in and about Clonmel that came from his store, and some of these show that at the time they were very richly gilded.

So far as I can gather, though my father liked the town of Clonmel itself, he had more friends in Waterford, and friends of a more cultivated and respectable class. I believe that, except a few old families in their country-houses, and retired officers in the outskirts of the town, there were few Catholic gentlefolk in or near Clonmel. It is probable that when my father opened his shop he was too well off to be patronised, and not quite respectable enough to be treated as an equal by the few old Catholic merchants. He kept pretty much among the priests and their set for social enjoyment, and avoided becoming intimate with those of his fellow-shopkeepers who had well-filled tills, or were fathers of pretty daughters. Seriously, I suspect that Mary Anne had taught him a lesson, that he had made up his mind to marry when he had acquired the means and the position to do so, and having thus decided, he put the matter out of his thoughts.

However, I have been told of a quasi love affair of my father's, which, on the whole, I am inclined to believe. He was once made welcome at a country house where there were daughters in the family. He asked permission to educate one of the girls, in order that in a few years' time she might become his wife. Permission seems to have been given, and she was placed in an Ursuline convent at Thurles, where she was to remain for a certain time. When she came out of the convent and went home to her father's house, unfortunately for Charles Bianconi she fell in love with a man whom everybody in Tipperary esteemed, the popular and handsome Martin Lanigan. My father saw the state of the case, and at once gave up all pretension to her hand. But the wedding was not to be. Mr. Lanigan died of injuries received during a contested election, and the young lady who had loved him devoted herself to his sister's children, and did not marry until late in life. Of love, in the way that many of us understand it, with romantic ideas and high passions, my father was hardly capable. His head was too full of the world and of the things of the world to have time to idealize a woman, or dally with a graceful image in his fancy, and find its realisation in some girl that he had chosen. He understood love-making in the foreign fashion, according to which, after a little private negotiation between the parents, everything might be comfortably arranged. And he had at that time the foreign idea of a home where the wife is not so fully a presiding deity as in the British household, but where the word "family" takes a wider meaning than with us. Abroad the ties between parents and children are stronger and more lasting, though the wife, as such, holds a place of lesser importance.

But I hear a story of a romance elsewhere. My father was, I am told, disposed to love another young lady, a playful young girl whom he always used to call by her pet name. This girl became a nun, and died shortly after she made her religious profession.

There always seems to have been an idea, equally prevalent among the most amiable and the most tyrannical rulers, that there is something mysterious in the way that Ireland ought to be governed, and that the ordinary principles of life will not hold good in that country. These notions my father would laugh to scorn. He not only believed them to be untrue, but he thought them worthless. He would proudly appeal to his own experiences as pedler, shopkeeper, car-owner, landowner, alderman, mayor, county magistrate, grand juror, deputy-lieutenant for his county—everything, in fact, but member of parliament; and on this theme he propounded the theory that the Irish people, rationally treated, were very much the same as any other race of men, and rather pleasanter to live with. He had mixed with men of every grade; his homelessness in his boyhood had opened to him the hearts and houses of Irish mothers of every class. Keeping his strong individuality and his national traits, the Lombard mountaineer had acquired in all else the feelings, passions, and prejudices of the people among whom his lot was cast. I can see now how, by slow and sure degrees, he inhaled, as the air that he breathed, the aspirations and the prejudices of his everyday neighbours. Doubtless, a common faith tended much towards the result.

My father had found many friends in Clonmel, especially among the clergy, and some of his greatest allies were the Franciscan friars. In the penal times, colleges of Irish Franciscans were founded on many parts of the Continent. Munster men especially affected those in Italy. St. Isidore's in Rome was ever a favourite resort of young Tipperary friars, who became very fond of their new country. Some of these returned to Clonmel, and became my father's chosen associates. For reasons that I cannot explain, among the disciples of St. Francis who re-transplanted themselves to the Irish soil, many "queer fellows," as the term was, seemed to flourish to an extent that that blessed man could never have foreseen. And it is noticeable among our countrymen, that the high animal spirits and strong sense of humour which constituted what long ago was called a "queer fellow," are a great help to an Irish priest in dealing with the people, and in helping him to bear up against the many discomforts of his holy office. Perhaps the Franciscan order is the most perfect example of democracy extant: no wonder then that its members threw themselves heart and soul into the great national struggle for civil and religious liberty in Ireland. From their order sprang the man who originated the temperance movement, and at one time almost divided with Daniel O'Connell himself

the popular hero-worship. This special friar, Father
Mathew, my father had known as a boy going to
school in Thurles, then a singularly handsome lad, and
of specially gentle and winning manners. My father,
who, I am bound to say, could not boast of so mild a
temper, became once engaged in a boxing match with
one of the day scholars, and in that youthful duel he
decidedly got the worst of it. The future Apostle of
Temperance acted as his second and bathed his bleeding
nose. The friendship thus made between the two boys
grew afterwards into strong intimacy, and will account
for the very affectionate tone of Father Mathew's
letters to my father.

There was something grand in hearing my father
draw comparisons between the present and the past. I
have often heard him speak well of individual parsons;
but if the disestablishment of the Irish Church had
meant the absolute quashing of Paganism, he could
not have exulted in it more triumphantly. He failed
to see how the working of the spirit of the age was
tending to sweep away all state religious endowments
and class privileges; he did not see this, but he rejoiced
in the removal of the badges of servitude. I must do
him the justice to say that he regarded the Land Bill
with great moderation. He did not join in the foolish
clamour of some landlords, nor did he, like others, hail
it as a positive boon, but simply thought it a wise measure, making landlords do what a man of honour ought
to do in ordinary circumstances. I do not think that
my father was as vehemently ardent on the wrongs of

tenants as he was about the wrongs of Papists. The
gross injustice of the tithes, and the still grosser abuses
in the manner of collection, were the points upon which
he was the most impetuous. I must note a curious
admission that once slipped from him. He then
acknowledged that such of the great Tory landlords as
were rich men and residents, were, in the main, good
landlords. This was an admission he was rather chary
of making, and on this occasion he dropped it by chance
rather than deliberately gave it in testimony.

In those days of the "Corner Shop" in Clonmel, Clonmel was the head-centre of the anti-Ascendancy party.
It was the town in which the revolution raged hottest
until the Roman Catholics ceased to be serfs. The agitation led by Daniel O'Connell was a mighty and peaceful
uprising of Catholic Ireland. The cautious middle
classes were the very bone and sinew of the movement.
The priests were O'Connell's lieutenants. For once
landlord and tenant, employer and employed, forgot all
mutual distrust, and Emancipation was at last carried.
In the Liberator's boyhood the penal laws had been
so far relaxed that the Catholics could take out long
leases, though it was not until later that a Catholic was
permitted to buy and become possessed of land. By a
still further relaxation of the penal laws, Catholics
were admitted to practice at the bar; but whatever
success they attained in their profession they were not
allowed to sit on the Bench. Parliament was closed
against them, as was every post of honour and emolument held under Government.

It is true that a price was no longer set upon the head of their priests ; it was no longer necessary that a Catholic who kept his faith should either quit the country, or hold his land through the courtesy of a Protestant who was the nominal owner, with power to foreclose at any moment. Catholics were no longer helots, but their position in the State was still so bitterly galling that Macaulay compares them to the plebeians in Rome under Volumnius.

Had my father been born and bred in Clonmel, he could not have thrown himself more vehemently heart and soul into the cause. In his later years, his politics toned down to a decorous and common-sense form of Whiggery, but that stage of development was far distant at the time of which I am speaking. In the early days of the Catholic Association, he glowed all over with a patriotic fervour, and his zeal was ardent rather than discreetly tempered by the loyalty of after years. I have reason to believe that the flame in his breast was kindled and fanned by the insolence of the Protestant shopkeepers, and the vexations these persons continued to inflict upon their Catholic rivals.

Nothing could exceed the spite and animosity that then showed itself almost hourly among the middle classes. The two parties,—Protestants and Catholics,— separated both by race and creed, hated each other with a raging enmity that had been handed down from one generation to another. The Catholics were just beginning to lift up their heads, though, as it has been said, it was a widow who first resisted the tax that the

Protestants in Clonmel had for a long time past imposed upon their neighbours. Joining together in one common cause, the Catholics began to feel that they were men ; they had leaders of their own faith who, struggling to obtain the brilliant prizes of political and judicial life, allied themselves with their brethren, the traders and the tillers of the soil.

Such was the little world in which Charles Bianconi, the "alien Papist," opened his Corner Shop. He used to say, sometimes, " While the big and the little were fighting together, I grew up amongst them."

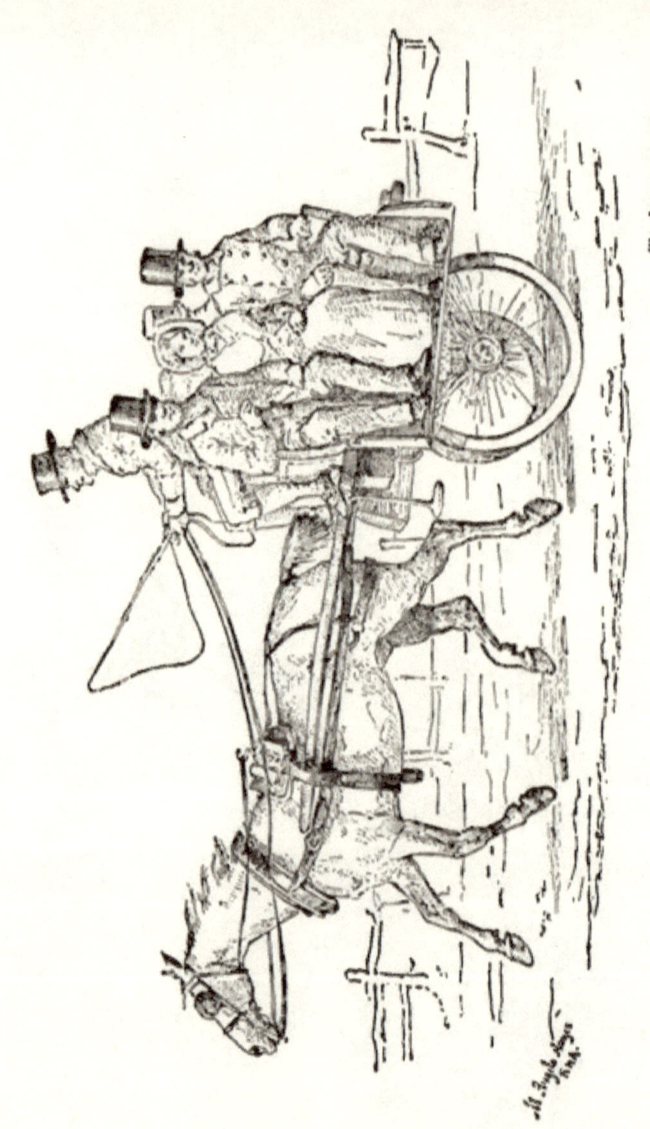

To face page 45.

CHAPTER IV.

"THE BIANS."

BY this homely and familiar title Charles Bianconi's once-famous cars were known all over Ireland, and he wished the chief chapter of this book to be so designated. It was between jest and earnest one evening, when my father was particularly well pleased with my labours, that he called out, " *We'll call the book ' Charles Bian-*" *coni, Car-Man ;' and we'll have a grand chapter on* " *the Bians."* I turned to my good friend Mr. Anthony Trollope for council,—the only man equally versed in books and in coaches to whom I could appeal. I asked him, very much in doubt, whether it would become a lady to head a chapter by what might seem to be a slang name. And he answered me : " Certainly call the cars the ' Bians.' The name became too well known to be slang." Thus encouraged, I have written the old familiar word in the post of honour ; though in deference to the wishes of my friends I have not put " Car-man " on the title-page.

I would crave the indulgence of my reader for the many deficiencies of this book. As I have said before,

I do not profess to any literary ability; but my short-comings, I fear, do not end there. I am quite unversed in horse-flesh and in book-keeping; and the many execrably badly written letters of my father's that I have had to wade through, have either touched upon portions of his life that would be uninteresting and unintelligible to strangers, or they have, as is too often the case, served only to give me a clue upon which to form my judgment of his many-sided existence. When his loving partiality made me what he called "an eldest son," it became a sacred duty for me to carry out his wishes concerning his written life. My own son, who is now only six years old, is the old man's sole male descendant; and as I could not avail myself of his assistance, I have single-handed been obliged to face the stable, the ledger, and the road,—thus trespassing on man's domain, simply because there was no one to take the work off my hands. "Needs must" has often carried many a diligent toiler safely to the goal. Assuredly, I began this task with no love of dabbling in ink, or for any unwomanly desire for notoriety; but simply to please my old father, and to help my husband, in whose hands the work would have been done far differently.

It was at first begun to beguile the tedium of a quiet winter in the country, continued half jestingly as a pleasant family occupation, set aside for awhile after my husband's death, then resumed in the hope of rousing my father's flagging energies,—again cast aside at his death, and then finally taken up and finished as a duty to be fulfilled. Such as it is, I have worked it out alone, uncheered by the help and sympathy which made its beginning so pleasant. Parts of it were written with fun and laughter, and parts of it were written with a sore heart. But through it all I have endeavoured, so far as it lies in me, to give an accurate picture of what my father was. Like other men he had his whims and his weaknesses, and these I have made plain, as I have also spoken of his kindliness of heart, his love of justice, and of the good that he strove to do to his fellow-creatures.

I was born just twenty years too late for my task; I have only the faintest memory of a journey on a long Bian. After I had written much about them, endeavouring to describe them as best I could from hearsay and from pictures, I judiciously put what I had written into the fire, as my artist friend, Mr. M. Angelo Hayes, has given me a much better description of the cars and of their manner of working than I could possibly have done. Mr. Hayes's narrative forms the subject of the following chapter; few men know the Bians better than he, for as a boy he lived exactly opposite to the old coach-office in Hearn's Hotel, in Clonmel.

Mrs. Cantwell, who now owns the inn that was once kept by Dan Hearn and his wife, has made many alterations and improvements in the old place. Railways have brought about a new state of things, and the daily bustle that was once watched by many a spectator in the old coachyard has since been moved to other places. During my visit to the old Bian premises I had much difficulty

in realising the contrast between the respectable, quiet
dulness of the main street of Clonmel, and the lively
scenes of noise and fuss it once presented. Waterford
rather benefited by the railways, but the trade of
Clonmel for a long time suffered much by the new
system of locomotion; there was a hardy colony of
bargemen altogether thrown out of employment. These
men had lived by conveying imported merchandise and
coals from Waterford through Carrick to Clonmel, and
by taking back the rich farm produce of Tipperary, Limerick, and Waterford counties. This traffic, which had
been large, dwindled down to a small trade in coal and
heavy exports. Kilkenny was sufficiently large, and was
so centrally situated as not to be much affected by the
change; but after the first train passed through Clonmel
the glory of the town departed. The 18 passenger cars,
the great reserve stables, the manufactories of coaches
and harness, the great smithies have all vanished. Clonmel is rather quieter now than when the lonely Italian
boy first walked under its quaint gateway towers.

Unlike many coach proprietors, my father had no
hotels of his own; but at Clonmel, Kilkenny, and
Waterford he adopted the following plan. He rented
large premises, reserving to himself the outer yards,
the great ranges of stables and corn storage, and he
sub-let the main houses, which he converted into hotels
for his agents; he simply charged them what he had
paid his landlord. In this way his property was
protected from all risks. Hearn's hotel in Clonmel
consisted of two or three private houses thrown into

one. Cummins's Hotel in Waterford is the charming old Georgian house of the Quan family, which my father took from Mr. Thomas Meagher, M.P. As Mr. Cummins, son of the late agent at Waterford, bought from my father a portion of the Bians, I was enabled to inspect the great old cars, and to see the arrangements. Portions of the vast storage have been turned to other uses. There were still great ranges of triple stores, and low, close, roomy stables. I made some remark about the hot air in the stables, but Mr. Cummins assured me that he pinned his faith to my father's axiom that a coach-horse cannot be kept too warm, for a horse comes in in such a heated-state from short but quick and heavy work.

I fancy that in Waterford I got some idea of the working of the large establishment. It was worked on a peculiar plan, and was, perhaps, the most perfect system that even Italian ingenuity ever suggested. Never was man better fitted than my father for perpetually watching and catching up ideas. His natural passion for rushing about, his extreme sharpness, the great quickness of his mind, of his hand, and of his eye, seemed to destine him specially for some such enterprise. I can never remember his staying an entire week at home, unless he happened to be ill.

There was Dan Hearn, the kindest and most genial of men, whose fine person and handsome face and mellow voice were the delight of my childhood. He had a peculiar and accurate knowledge of horses, knowing all their points, and being able to tell nearly at a glance how far such and such a beast would be serviceable. He was my father's right-hand man, endowed with almost unlimited powers, subject only to my father's somewhat autocratic changes. Many a time after he had gone through a whole district, casting screws, adjusting the teams, making and testing his new purchases, my father would swoop down after him and upset all his nice arrangements. Mr. Hearn was, in a word, the head agent, responsible to no one but my father. His salary was,—what would be now thought small,—£120 a-year; but my father "made it up to him" in other ways. Dan Hearn, alone of all the agents, had the power to draw cheques; he purchased most of the horses and nearly all the fodder. There were three other agents, or inspectors, paid at the same rate; but the principal resident agents seldom received more than from £52 to £72 a-year. In the smaller towns the agents were generally shopkeepers, and they received a commission of five per cent. on the money that passed through their hands.

The drivers, whose perquisites in some cases were very considerable, were paid in inverse ratio to the profits,—whence my father's standing joke, that the better a driver was, the more he reduced his wages. Some of the famous coachmen only received 2s. 6d. a week. On the night mails and the unfrequented roads their wages went up to 15s. The reader will, of course, recollect that 15s. a-week in Ireland, thirty or forty years ago, meant a great deal more than it would now. The helpers in the stables were paid from 10s. to 15s.

Some of them were at work all night, as the mail traffic was mostly carried on during the night; these men were at work from six in the evening to six o'clock in the morning. All the helpers had hard work: they usually had each five horses to clean and feed, to harness and unharness; the drivers had to drive them and to look after the vehicle.

In 1865, the year of the transfer of the establishment from my father's hands, there were 130 agents, 85 drivers, and 200 helpers. The four travelling agents, Mr. Hearn and his three colleagues, used to look after the horses, see what horses were running on what lines, make themselves acquainted with their condition, as to how far they were good or bad, how they did their work, and they had to keep each district supplied with forage. In Clonmel, Sligo, and Galway, the three great central depôts, there were car factories, with about twenty hands constantly employed in each. Besides these there were the smiths and coach-builders; but these latter were only engaged for coach-building purposes; and in each of these towns there were two harness-makers belonging to the establishment. It was always a practice of my father's to give out the shoeing of the horses to the local blacksmiths.

Besides the ordinary duties of booking passengers, receiving and remitting fares, the agents had to submit to a complicated system of way-bills. The agent handed to each driver every morning a way-bill, showing on the first page the driver's name, the name of the horse or horses that ran in the car, of the towns passed through, and the hours of arrival or departure at each place. On the second and third pages the names of the passengers were entered, showing where they started from and their place of destination, and the amount of fare paid; the total sum of these various amounts was of course filled in at the bottom. At the side of the page were the agent's initials, and underneath the particularities of the goods conveyed were entered together with the charges of transport, and to these the agent's initials were also placed. These way-bills the agents had to copy out into their day-books, and every three days they were sent to the head office at Longfield, where my father lived after he left Clonmel. Each agent had also to furnish monthly accounts of receipts and expenditure, and these were compared with the books in the office at Longfield, into which all the way-bills had been previously copied. Here all the accounts of the establishment were duly checked, being posted into a large ledger, showing at a glance in its many columns the daily and the monthly receipts at every car-office. Every ten days the agent had to furnish an account of the consumption of straw, hay, and oats, with further particulars of the number of horses, each animal's consumption, and the total quantity consumed during the period, and the balance in hand. From this it will be seen to what an elaborate system of checks and counter-checks the agent had to submit. My father's minute code of precautions even extended to forbidding a groom's wife to keep hens, lest the oats should find a wrong destination. Each horse was allowed daily 15 lbs. weight of oats, in three equal feeds, 16 lbs. of hay, and 8 lbs. of straw for bedding. My father held that too much hay meant broken-windedness, and that the very small allowance of litter was sufficient for practical uses. The slightest excess in the consumption was charged to the agent, which in one way or another he had to refund. One of the best and most trusted agents in the western district was once short of 28 barrels of oats, and he had to supply the deficiency at his own cost, though there was no suspicion of dishonesty attaching to him.

The most irksome portion of the agent's duty was the night work, as he was obliged to take the way-bills from the driver. The driver of a mail car first drove to the post-office and delivered his mails, and then proceeded to the car-office, where the agent had to take charge of the parcels and write up the way-bill; he was, in fact, expected to be at his post at the departure and on the arrival of every car. And where female labour was employed the work was the same. The women were generally the wives or daughters of deceased agents. My father was not at all averse to allow women to occupy these posts; he piqued himself upon his power of reading faces, and he occasionally chose a woman in preference to a man. He was not moved by a pretty face or by any softness on the woman's part, for in general he was very indifferent to female charms; but he made his choice where he perceived a general air of intelligence and tact. At one time he had as many as twenty female agents.

In his own private office behind the dining-room his excellent old secretary, Mr. Denis Francis O'Leary, always sat at the desk opposite to my father. And Dan Hearn, who scorned literary luxuries, used to pull a chair towards the side of the table between them, and with a stumpy bit of a quill pen, such as no one else could have held in his hand, he wrote his business letters—concise, pithy, and often humourous, but the writing itself looked like the characters on a tea-chest. Then there was the back office in a building in the house yard. There six or seven desks were kept at work, one posting up the way-bills, another at the expense account, a third at the ledger, two at the forage returns, and two more at the index and the omissions. My father's last private clerk, Denis Dwyer, has furnished me with some particulars, and he showed me in a few moments in one of those huge leather-bound volumes that in the last year but one of my father's ownership—in 1864—the passenger traffic realised the sum of £27,731, the mail contracts paid £12,000; making altogether £39,731.

With all the avowed and acknowledged supervision, my father had additional reports from spies; these men were supplied with money not merely to pay their fares, but to tip the drivers. There was the spy proper who was solely employed for the purpose until he became too well known; one of these ingenious gentlemen was betrayed by his carpet-bag bursting and a quantity of bran rolling out of it. Then there were occasional spies, often schoolmasters out for a holiday, who were glad enough of an opportunity of getting a free outing; many and wondrous were the effusions of these pedagogues. There was an old bookseller traveller who used to report in return for his free transit, and there were sundry other similar characters who were paid for their services in various ways. But there were always two official spies regularly upon the staff of the establishment. These "very much dreaded officials," as my father's clerk styles them in the paper I am now condensing, had to report the number of passengers, which was invariably compared with the number marked on the way-bills; they also reported upon the state of the horses, of the harness and the vehicles, the behaviour of the agents, drivers, helpers, and especially the demeanour of the agent towards the public. Civility, attention, and punctuality were always rigidly enforced, and anything calculated to offend the public was always punished. If there was any discrepancy between the report given by a spy, and the number of passengers, &c., marked on the way-bill, the matter was immediately investigated, and an agent detected in falsifying a way-bill was at once dismissed. The spies were obliged to assume sundry *aliases*, and, I fear, to tell many untruths. They always had decent-looking luggage, even though hay, bran, and stones were often the contents of their bags. The drivers were ever on the look out for them, and they displayed a marvellous ingenuity in detecting their presence and in telegraphing the news along the line.

How my father contrived to keep up the close and intimate knowledge of every man and horse in his great enterprise was a puzzle to everybody. He had beyond doubt the best memory for faces that I ever knew;—it was quite equal to what we hear of George III. The very gradual growth of the establishment, of course, helped this. It began with one ordinary jaunting-car, and then it increased and multiplied, and took all sorts of shapes and forms. I stoutly maintain my father's great strength lay in his power of adaptability; he was not a discoverer, hardly an inventor, but no man was quicker or keener to grasp all the bearings of a subject and mould them to his own uses.

There is one circumstance told me by Father John Ryan, P.P., who had heard it from my father, that I must insert here. My father had begun his enterprise with a very small capital; though he rapidly and steadily increased his traffic the great expenses he incurred by that very extension prevented much accumulation of profit. Fodder for the horses, after the "war prices" had gone down, was very cheap, and a spare £1,000 would have given him a perfect command of the market. That spare £1,000 came to him in the following way. I quote Father John's own words:—

" The first thing that crops up here in my memory " is his connection with the historic Waterford election. " This was in 1826. The popular party had at first " no idea of starting a candidate in opposition to the " Beresford party, which was then considered all-power- " ful, and Bianconi's cars were engaged by them. By-

" and-by Villiers Stuart decided upon allowing himself
" to be put in nomination, and Bianconi was then
" applied to, as without his aid success was impossible.
" The morning after this application he was pelted with
" puddle. Coming up from the Friary Chapel, one or
" two of his cars and horses were heaved over the
" bridge, and he wrote to Beresford's agent stating that
" he could not risk the lives of his drivers and his own
" property on their side, and declaring off. He then
" engaged with the popular party, and certainly enabled
" them to gain the glorious victory they achieved. This
" election lasted for several days. At its termination
" the sum of £1,000 was paid to him. Before this he
" was always at the mercy of the market; with that
" amount of ready cash,—oats were then as low as 6d. a
" stone, and hay and other provisions at a corresponding
" low price,—he bought up and laid in such a quantity
" of forage of every sort, as kept him independent of
" the market for the future. Immediately after this he
" got married, and the money that he thereby acquired,
" made him still more able to command the market. I
" should also place on record that Mr. Bianconi always
" allowed a suitable pension to the wife, or mother, or
" children of any man who lost his life or his health
" in the establishment as helper, or groom, and some-
" times as driver; and should also mention that he
" allowed half-a-crown to every patient leaving the
" fever hospital, who presented at the office a certificate
" from his clergyman—no matter of what religion.
" Though he was very generous in his charities, he

" was most punctual and exact in his money dealings.
" He went into Hearn's Hotel one day and said to the
" barmaid, ' Judy, I was in London last week, and I
" 'did not forget you.' She thanked him. 'I brought
" ' you a tea-urn,' he said. He sent the urn to the hotel
" that evening, and a day or two after he called and
" said to the girl, ' Judy, you owe me 5s. 9½d.' 'What
" 'for, sir ?' 'For the tea-urn I brought you.' 'Oh, sir,
" ' I thought that was a present you sent us.' 'Come,
" ' come, no talk, but pay me what you owe me.' She
" gave him 5s. 8d., all the money that was in the till.
" On the day following he called again at the inn, and
" said, 'Judy, you owe me three half-pence of the
" 'price of the tea-urn.' Judy paid him the money,
" but kept telling the story for some time afterwards."

I have invariably heard my father say that no man
was better served than he was.   His rule was a patriarchal despotism ; his orders were to be obeyed without
a murmur of dissent, he had a horror of men who asked
why and wherefore.   Provided that he was obliged
briskly and thoroughly, he tolerated a considerable
liberty of speech.   Many a time I have heard him
laugh at a saucy answer ; certain cranky helpers invariably swore at him when he made them do what they
did not like.

English tourists have often told me what delightful
opportunities of seeing the people and the country his cars
have afforded them. Though the drivers had orders to fill
all the vacant places with poor people, especially women
carrying babies on their backs, still they very gene-

rally succeeded in separating the poorer from the better classes. In nothing is the Celtic quickness more remarkable than in the prompt discrimination of classes, and the faculties of these men became sharpened by long practice. Still it did sometimes happen that a disciple of daily scrubbing and tubbing found himself in closer quarters than was pleasant with a poor harvester or a female tramp, whose clothing was not of the nicest kind. My father at first evidently only contemplated carrying the poorer people; there was the lordly mail coach for the " quality." Had he possessed a spirit of artistic keeping he would have eschewed coaching altogether, and kept to his own peculiar line. But circumstances were too strong for him, and he became a great coach-owner, both in partnership with others and on his own account. He purchased the great coaching business of the Hartleys and the Bournes. He had also been a partner with the late John Talbot, of Ballybrent, as fine a specimen of an old Irish gentleman as the heart of man could desire. My father always maintained that he was the rightful Earl of Shrewsbury, and my husband, who had been in the House of Commons with him, more than confirmed my father's eulogies on Mr. Talbot.

My father was an old servant of the post-office, for which department he entertained a great regard. Judging by the vast pile of post-office letters I have found in his pigeon-holes, and the somewhat grumbling tone of many of them, I should imagine him to have been a loyal but a very turbulent vassal. If he liked and trusted the post-office surveyor he would help him to get the public well served. Once when a most special friend of his found himself obliged to provide mail contractors in the north without adequate means from head-quarters, my father got him nobly out of the difficulty by threatening the northern monopolists to come down upon them with half his forces and contest the road;—a threat which procured the required accommodation on fair terms, but which " the wily Italian," as certain Clonmel folk called him, warned his friend was solely a threat, and that he never really intended to do the thing.

In the spring of this year I visited Waterford, and was of course charmed with the beauty of the place, and with hearing the tales of bygone days. In the room I occupied there hung a fine old print, the frame of which had been gilded by my father, and given by him to old Mrs. Cummins. And I got some information from her son, Father George Cummins, who recollected the names and reputation of the coachmen on the road when he was a boy at school. I will now let him tell his own story.

" Cummins's Hotel stands about in the middle of the " quay at Waterford, and there every day at three " o'clock in the afternoon there used to be a scene of " business and bustle, not unmixed with merriment, " that never failed to attract a crowd to see the start- " ing of the Bians. At two o'clock the preparations " began ; the huge vehicles were drawn out before the " door of the hotel, and luggage from all quarters " came down on trucks, or on the backs of men

" and of boys. And from the hotel, whilst impatient
" and business-like commercial men were providing, at
" the ample table d'hôte, against the hardships of the
" road, that valuable servant the ' boots ' might be seen
" bearing case after case of heavy luggage to be stowed
" in the well or piled up on the top of the car. Then
" came the cynosure of many eyes, the coachman, fol-
" lowed by a boy carrying his whips,—for the coach-
" man who thought well of himself always carried a
" spare tormentor. He walks along slowly, bending
" under the burden of many caped coats and rugs, and
" as each driver arrives his merits are criticized and
" decided upon by the knowing ones who are skilled in
" horse-flesh. Already ' boots ' has secured the post of
" vantage—the box-seats—for his favourites, and dan-
" gling down may be seen the flash rugs of well-known
" commercial men in evidence of possession gained. As
" the hour approaches the guests come forth from the
" hotel dressed in all the varied fashion of travelling
" costume, fur rugs, glaring mufflers, wonderful top-
" coats, and cunning devices of all kinds for keeping out
" the cold or keeping in heat. Tobacco-pipes of curious
" and grotesque patterns astonish and delight the inqui-
" sitive lookers-on, and many an apprentice, who lingers
" in open-mouthed admiration at the travellers, wonders
" if it shall ever be his good fortune to get on ' the road.'
" The packing of the luggage on these cars was a work
" demanding skill and experience, and it not infrequently
" happened that some one, anxious to reach his home,
" would gladly accept a seat on the ' well,' on the top

" of the piled-up packages, when a place upon either
" side of the car was not to be had.   The principal
" attraction, however, was the arrival of the horses, and
" for many years the skill and coolness of Pat Dillon
" was the delight of the passengers on their journey,
" and of the crowd who watched him handle the reins
" at starting.   The Clonmel car was known by its grey
" horses, and by its prominent position in the group.
" For many years a very remarkable horse named
" Pender ran the lead in this conveyance, and though
" he was stone blind, and was very spirited and impa-
" tient, the masterly Pat Dillon could steer him without
" a mistake through the country carts, and around
" sharp and ugly corners.   Pender could never be put
" to until the moment of the start ; he was always led
" up and down, and was the cause of much admiration
" among the bystanders.   He was a grey horse of the
" most perfect symmetry, stout of limb, and well rounded
" at the quarters, and had none of the lankiness so
" often seen in coach-horses.   Not until after Dillon
" had seated himself, and given a complacent look
" round at the well-filled car, which represented to him
" perquisites to the amount of ten or fifteen shillings,
" and he had received the way-bill from the bustling
" agent, and had assured himself that the wheelers
" were all right,—it was not until then that Pender
" could be run into his place.   In a second the reins
" were passed by two attending grooms up to the box,
" and the eager horse, rearing with impatience, started
" off admidst the plaudits of the crowd. ' Now for

" ' Kilkenny !' cries out the agent ; and all eyes were
" withdrawn from the receding Clonmel car to the one
" about to start for Kilkenny. Among the coachmen of
" the day there was no one more popular on the road
" than William Mullaly. He was a young man whose
" family connections and his education entitled him to
" a more respectable position, but his love of horses,
" and his desire for ' fingering the ribbons ' led him to
" adopt as a trade what he had practised as an amateur.
" The perquisites on the Waterford and Kilkenny line
" were generally good, and that no doubt proved a strong
" argument with him. Mr. Bianconi, for many years,
" was opposed by a rival car-owner in a very spirited
" manner on this line. That afforded to Mullaly many
" opportunities of displaying his daring and his skill in a
" manner not always pleasant to travellers ; yet, though
" he never allowed himself to suffer a ' go-by,' he was
" never known to have met with a serious accident.
" And there was Tom Keogh, too,—a name familiar to
" all who knew the Bianconi establishment,—who spent
" over thirty years on the box-seat of the ' Dungarvan.'
" As remarkable for his politeness to ladies, and his ten-
" derness to weakness in distress, as he was for his
" brusqueness to the rougher sort of customers on his
" drive, he was a general favourite with all decently
" behaved people, and he was the terror of the sailors
" who travelled much upon his road. Poor Tom clung
" so affectionately to his accustomed occupation that at
" last he had literally to be lifted down from his seat.
" For no amount of telling was of any avail, even after

" he had got old, and had become incapable through
" weakness.

" Mr. Edward Cummins, the proprietor of Cummins's
" Commercial and Family Hotel, was Mr. Bianconi's
" agent at Waterford. This connection dates back to
" the year 1821 or 1822, and was continued through
" the Cummins family up to the period of the selling
" of the establishment, when the Dungarvan, Passage,
" and New Ross lines passed by purchase to Messrs.
" W. K. and P. Cummins. In the heyday of the estab-
" lishment, Waterford was one of the most important
" depôts in the country. On Sundays, when all the
" horses working into that city were resting, the stables
" usually contained forty animals. The hotel being
" the centre of this traffic, was naturally a place of
" great business and bustle. Mrs. Cummins, who
" directed and managed the affairs of the house, com-
" bined all her native quickness, intelligence, and
" energy, together with a certain motherly tenderness
" and matronly dignity. She was well and extensively
" known; and the hospitality that was gracefully and
" generously dispensed by her gave to the hotel a cha-
" racter of homeliness almost peculiar to it. Among the
" patrons and staunch friends of Mrs. Cummins there
" was no one who esteemed her worth or appreciated
" her more truly than Mr. Bianconi. His plate-chest, in
" the early days of her housekeeping, was always at her
" command, when some unusual thronging at assizes or
" elections, in those stirring days of the Agitation, made
" more than usual demands upon the resources of her

“ establishment. When he visited Waterford in after
“ times, it was his delight to accept the hospitality of
“ the house, to take an interest in the family affairs,
“ and to talk pleasantly over old scenes and acquaint-
“ ances. He consented to be a sponsor for one of Mrs.
“ Cummins's children, and on the day of the baptism
“ he deposited £50 in the National Bank, in the name
“ of his god-child, which, with the interest thereon,
“ was to be given to him on his twenty-first birthday.
“ It was amusing to note the little contrivances that
“ the ingenuity of his hostess discovered to gratify the
“ fancies of her kind patron. Mr. Bianconi, though
“ by no means a gourmand, was well known to have
“ his little peculiar tastes. Things usually disregarded
“ or despised by the lovers of good living were to him
“ the greatest treats. He could make a feast upon
“ cockles, and pig's head was a rarity that he looked
“ forward to with great pleasure. Young veal, which is
“ humorously called ‘staggering Bob,’ was to him quite
“ a *bonne bouche*, and he also confessed to a weakness
“ for tripe. In Waterford he used to revel in all these
“ whims, much to his own and his friends’ amusement.
“ In the season he always took home some of the pecu-
“ liar pickled cockles of the place.”

I will here insert the narrative of Mr. John Walsh,
who first entered into my father's service as a boy, just
after he had left the National School, and who is now
so deservedly respected by all that know him, that any
further praise of mine would be needless. He and his
partner, Mr. Kennedy O'Brien, who was literally born

in the establishment, purchased the Western lines from
my father.

"SLIGO, January 15th, 1876.

"DEAR MRS. O'CONNELL,—In compliance with your
" wish, I now give you a brief sketch of my connection
" with the late Mr. Bianconi, whose death I deeply
" deplore; for, though he was kind to all, he seemed to
" take quite a fatherly interest in me.

"On this day twenty-six years ago my father took
" me to Longfield. I was then only a boy, not sixteen
" years old. I was shown into the parlour where Mr.
" Bianconi was alone, and he said to me, 'John, I am
" going to send you to Clonmel to learn the business,
" and I will make a man of you. The first thing you
" will do when you go there is to buy a saucepan.
" You will see the women going round the town every
" morning with cans of milk on their heads; buy a
" pennyworth of new milk and add a mug of water to
" it; boil that and get a twopenny loaf; and, By the
" Hokey! you will have a breakfast fit for any man.
" Now, as to wages, I will not give you much money,
" as it would only spoil you: I will give you half-a-
" crown a-week, to begin with!'

"It was with feelings of delight I started the next
" morning on the early car. I was free, and would
" have to go to school no more, little dreaming I had a
" great deal more to learn. I arrived in Clonmel in due
" time, and after going through a few streets, we pulled
" up at the office, next to Mr. Hearn's Hotel. My ideas
" of the establishment became at once confused, and I

" was lost in amazement at the magnitude of the
" place, as I was shown round it. At the back of the
" hotel and office was a large yard; on the right was
" the harness-room, where five men were busy work-
" ing; higher up there were three forges with eight
" smiths, all of them busy with their irons; on the left
" was the timber-shop, where a foreman and his wheel-
" wrights were engaged; above that were the hospital
" stables, capable of holding sixteen horses; and in a
" loft over the stables and timber-shop two men were
" always at work making new cars, and another man
" painting them. Mr. Quirk, a good and kind man,
" superintended this department. I was next brought
" to a square yard on the other side of the street, where
" forty horses stood in charge of six grooms; and I
" soon afterwards learned that all these horses went
" out every day and others came back in their places.
" Cars drawn by three and coaches drawn by four
" horses came in and went out so fast, that for days I
" was bewildered and did not know what to think.
" There were four came from and went out to Water-
" ford, three to Tipperary, three to Gooldscross, one to
" Cork, one to Kilkenny, one to Youghal, and one to
" Fethard.

" I must candidly acknowledge that I did nothing,
" nor was I able to do anything for a long time,
" though in about a fortnight Mr. Bianconi told my
" father I was a great fellow, and that my wages were
" to be doubled from that day. Soon after I was raised
" to eight and then to ten shillings, for merit I did not

" possess.   And as I became useful, on the retirement
" of Mr. Quirk to Mount Mellery, I was raised to twelve
" shillings a-week, at which it remained for a long time.

   " The opening of the railway from Tipperary to
" Clonmel, and ultimately to Waterford, reduced us so
" much, that the agent, Mr. Connell, retired.   The
" whole management was then entrusted to me.   In
" about four months, thinking I was forgotten, I told
" Mr. Bianconi that when I was no good he raised my
" wages fast enough, but now when I was doing every-
" thing he forgot me.   He said to me, 'I am glad you
" reminded me of it; you will now have fifteen shillings
" a-week from the time Mr. Connell left.'

   " On the 24th of April 1854, I was sent as agent to
" Athenry, in the county Galway, at £1 a week, where
" an immense trade was done on the Westport line
" with passengers, parcels, and fish.   I was very con-
" tented for about eighteen months, when I applied for
" a change, and was promised Sligo.   But Mr. Bianconi
" was induced to change his mind, and he told me in
" Longfield I was to go back again to Athenry, which
" I refused to do.   He insisted that I should, and that
" I should have an increase of pay from the time I was
" twelve months there.   I asked how much, but he
" would not tell me until I should be there two years.
" Of course I went back, and when the time had
" expired, I had a letter to say that my salary was to
" be £60 a-year, to date from a twelvemonths after I
" had been there.

   " On one of my visits afterwards to Longfield, Mr.

" Bianconi asked me if it was true that I was going to
" be married. I told him it was not. He then asked
" was there anything about a certain lady, and if she
" had a lot of money. I said she had money. 'But
" you would not marry her,' he said. I said, 'No.'
" 'That's right,' said he; 'never marry for money, but
" marry for love.'

" My long and faithful service at that station,—five
" years,—was rewarded. In 1859 I did get married, and
" was then moved to Sligo, where a large field was open
" to me. We had thirty-three horses standing in charge
" of six grooms; a long car came from and went out
" daily to Enniskillen, one to Strabane for Derry, one
" to Westport, one to Bellaghy, and three coaches to
" Mullingar and Longford, meeting the train to Dublin,
" on one of which the far-famed guard, M'Clusky, tra-
" velled. I could not attempt to describe the ready
" wit or the good-humoured jokes with which he made
" up stories suitable for his passengers. For the days
" that he was to be on the coach seats were often secured
" a week beforehand, so popular was he with the tra-
" vellers.

" In July, 1862, the workmen were removed from
" Longford to Sligo; and, as I had always made strong
" representations against building the cars so heavy, I
" hoped to be able to remodel them; but, strange to
" say, Mr. Bianconi would not consent, and it was only
" in May, 1865, when he saw one of a light weight that
" I had just finished building, and I had proved to him
" that it was as strong as one of the old kind, which

" was once and a half as heavy, that he consented to
" have all the others made lighter. The opening of
" the railway from Longford to Sligo did away with
" our coach line, but I soon found that it made an
" opening for a summer car to Bundoran; and having
" put my views before Mr. Bianconi, he immediately
" sent me the horses asked for, and was so well pleased
" with the result that he ordered me to charge him with
" commission on the receipts in addition to my salary,
" —a thing unprecedented in the establishment. In
" the year 1866 he wrote to Mr. O'Brien, the travelling
" agent, to meet him here in Sligo; and when we had
" talked over business, he said, 'I have brought ye
" together to know would ye buy all my establishment
" to the north and west of the line between Dublin and
" Galway.' We agreed to do so, but his own accident,
" which happened soon afterwards, put an end to the
" arrangement. However, he sent for us in March,
" 1867, and sold to us the portion we each required at
" our own price. Mine extended from Westport, in
" Mayo, to Letterkenny, in County Donegal; and after
" the purchase was made out, Mr. Bianconi said his
" terms were half the money in hand, and the other
" half in monthly instalments. I told him that in that
" case I could not treat with him. He said, 'What do
" you mean? You have money.' I said, 'If I have,
" I am not going to give it to you. If you expect ever
" to be repaid you must not only trust to our word, but
" you must give us plenty of money to work the lines.'
" He paused for a long time, and kept looking at me.

"Then he said, 'John, you are right; it shall be as
"you say.' It is needless to add that he did so, and
"long after I had paid him back he would try to force
"me to take money I did not want, and he always
"manifested that interest in my business which caused
"me to apply to him in any cases of difficulty for his
"advice, which was cheerfully given, and which I am
"sorry to say I shall miss for the future.

"I must apologize, dear Mrs. O'Connell, for the
"length of this letter, but I had to touch on the various
"stages to show that he fulfilled his promise when he
"said that he would make a man of
"Your faithful servant,
"JOHN WALSH."

The following is an extract from Mr. Anthony Trollope's History of the Irish Post-office, published in the
Postmaster-General's Report for 1857 :—

"In 1827, and for many years previously, the payment for carrying the mails was 5*d*. the double Irish
mile. The average is still much the same, being 2*d*.
the English mile, which is within a fraction equal to 5*d*.
the double Irish mile. But though the work done is no
cheaper, it is much better. The old system of getting
the cross mails carried by any animal that the conscience
of the local postmaster thought good enough for such a
service does not, however, appear to have been interfered
with by the authorities, but to have been gradually
amended by the commercial enterprise of a foreigner.

"In 1815 Mr. Bianconi first carried his Majesty's mails in Ireland, but he did so for many years without any contract. He commenced in the County Tipperary, between Clonmel and Cahir, and he then made his own bargain with the postmaster, as he did for many subsequent years. The postmaster usually retained one moiety of the sum allowed as his own perquisite, and Mr. Bianconi performed the work for the remainder. The sum that Mr. Bianconi received was thus very small, and therefore he could not, and would not, run his cars at any hours inconvenient to his passenger traffic, or any faster than was convenient to himself.

"From 1830, when the English and Irish Post-offices were amalgamated under the Duke of Richmond, the public, as Mr. Bianconi says, got something like fair play, and he and others were allowed to carry the mails by direct contract with the Post-office.

"From that time till 1848 Mr. Bianconi continued to increase his establishment, and in latter years he had 1,400 horses, and daily covered 3,800 miles. The opening of railways has, however, so greatly interfered with his traffic as to expel his cars from the main lines. But Mr. Bianconi has met the changes of the times in a resolute spirit. He has always been ready at a moment's notice to move his horses, cars, and men to any district, however remote, where any chance of business might show itself. And now, in the winter of 1856 and 1857, he still covers 2,250 miles, and is the owner of above 1,000 horses, working in the four provinces from the town of

Wexford in the south-east to the mountains of Donegal in the north-west. Mr. Bianconi has done good service. By birth he is well known to be Italian; but he is now naturalised, and England, as well as Ireland, should be ready to acknowledge his merits. It may perhaps be said that no living man has worked more than he has for the benefit of the sister kingdom.

"While on the subject of the conveyance of mails, it may be well to point out that it was reported in 1829 by the Commissioners, who had then for many years been inquiring into the Irish Post-office, that the night mail-coaches then working, and which covered 1,450 miles, cost upwards of £30,000, whereas the same conveyance over the same distance in England would, according to the evidence of Mr. C. Johnson, the English superintendent of mail-coaches, have cost only £7,500. This was the more singular, as forage and labour were much cheaper in Ireland than in England. But it was accounted for by the fact that the whole business was in the hands of a very few persons, and that the local innkeepers could not be induced to embark in the trade. To that cause may probably be added this other, that at the period in question jobbing was not yet extinct in Ireland. The excess has, however, entirely disappeared. Indeed, in Ireland the work is now done cheaper than in England,—the cost in England being $2\frac{1}{4}d.$ a mile; in Scotland, $2\frac{1}{2}d.$; in Ireland, $2d.$*

"In no part of the United Kingdom has more been

---

* These were the rates in 1855. But in 1856 the rates were, in England, $2\frac{1}{2}d.$; Scotland, $3d.$; Ireland, $2d.$

done for the welfare of the people by the use of railways for the carrying mails, and by the penny post-
age, than in Ireland. In 1784 there were then posts
six days a week on only four lines of road, letters to all
other places being conveyed only twice or thrice a
week. Now there are daily posts to almost every
village, and I know of but one important town that has
not two daily mails both with London and Dublin. I
think this proves, as regards the Post-office, that the
Government has not forgotten its paternal duties.

" ANTHONY TROLLOPE."

The following papers give some statistics of my
father's coach and car establishment. They are a
collection of papers read at meetings of the British
Association for the Advancement of Science, and of
the National Association for the Promotion of Social
Science. They were published collectively in Dublin
in the year 1869, and by my father's express wish I
now here reproduce them.

I.—PAPER READ BY MR. BIANCONI AT THE CORK MEETING
OF THE BRITISH ASSOCIATION FOR THE ADVANCE-
MENT OF SCIENCE, August 19th, 1843.

Up to the year 1815, the public accommodation for the
conveyance of passengers in Ireland was confined to a
few mail and day coaches on the great lines of road.

From my peculiar position in the country, I had
ample opportunities of reflecting on many things, and

nothing struck me more forcibly than the want of a cheap and easy means of locomotion. The inconvenience felt by this want of more extended means of intercourse, particularly between the different market towns, gave great advantage to the few at the expense of the many; and it also caused a great loss of time. For instance, a farmer living twenty or thirty miles from his market town spent the first day in going there, a second day in doing his business, and a third day in returning.

In July, 1815, I started a car for the conveyance of passengers from Clonmel to Cahir, which I subsequently extended to Tipperary and Limerick. At the end of the same year I started similar cars from Clonmel to Cashel and Thurles, and from Clonmel to Carrick and Waterford ; and I have since extended my establishment into the most thinly populated localities. I have now cars running from Longford to Ballina and Belmullet, which is 201 miles north-west of Dublin, from Athlone to Galway and Clifden, 183 miles due west of Dublin, from Limerick to Tralee and Caherciveen, 233 miles south-west of Dublin. There are now in the establishment 100 vehicles, including mail-coaches and different-sized cars, capable of carrying from four to twenty passengers each, and travelling eight or nine miles an hour, at an average of one penny farthing per mile for each passenger, and which in all perform daily 3,800 miles, pass through over 140 stations for the change of horses, and consume from 3,000 to 4,000 tons of hay, and from 30,000 to 40,000 barrels of oats, annually, both of which are purchased in their respective localities.

The establishment is not at work on Sundays,—with the exception of those portions of it as are in connection with the Post-office or canals,—for the following reasons: first, the Irish being a religious people, will not travel on business on Sundays; and secondly, experience teaches me that I can work a horse eight miles per day, six days in the week, much better than I can six miles for seven days; and by not working on Sundays, I effect a saving of 12 per cent.

The advantages derived by the country from this establishment are almost incalculable; for instance,—the farmer who formerly drove, spent three days in making his market, can now do so in one, for a few shillings; thereby saving two clear days, and the expense and use of his horse.

The example has been generally followed, and cars innumerable leave the interior for the principal towns in the south of Ireland, which bring parties to and from markets at an enormous saving of time, and in many instances cheaper than they could walk.

The establishment has been in existence twenty-eight years, travelling with its mails at all hours of the day and night, and has never met any interruption in the performance of its arduous duties. Much surprise has often been expressed at the high order of men connected with it, and at its popularity: but people who thus express themselves forget, I think, to look at Irish society with sufficient grasp. For my part, I cannot

better compare it than to a man becoming convales-
cent after a serious attack of malignant fever, and
requiring generous and nutritious food, in place of
medical treatment. I take my drivers from the lowest
grade of the establishment; they are progressively
advanced according to their respective merits, as
opportunity offers, and they know that nothing can
deprive them of these rewards, and also of a pension of
their full wages in case of old age or accident, unless
it be their own wilful and improper conduct. As to
the popularity of my service, I never yet attempted to
do an act of generosity or common justice, publicly or
privately, that I was not met by manifold reciprocity.

I regret that my friend Dr. Taylor should have so
suddenly called upon me to take part in this Association, instead of giving me an opportunity to prepare
a document worthy of their acceptance; but such as
this is, it is perfectly at their service, and with my best
wishes.

In reply to a question as to the number of persons in
his employment, Mr. Bianconi said that, before answering the question, he would illustrate his mode of manag-
ing the establishment. Any man found guilty of
uttering a falsehood, however venial, was instantly
dismissed; and this, consequently, insured truth, accuracy, and punctuality. This being his fundamental
principle of management, he himself would not venture
on returning a positive answer to the question. They
could judge how many men were employed, when he
stated that there were 140 stations, and that each

station had from one to six, or even eight, grooms; there were about 100 drivers, and about 1,300 horses. The rate of travelling was from eight to nine miles an hour, including stoppages; and as for remuneration, in proportion as he advanced one of his drivers, he lowered his wages. This might seem wonderful, but such was the fact. He advanced his driver by placing him on a more lucrative line, where his certainty of receiving fees from the passengers was greater. The drivers on the least paying roads received higher wages, their fees being low. He said that he would have referred more to the innate sense of morals common to the people of Ireland, in order to exhibit how easy it was for him to manage with facility and success such an extended establishment, were he not afraid of English criticism. He could not personally inspect each station, —a year would be employed in that alone,—but he acted to those he employed as he would wish them to act towards him,—he made them believe they were not his slaves, but fellow-citizens, differing from him only in gradation. He also made them feel that in doing their work they conferred on him a greater benefit than he did on them by payment of wages. He asserted, in answer to a question put, that his cars had never once been stopped, and that even in the time of the Whiteboy insurrection, and when Kilkenny was disturbed, though he had the carriage of a most important mail— the Dublin mail—for a part of the road, he was never interrupted; he repeatedly passed hundreds of the people on the road at night and yet not one asked

him where he was going.   This showed the high
bearing of the people, and the respect they had for the
laws of their country.

II.—Paper read by Mr. Bianconi at the Dublin
Meeting of the British Association for the
Advancement of Science, August, 1857.

Referring to the synopsis of my establishment, sub-
mitted in a concise form to your Association at its
session in Cork, in 1843, I now take the liberty of
submitting some further particulars, embracing its
origin, with its present condition, and the extent of
its operations. My establishment originated immediately after the peace of 1815, having then had the
advantage of a supply of first-class horses intended for
the army, which I bought from ten to twenty pounds
apiece,—one of which drew a car and six persons with
ease at the rate of seven miles an hour. The demand
for such horses having ceased, the breeding of them
naturally diminished, and, after some time, I found it
necessary to put two inferior horses to do the work of
one. Finding I thus had extra horse power, I increased
the size of the car which originally held six passengers,
—three on each side,—to one capable of carrying eight ;
and in proportion as the breed of horses improved, I
continued to increase the size of the cars for summer
work, and to add to the number of horses in winter, for
the conveyance of the same number of passengers, until
I converted the two-wheeled two-horse cars into four

wheeled cars drawn by two, three, or four horses,
according to the traffic on the respective roads, and the
wants of the public. The freedom of communication
has greatly added to the elevation of the lower classes;
for in proportion as they found that travelling on a
car with a saving of time, was cheaper than walking
with a loss of it, they began to appreciate the value of
speedy communication, and hence have been, to an
almost incalculable extent, travellers by my cars,
whereby they were enabled to mix with the better
orders of society, and their own moral elevation has
been of a decided character. As the establishment extended I was surprised and delighted at its commercial
and moral importance. I found, as soon as I had
opened communication with the interior of the country,
the consumption of manufactured goods greatly increased. The facility for conveying goods enabled the
consumer to buy his wares more directly from the
manufacturer, and he consequently bought them cheaper
than when they had passed through the hands of many
retail dealers. For instance, in the more remote parts
of Ireland, before my cars ran from Tralee to Caherciveen in the south, from Galway to Clifden in the
west, and from Ballina to Belmullet in the north-
west, purchasers were obliged to give eight or nine
pence a yard for calico for shirts, which they afterwards
bought for three and four pence. The poor people,
therefore, who previously could ill afford to buy one
shirt, were enabled to buy two for a less price than they
had paid for one, and in the same ratio other commo-

dities came into general use at reduced prices. The formation of my first car conveying passengers back to back, on the principle of the outside car now so much used in Dublin, was admirably adapted to its purposes, and it frequently happened that, whilst on one side were sitting some of the higher classes, the poorer people would seat themselves on the other. Not only was this unaccompanied with any inconvenience, but I consider its effects were very salutary; as many who had no *status* were, by coming into communication with the educated classes, inspired with the importance of, and respect for, social position. The growth and extent of railways necessarily affected my establishment and diminished its operation, by withdrawing from it ten two-wheeled cars, travelling daily 450 miles; twenty-two four-wheeled cars, travelling daily 1,620 miles; five coaches, travelling daily 376 miles,—thus making a total falling off of thirty-seven vehicles, travelling daily 2,446 miles. Notwithstanding the result of the extension of railways, I still have over 900 horses, working thirty-five two-wheeled cars, travelling daily 1,752 miles; twenty-two four-wheeled cars, travelling daily 1,500 miles; ten coaches, travelling daily 992 miles,—making in the whole sixty-seven conveyances, travelling daily 4,244 miles, and extending over portions of twenty-two counties, viz :—Cork, Clare, Carlow, Cavan, Donegal, Fermanagh, Galway, King's County, Kilkenny, Kerry, Limerick, Longford, Leitrim, Mayo, Queen's County, Roscommon, Sligo, Tipperary, Tyrone, Waterford, Wexford, and Westmeath. Anxious to aid as well as I could the resources of the country, many of which lay so long unproductive, I endeavoured, as far as it was practicable, to effect so desirable an object. For instance, I enabled the fishermen on the western coast to avail themselves of a rapid transit for their fresh fish, which, being a very perishable article, would be comparatively profitless unless its conveyance to Dublin and other suitable markets could be insured within a given time. So that those engaged in the fisheries of Clifden, Westport, and other places, sending their produce by my conveyances on one day, could rely on its reaching its destination the following morning,—additional horses and special conveyances being provided and put on in the proper seasons. The amount realised by this valuable traffic is almost incredible, and has, in my opinion, largely contributed to the comfort and independence of the people now so happily contrasting with the lamentable condition of the west of Ireland a few years since. I shall conclude with two observations, which, I think, illustrate the increasing prosperity of the country, and the progress of its inhabitants. First, although the population has so considerably decreased by emigration and other causes, the proportion of travellers by my conveyances is greater,—thus demonstrating that the people appreciate, not only the money value of time, but also the advantages of an establishment designed and worked for their particular use and development, now forty-two years in operation. Secondly, the peaceable and high moral bearing of the

Irish people, which can only be known and duly felt by those who live amongst them, and who have had long and constant intercourse with them. I have therefore been equally surprised and pained to observe in portions of the respectable press, both in England and Ireland, repeated attacks on the morality of our population, charging them with a proneness to violate the laws, and with a disregard of private property. But as one plain truth is worth a thousand bare assertions, I offer in contradiction of those statements this indisputable fact :—
My conveyances, many of them carrying very important mails, have been travelling during all hours of the day and night, often in lonely and unfrequented places, and during the long period of forty-two years that my establishment is now in existence, the slightest injury has never been done by the people to my property, or that intrusted to my care ; and this fact gives me greater pleasure than any pride I might feel in reflecting upon the other rewards of my life's labour.

III.—Paper read by Mr. Bianconi at the Dublin Meeting of the National Association for the Promotion of Social Science, August, 1861.

Having in 1843 and in 1857 presented to the British Association, at the sessions in Cork and Dublin, a synopsis of my establishment in Ireland, which was received with a degree of interest to which I could have scarcely deemed it entitled, I now venture for the third, and perhaps the last time, to refer again to the subject, because I think it bears on the rise and progress of the social condition of this country.

In 1807-8 I was living at Carrick-on-Suir, distant from Waterford, by road sixteen, and by the river Suir about thirty miles; and the only public mode of conveyance for passengers between these two places, together containing a population of between thirty and forty thousand inhabitants, was Tom Morrissy's boat, which carried from eight to ten persons, and which, besides being obliged to wait the tide, took from four to five hours to perform the journey, at a fare of sixpence halfpenny of the then currency. At the time the railway opened, in 1853, there was between the two towns horse-power capable of conveying by cars and coaches one hundred passengers daily, performing the journey in less than two hours, at a fare of two shillings, thus showing that the people not only began to understand the value of time, but also to appreciate it.

However strange it may appear, I have always entertained the belief that my having come to this country without a knowledge of the language was of advantage to me. I had more time for observation and reflection, by which I was impressed with the great want of such an establishment as I originated, and to the formation of which two circumstances mainly contributed.

Firstly, the tax on carriages, by which the middle classes were precluded from using their own vehicles.

Secondly, the general peace that followed the battle

of Waterloo, and by which a great number of first-class horses, bred for the army, were thrown on the market with very little competition existing for their purchase.

The family outside jaunting-car, thus expelled from general use by a carriage-tax, suggested itself to me as being admirably adapted for my purpose; and I was enabled to procure these vehicles on very moderate terms. The state of the roads was such as to limit the rate of travelling to about seven miles an hour, and also obliging the passengers to walk up the hills. Thus all classes were brought together, and I have felt much pleasure in believing that the intercourse thus created tended to inspire the higher grades with respect and regard for the natural good qualities of the humbler people, which the latter reciprocated by a becoming deference and an anxiety to please. Such a moral benefit appears to me worthy of special notice and congratulation.

At the commencement of my establishment in 1815, which was principally confined for several years to the south of Ireland, the conveyance of the cross mails was confided to local postmasters, who generally farmed them out, and the duty was performed by men who rode on horseback, or else walked. On the 6th of July 1815, I had the pleasure of being the first to establish the conveyance of the cross mails by cars, having undertaken to carry the Cahir and Clonmel mail for the postmaster of Cahir, for half the amount he was himself paid for sending it, by a mule and a bad horse alternately. I subsequently became a contractor for the conveyance of several cross mails at a price not exceeding half the amount the Government had paid the post-masters for doing this duty; and it was not until Lord O'Neill and Lord Ross ceased to be Postmasters-General of Ireland, and that the Duke of Richmond became the Postmaster-General of the United Kingdom, under the Government of Lord Grey, and that the local postmasters were no longer appointed exclusively from one section of the community, that the conveyance of all the cross mails was set up to public competition, to be carried on the principle of my establishment. It is impossible to over-estimate the advantage derived by the public from this change; for the local postmasters, who dared not report their regularity of their own contractors in the performance of their duty, became extremely strict in seeing that the new contractors performed their duties regularly, and by this new system the public received their letters upon an average of nearly thirty per cent. saving of time.

As railways may now be said to be the great civilisers of the age, by bringing people into communication, who, but for the facilities of travelling, would be unknown to each other, so my cars, at an earlier period, opened between different parts of Ireland an intercourse which had not previously existed.

Notwithstanding the inroads made on my establishment by the railways, and which displaced over 1,000 horses, and obliged me to direct my attention to such portions of the country as had not before the benefit of my conveyances, it still employs about 900 horses, travelling over 4,000 miles daily, passing through twenty-three counties, having 137 stations, and working twelve mail and day coaches 672 miles; fifty four-wheeled cars, with two and more horses, travelling 1,930 miles; and sixty-six two-wheeled one-horse cars, travelling 1,604 miles.

The commencement of my car establishment in the county of Tipperary, in the year 1815, was a matter of great surprise to many, as at that time the country was much disorganized, owing principally to the maladministration of the laws, and to the almost total severance of the bond which ought to have united the upper and humbler classes of society. This sad state of things was afterwards improved by the efforts made to obtain Catholic Emancipation, which the people were taught to believe could only be obtained by obedience to the laws and by self-reliance, both of which were respected by the increasing liberality of public opinion.

The benefits conferred by the establishment of petty sessions cannot be over-estimated; they soon proved most salutary in inspiring the people with respect for the law; for as power was deputed to these local courts from the quarter sessions, and to the latter from the superior courts, not only was confidence in the administration of justice strengthened and more diffused, but the evil of consigning great numbers untried from one assizes to another, to the demoralizing influence of the gaol, thereby exposing those who might be innocent to certain degradation, and rendering the guilty more depraved, was in a great degree obviated. Nor can I avoid reference to the visible effects produced by education and the Reformatory movement, so admirably calculated to check crime in its infancy, and to restore to society those who would, under the old system, have crowded the public prisons, have been lost to themselves, and have become a curse to the community. I have ever regarded the impartial and regular discharge of the duties at petty sessions as one of the most useful aids in tranquillising the country and improving the habits of the people, which, in Ireland, I rejoice to say, can now bear comparison with those of any other nation.

I shall conclude with a hope that the Social Science Association may often receive a deserved welcome in this my adopted country, and that on each recurring visit, it will have to place on its records satisfactory proofs of the moral, intellectual, and physical progress of Ireland.

IV.—PAPER READ BY DR. NEILSON HANCOCK AT THE BELFAST MEETING OF THE NATIONAL ASSOCIATION FOR THE PROMOTION OF SOCIAL SCIENCE, 1867.

AT several meetings of the British Association for the Advancement of Science, and the National Association for the Promotion of Social Science in Ireland, Mr. Bianconi has attended, and has given some Statistics of the progress of his enterprise. He has unfortunately been prevented in this instance by an accident from being present,* but has placed the Statistics up to the period of his retiring from business in my hands, and I have embodied the results in the following paper.

Doubts are frequently expressed as to whether the scarcity of manufactures in the south and west of Ireland arises from the absence of coal and iron, or from some defect in the people which mars enterprise, however well conceived or well planned.

For the solution of such a question,—the most important that can occupy a Social Science Congress in Ireland,—a good test to apply would be the observation of some enterprise conducted on the same principle in different parts of Ireland, conducted too on a sufficiently large scale, or for a sufficient length of time, to afford satisfactory evidence of its success or failure.

Now, the statistics of such an enterprise have been placed in my hands. I have examined them, and I propose to submit to this department the results of that examination.

Mr. Bianconi, the great coach and car proprietor, has recently handed over to his agents on very liberal terms the different lines he was working.

He commenced operations as a car proprietor in 1815, and after the lapse of half a century, has retired from a thriving and prosperous business, having at the time he retired a traffic extending over 2,506 miles worked daily.

* Mr. Bianconi broke his thigh on the 5th October, 1866, and has consequently been confined to his room for the greater part of the past year, during which he was obliged to retire from business altogether.

The regular progress by which the traffic was produced, is indicated by the following figures:—

Established.					Miles Worked Daily.
1815 to 1825	.	.	.	.	1,170
1826 to 1835	.	.	.	.	1,064
1836 to 1845	.	.	.	.	1,032
					——
Established before Railways.					3,266
1846 to 1855	.	.	.	.	2,656
1856 to 1865	.	.	.	.	938
					——
Established since Railways .					3,594
					——
Total Established	.				6,860

It might be expected that railways would injure if not overthrow the traffic, but in the enterprising hands of Mr. Bianconi it only changed its direction.

The judgment with which the earlier lines were planned, is shown by the small number discontinued before the introduction of railways.

Lines Discontinued.					Miles Worked.
1815 to 1825	.	.	.	.	Nil.
1826 to 1835	.	.	.	.	Nil.
1836 to 1845	.	.	.	.	76
					—
Discontinued before Railways .					76
1846 to 1855	.	.	.	.	2,214
1856 to 1865	.	.	.	.	2,064
					——
Discontinued since Railways	.				4,278
					——
Total Discontinued	.		.		4,354

If we deduct the total number of miles discontinued (4,354) from the total number ever established (6,860), we get 2,506, the number of miles in 1865, which is only 684 below the maximum number (3,190) in 1845, before railways interfered with the traffic.

The next matter to notice is the character of the traffic.

Mr. Bianconi's great idea was that we never should despise poor people, or apparently small interests. His great enterprise arose from the problems:—how to make a two-wheeled car pay while running for the accommodation of poor districts and poor people, as regularly as the mail coaches did for the rich; and when that was solved, how to regulate a system of traffic by a network of cars,—the cars increasing in size as the traffic required, from the short two-horse car holding six people, to the long four-horse car holding twenty people.

His use of stage coaches arose altogether from the mail contracts, and not from any want of confidence in the car system. To the last Mr. Bianconi never despised the two-wheeled car, for to this he owed his fortune.

The traffic amongst the conveyances is thus distributed :—

	Miles ever Worked.	Final Traffic.
Two Wheels	1,286	802
Four Wheels	3,988	1,396
Coaches	1,586	308
Total	6,860	2,506

The extent of Ireland over which the traffic was diffused when Mr. Bianconi retired, may be judged by the fact that we find his conveyances at Dungarvan,

Waterford, and Wexford, on the east coast; at Tralee,
Galway, Clifden, Westport, and Belmullet, in the
west; at Bandon, Rosscarbery, Skibbereen, and Caherciveen, in the south; and at Sligo, Enniskillen, Strabane, and Letterkenny, in the north; whilst in the
centre of Ireland we find the towns of Clonmel, Thurles,
Kilkenny, Birr, and Ballinasloe.

The history of Mr. Bianconi's establishment dis-
closes some interesting results in Social Science. It
appears that he organized his establishment on a
system of promotion and pensions rarely adopted
except in public departments. His drivers, being
taken from the lowest grade of the establishment, and
progressively advanced according to their respective
merits as opportunities offered, were allowed to retire
on pensions either from old age, incapacity, or sickness,
and the orphan children of the grooms and others were
educated by him, and afterwards filled the situation of
their deceased parents.

The great experience of Mr. Bianconi from the dura-
tion of his undertaking, and the extent of the country
over which it extended, makes his testimony as to the
conduct of the people towards himself most valuable.
He has informed me that he could repeat now what he
said at the British Association in 1857:

"My conveyances, many of them carrying very important mails,
have been travelling during all hours of the day and night, often in
lonely and unfrequented places, and during the long period of forty-
two years (now fifty-two, in 1867) that my establishment is now in
existence, the slightest injury has never been done by the people to
my property, or that intrusted to my care; and this fact gives me

greater pleasure than any pride I might feel in reflecting upon the other rewards of my life's labour."

He wishes, too, to repeat what he said at the British Association in Cork, in 1843:

"That he never yet attempted to do an act of generosity or common justice, publicly or privately, that he was not met by manifold reciprocity."

The Official Statistics of Crime corroborate Mr. Bianconi's evidence as to the suggestive absence of crime connected with opposition to trade or manufacture in Ireland.

Mr. Bianconi has now retired from active life at the age of eighty, after a long and honourable career. He came to this country—a young foreigner—in 1802. He commenced his great enterprise in 1815, and he suffered from the legal disabilities then imposed on foreigners. The support of Sir Robert Peel, when Home Secretary, was unable to secure him letters of naturalisation when he first applied for them to the Privy Council in Ireland, and it was not until he had been resident in Ireland for twenty-nine years, that in 1831 this recognition of citizenship was at length granted, during the administration of Earl Grey, his application being supported by the Grand Jury of Tipperary, where he resided.

His history, I think, shows that foreigners may succeed in Ireland as well as natives.

We may congratulate Mr. Bianconi on his retirement in having truly served his adopted country, not only by the great system of traffic which he organized and developed, but on his having afforded the strongest

proof that there is nothing in the character of the
inhabitants of the most Celtic districts in Ireland to
prevent the success of any enterprise, however extensive, which is conducted with such energy, ability,
good feeling, and sound sense as he has displayed.

He has shown, too, that we must look for the causes
of the scanty development of manufactures in the south
and west of Ireland to the want of coal and iron and
flax, and to the absence of the advantages which the
long possession of the facilities for obtaining these has
given to more favoured countries, rather than to the
theories hitherto prevalent about the unsuitabilities of
the Irish people for such labour:

STATISTICS OF LINES ESTABLISHED.

Lines Established.	Distance.	Date when Established.	No. of Miles Worked Daily.	Two-wheeled Cars.	Four-wheeled Cars.*	Coaches.
Clonmel and Limerick	50	1815	100	...	100	...
Clonmel and Thurles	31	1815	62	...	62	...
Clonmel and Waterford, 10 o'clock	32	1816	64	...	64	...
Waterford and Ross	15	1818	30	...	30	...
Waterford and Wexford	40	1819	80	...	80	...
Waterford and Enniscorthy	36	1819	72	...	72	...
Clonmel and Waterford (Regulator)	32	1820	64	...	...	64
Clonmel and Waterford (Telegraph)	32	1821	64	...	64	...
Clonmel and Cork	65	1821	130	...	130	...
Clonmel and Kilkenny	33	1821	66	...	66	...
Kilkenny and Waterford	32	1822	64	...	64	...
Clonmel and Thurles	31	1822	62	...	62	...
Thurles and Kilkenny	31	1822	62	62	...	...
Roscrea and Portumna	28	1822	56	56	...	...
Tipperary and Cashel	13	1824	26	...	26	...
Waterford and Dungarvan	28	1824	56	...	...	56
Dungarvan and Lismore	16	1824	32	32	...	...
Wexford Mail	40	1825	80	...	80	...
Total	585		1,170	150	900	120
Thurles and Roscrea	23	1826	46	...	46	...
Tipperary and Clonmel, 3 o'clock	30	1828	60	...	60	...
Tipperary and Clonmel Night Mail	30	1828	60	60	...	...
Limerick and Cork	40	1830	80	...	80	...
Clonmel and Dungarvan	26	1831	52	...	52	...
Athlone and Longford	24	1831	48	48	...	...
Waterford and Kilkenny	32	1831	64	...	64	...
Birr and Ballinasloe	26	1831	52	52	...	...
Sligo and Longford	56	1832	112	...	112	...
Limerick and Tralee Car	62	1833	124	...	124	...
Limerick and Tralee Coach	60	1833	120	...	...	120
Ross and Carlow	22	1833	44	...	44	...
Limerick and Galway	64	1834	128	...	...	128
Kilkenny and Mountmellick	37	1835	74	...	74	...
Total	532		1,064	160	656	248
Killarney and Caherciveen	37	1836	74	74	...	...
Tralee and Caherciveen	16	1836	32	32	...	...
Ballinasloe and Westport	75	1836	150	...	150	...
Ballinasloe and Galway	34	1836	68	...	68	...
Mitchelstown and Mallow	21	1837	42	...	42	...
Longford and Castlerea	27	1837	54	...	...	54
Galway and Clifden, 9·30 o'clock	50	1837	100	...	100	...
Limerick and Killarney	15	1839	30	...	30	...
Ballinasloe and Athlone	15	1839	30	...	30	...
Ross and Fethard	20	1840	40	40	...	...
Longford and Ballina	71	1840	142	...	142	...
Clonmel and Roscrea	56	1842	112	...	112	...
Ennis and Ballinasloe	38	1844	76	...	76	...
Ballina and Belmullet	41	1844	82	...	82	...
Total	516		1,032	146	832	54
Total before Railways	1,633		3,266	456	2,388	422

* The lines upon which four-wheeled cars came to be used are so classed, though in many cases they were commenced with two-wheeled cars.

STATISTICS OF LINES ESTABLISHED.

Lines Established.	Distance.	Date when Established.	No. of Miles Worked Daily.	Two-wheeled Cars.	Four-wheeled Cars.	Coaches.
Mullingar and Longford	26	1848	52	...	52	...
Westport Mail	62	1849	124	...	...	124
Mullingar and Sligo Mail	82	1849	164	...	...	164
Mullingar and Sligo Day	82	1849	164	...	...	164
Mullingar and Galway Mail	70	1849	140	...	...	140
Mullingar and Galway Day	70	1849	140	...	...	140
Mullingar and Carrick-on-Shannon	50	1849	100	...	...	100
Waterford and Gooldscross	51	1849	102	102	...	...
Templemore and Athlone	51	1849	102	...	102	...
Clonmel and Gooldscross	21	1849	42	42	...	...
Clonmel and Gooldscross Coach	21	1849	42	...	...	42
Gooldscross and Cashel, 6 o'clock	6	1849	12	12	...	...
Athlone and Ballina	70	1851	140	...	...	140
Galway and Boyle	50	1851	100	...	100	...
Athlone and Roscommon	19	1851	38	...	38	...
Galway and Westport	52	1851	104	...	...	104
Limerick and Tipperary	23	1851	46	...	...	46
Galway and Clifden Mail	50	1851	100	100	...	...
Limerick and Ennis Mail	22	1852	44	...	44	...
Sligo and Strabane	71	1852	142	...	142	...
Sligo and Enniskillen	30	1852	60	...	60	...
Sligo and Westport	62	1852	124	...	124	...
Tuam and Claremorris Day	17	1852	34	34	...	...
Tuam and Claremorris Mail	17	1853	34	34	...	...
Kilkenny and Durrow	16	1853	32	...	32	...
Athenry and Westport	61	1853	122	...	122	...
Waterford and Maryborough	62	1853	124	...	124	...
Limerick and Ennis Day	22	1854	44	...	44	...
Killarney and Mallow	41	1854	82	82	...	...
Tralee and Mallow	51	1854	102	...	102	...
Total	1,328		2,656	406	1,086	1,164
Westport and Newport	8	1857	16	16	...	...
Strabane and Letterkenny	15	1857	30	30	...	...
Bandon and Skibbereen Mail	33	1857	66	...	66	...
Bandon and Rosscarbery	20	1857	40	...	40	...
Ballinasloe and Ballybrophy	48	1858	96	96	...	...
Ennis and Oranmore	36	1859	72	72	...	...
Enniskillen and Omagh	64	1860	128	...	128	...
Enniskillen and Bundoran	30	1861	60	...	60	...
Tuam and Dunmore	10	1861	220	220	...	...
Castlebar and Ballina	26	1862	52	...	52	...
Kilkenny and Urlingford	16	1862	32	...	32	...
Waterford and Passage, 6 o'clock	8	1863	16	...	16	...
Waterford and Passage, 3 o'clock	8	1863	16	...	16	...
Castlerea and Ballina	43	1864	86	86	...	...
Westport and Swinford	27	1864	54	54	...	...
Letterkenny and Strabane	15	1864	30	...	30	...
Ross and Wexford	25	1864	50	50	...	...
Killarney and Caherciveen	37	1865	74	...	74	...
Total	469		938	424	514	
Total after Railways	1,797		3,594	830	1,600	1,164
Total before Railways	1,633		3,266	456	2,388	422
General Total	3,430		6,860	1,286	3,988	1,586

STATISTICS OF LINES DISCONTINUED.

Lines Discontinued.	Date when Discontinued.	No. of Miles Worked Daily.	Two-wheeled Cars.	Four-wheeled Cars.	Coaches.
Waterford and Ross ...	1836	30	...	30	...
Thurles and Roscrea ...	1842	46	...	46	...
Total before Railways		76		76	
Wexford Mail ...	1846	80	...	80	...
Tipperary and Cashel	1847	26	...	26	...
Clonmel and Limerick	1849	100	...	100	...
Clonmel and Thurles	1849	62	...	62	...
Tipperary and Clonmel Night Mail	1849	60	60	...	...
Limerick and Cork ...	1849	80	...	80	...
Clonmel and Roscrea	1849	112	...	112	...
Ennis and Ballinasloe	1849	76	...	76	...
Kilkenny and Waterford	1851	64	...	64	...
Longford and Castlerea	1851	54	...	...	54
Ballinasloe and Athlone	1851	30	...	30	...
Longford and Ballina	1851	142	...	142	...
Tipperary and Clonmel, 3 o'clock ...	1852	60	...	60	...
Kilkenny and Mountmellick	1852	74	...	74	...
Mullingar and Galway Mail	1852	140	...	...	140
Mullingar and Galway Day ...	1852	140	...	...	140
Clonmel and Gooldscross Coach	1852	42	...	...	42
Clonmel and Waterford, 10 o'clock	1853	64	...	64	...
Clonmel and Waterford Regulator	1853	64	...	...	64
Clonmel and Waterford Telegraph	1853	64	...	64	...
Clonmel and Cork	1853	130	...	130	...
Waterford and Kilkenny	1853	64	...	64	...
Limerick and Tralee Coach ...	1853	120	...	...	120
Ballinasloe and Westport	1853	150	...	150	...
Ballinasloe and Galway	1853	68	...	68	...
Limerick and Killarney	1853	30	...	30	...
Clonmel and Kilkenny	1854	66	...	66	...
Mullingar and Longford	1855	52	...	52	...
Ross and Fethard	1856	40	40	...	...
Roscrea and Portumna	1857	56	56	...	...
Templemore and Athlone	1857	102	...	102	...
Mitchelstown and Mallow ...	1858	42	...	42	...
Athlone and Ballina ...	1859	140	...	...	140
Athlone and Roscommon	1859	38	...	38	...
Limerick and Ennis Day	1859	44	...	44	...
Ross and Carlow	1860	44	...	44	...
Sligo and Longford ...	1861	112	...	112	...
Galway and Boyle ...	1861	100	...	100	...
Galway and Westport	1861	104	...	...	104
Limerick and Tipperary	1861	46	...	...	46
Athenry and Westport	1861	122	...	122	...
Mullingar and Sligo Mail	1862	164	...	...	164
Mullingar and Sligo Day	1862	164	...	...	164
Waterford and Gooldscross ...	1862	102	102	...	...
Waterford and Maryborough	1862	124	...	124	...
Mullingar and Carrick-on-Shannon	1863	100	...	...	100
Killarney and Mallow	1864	82	82	...	...
Tralee and Mallow ...	1864	102	...	102	...
Athlone and Longford	1865	48	48	...	...
Kilkenny and Durrow	1865	32	...	32	...
Ballinasloe and Ballybrophy	1865	96	96	...	...
Enniskillen and Bundoran ...	1865	60	...	60	...
Total after Railways ...		4,278	484	2,516	1,278
Total before Railways		76	...	76	...
General Total ...		4,354	484	2,502	1,278

FINAL TRAFFIC.	Date when Established.	No. of Miles Worked Daily.	Two-wheeled Cars.	Four-wheeled Cars.	Coaches.
Waterford and Wexford	1819	80	...	80	...
Waterford and Enniscorthy	1819	72	...	72	...
Clonmel and Thurles	1822	62	...	62	...
Thurles and Kilkenny	1822	62	62	...	...
Waterford and Dungarvan	1824	56	...	...	56
Dungarvan and Lismore	1824	32	32	...	...
Total		364	94	214	56
Clonmel and Dungarvan	1831	52	...	52	...
Birr and Ballinasloe	1831	52	52	...	...
Limerick and Tralee Car	1833	124	...	124	...
Limerick and Galway	1834	128	...	...	128
Total		356	52	176	128
Killarney and Caherciveen	1836	74	74	...	...
Tralee and Caherciveen	1836	32	32	...	...
Galway and Clifden, 9.30 o'clock	1837	100	...	100	...
Ballina and Belmullet	1844	82	...	82	...
Total		288	106	182	
Total before Railways		1,008	252	572	184
Westport Mail	1849	124	...	...	124
Clonmel and Gooldscross	1849	42	42	...	...
Gooldscross and Cashel, 6 o'clock	1849	12	12	...	...
Galway and Clifden Mail	1851	100	100	...	...
Limerick and Ennis Mail	1852	44	...	44	...
Sligo and Strabane	1852	142	...	142	...
Sligo and Enniskillen	1852	60	...	60	...
Sligo and Westport	1852	124	...	124	...
Tuam and Claremorris Day	1852	34	34	...	...
Tuam and Claremorris Mail	1853	34	34	...	...
Total		716	222	370	124
Westport and Newport	1857	16	16	...	...
Strabane and Letterkenny	1857	30	30	...	...
Bandon and Skibbereen	1857	66	...	66	...
Bandon and Rosscarbery	1857	40	...	40	...
Ennis and Oranmore	1859	72	72	...	...
Enniskillen and Omagh	1860	128	...	128	...
Tuam and Dunmore	1861	20	20	...	...
Castlebar and Ballina	1862	52	...	52	...
Kilkenny and Urlingford	1862	32	...	32	...
Waterford and Passage, 6 o'clock	1863	16	...	16	...
Waterford and Passage, 3 o'clock	1863	16	...	16	...
Castlerea and Ballina	1864	86	86	...	...
Westport and Swinford	1864	54	54	...	...
Letterkenny and Strabane	1864	30	...	30	...
Ross and Wexford	1864	50	50	...	...
Killarney and Caherciveen	1865	74	...	74	...
Total		782	328	454	...
Total after Railways		1,498	550	824	124
Total before Railways		1,008	252	572	184
General Total		2,506	802	1,396	308

I will conclude this chapter with some extracts from my father's Bian correspondence. I found two tin cases full of his letters (the deciphering of which cost his last clerk and me three months' hard labour) written during our three years' sojourn abroad, when my father spent at least the half of each year with his dying daughter. Nothing ever gave me a better idea of his extraordinary power of minute detail and comprehensive schemes. To get the full value out of his postage-stamp he wrote letters of more than double the length of those he usually wrote when at home; and though these letters extend only over a period of three years, what he says about the Bian establishment would apply equally well to any other time.

He had instructed his agents—Mr. Hearn, Mr. Carrigan, and Mr. O'Leary—to hold a congress at stated periods, in his absence; and his letters, though usually addressed to Mr. O'Leary, were meant to be shown to his two colleagues.

" I hope that your having only twenty-six barrels of
" oats at Clifden, in place of thirty or forty barrels,
" may be a clerical mistake, as there can be no excuse
" for so serious a deficiency. How do you account for
" Mr. Hearn's liberality to Mr. Feeny? He ought to
" have bought his old screws for £8 or £10 apiece.
" As for cars, we are swamped with machinery all over
" the country that will never yield us anything. Your
" index for March is very good. . . . . In reference
" to the pump at Gooldscross you and Mr. Hearn are
" wrong, as I intend to have a force-pump against the

" wall, and a lead-pipe down from that into the well.
" When next you see our respected friend, Father
" Kirwan, P.P., tell him that he had a great loss in
" not seeing the world's sight in the extraordinary con-
" gregation lately assembled in the Exhibition, and we
" hope he will not forget his promise of calling at
" Longfield.　I fear that, from the weakness of my
" daughter's health, I shall be delayed here until Mon-
" day. . . . . While Messrs. Hearn and Carrigan are
" with you, impress on Mr. Carrigan the necessity of
" dividing the stations into districts, and then appoint
" one from among the travelling staff to each district,
" and in no time they will have our stock complete.
" On no account allow any agent to buy even one
" barrel of oats, as I have before so frequently ex-
" plained.　In the face of this I find Mr. Carrigan
" dashing off cash to them. . . . . By all means go
" fully into the charge of immorality against F——;
" if guilty, he must be forthwith dismissed, and no
" quarter given.　Mr. Hughes is to take his place.
" Be sure no quarters are given to any one found in
" the least out of order, either in honesty or discipline.
" Rely on it we are greatly to blame for allowing the
" whole of the north and the north-western districts to
" run wild, as we have done for the want of one or
" two commissioners being sent amongst them.　I have
" the greatest confidence in Mr. Carrigan's honesty and
" zeal, but none at all in his craft. . . . .

　" Mr. Carrigan must turn his attention seriously to
" what I believe has escaped us all in his district: the

" care of washing and oiling the respective cars and
" coaches by the respective drivers; and he shall be
" held responsible for the cars in his district. From
" the state of the badly worn-out arms of axles we
" lately had to replace in these districts, I am only sur-
" prised how our horses were able to move along with
" them; therefore let you all look sharp at this, and make
" a general rout about it, to agents, drivers, &c. . . . .

" When next you see Mr. Hearn and Mr. Carrigan
" you must make arrangements to put a proper person
" to travel for us in place of ——, who is known to
" everybody; otherwise all our men, particularly those
" far west, will become demoralised. This is most
" essential, and it must be looked to at once. Do you
" compare the secret report with the way-bills? If so,
" why don't you say something? In reference to Mr.
" Cusack and Mr. Connell, and the keeping of the
" accounts, I shall be satisfied with any arrangement
" your congress may come to. . . . . .

" I am indignant at the humbugging of Sim Ryan,
" who knew how badly he was wanted at Bagnalstown
" as well as in the west, and who frittered away his
" time wantonly at Kilkenny and at Carlow. Write to
" Mr. Hearn at Callan, saying that we take the ten tons
" of hay at his price—21s. per ton—and he shall have
" the Kilkenny price for his oats, which he may com-
" mence issuing from and after the first of next month.
" And be sure you write a conciliatory letter to him to
" make amends for the improper conduct of Mr. Ryan
" towards so respectable a man. . . . . .

"Why did not the train stop a few minutes for our
"coach on the 30th ult.? See the agent at Goolds-
"cross about this; that's not the way we would treat
"them. Your unpaid letter of 13th has cost me more
"than if you had prepaid it. . . . .

"Credit Post-office cross mileage £730 17s. 8d.;
"direct mileage, £1,188 2s. 6d., and which is falling
"off £519 8s. 0d. since last quarter, and will soon be
"about £500 less than the past quarter,—so much for
"railroad economy. Credit Grand Canal £83 6s. 8d.,
"being two months' boating,—the last of our contract
"after a connection of nearly twenty years on the most
"honourable and best understanding. Debit Dublin
"Bank for these sums which will be paid them by next
"Saturday. Credit Dublin Bank £600. Debit Mr. T.
"Hayes, of Dublin. Credit Dublin Bank £475, and
"Mr. T. Hayes £40. Debit nurse £17 10s. 0d. in full
"of all wages due. . . . ."

Here is another point on which he laid great
stress :—

"I am much alarmed at finding in the index some
"of the cars transposed from one number to another,
"which must have the effect of falsifying the general
"car-book, and specially my statistics of 1851. . . . ."

My father attached great importance to his guards,
and here he speaks of John O'Mahony, one of his
favourites :—

"I hope John O'Mahony has been put upon higher
"wages, and on a proper line, as much depends upon
"the guards. I fear they are not sufficiently interested

" for us, nor of the class we ought to get, as they rob
" us with impunity when the agents are too slothful to
" get up at night to see after their business. I wrote
" twice to put an agent at Tuam in place of ——, if he
" did not attend better. . . . .

" We ought to take up the Tralee coach; and ask
" Mr. Hearn what we should do about the Dingle one.
" Suppose we make the first from Ballina to Sligo for
" fish at 1d. per lb.; it may be small, but still worthy
" of our consideration. But they should pay us at
" Ballina, and give us no trouble after. . . . .

" I am glad to see from your letter that you are
" greatly improved in business in the back office. I
" am glad you did so well in the oats account. You
" ought to open a banking account by Mr. Hearn
" giving you an account every week or ten days of all
" the cheques he draws, and see that the agents give
" credit for these regularly, which will also add to the
" facility and care of the oats account. . . . .

" Let Kilkenny supply Jerpoint with hay and oats
" for the future, in order to prevent Mr. Devine
" swamping us entirely, as I don't understand what
" we are about there. Write to Mr. Dobbin that on
" my return his account shall have my first attention,
" and be sure that Mr. R. Dobbin, of Tipperary, shall
" get £20 monthly, but on account. Send the follow-
" ing sums to Clonmel:—£2 to St. Vincent de Paul,
" £3 to Sisters of Charity, &c. . . . ."

Nothing could exceed my father's horror of agents
buying oats. This was the province of Mr. Hearn and

his two subordinate inspectors.　Here is a little lecture
on the subject :—

"You are aware of my great objection to agents
" buying oats, and the extraordinary expense I have
" gone to in a new staff of men to do so for the agents ;
" and in the face of all this, I find that we are out of
" oats at Sligo, and at Boyle.　The agent is made to
" do the duty of the new staff ; that is such a loss to the
" establishment.　Show this to Messrs. Hearn and
" Carrigan, and make the latter explain to me the
" reason of it. . . . . You must not on any account
" allow any agent to keep one penny balance under
" any pretence, as the oats and beans must be supplied
" only by Mr. Hearn.　Allow no person to draw money
" from any of the agents, and dismiss any one who does
" not act up to the letter of our orders. . . . .

" Since I wrote to you on the 14th I got yours of the
" 4th, and of the 14th.　Ask Father Kirwan if he
" thinks young ——, now in the back office, sufficiently
" honest to be trusted in money matters.　Would he
" receive our cash, say £1, £2, or £10, and put it
" without compunction into his pocket ?　I think not.
" If Father Kirwan is also of the same opinion, that he
" is honest, send him off on receipt of this to replace
" ——, who shall be forthwith dismissed. . . . .

" Many thanks for yours of the 5th instant, received
" since I wrote to you on the 14th.　Tell Mr. Hearn I
" don't agree with him about young Long, who would
" soon become most useful under Mr. Tobin.　And if
" Mr. F—— had our business at heart, or understood

" it, he would not allow the stable to be without a
" proper sconce, and thereby prevent the men from
" sticking candles to the walls.   Besides, he is throwing
" away his time with us, as well as being in our way,
" and his father ought to insist on his going out to
" the gold diggings.   So I hope Mr. Hearn will take
" courage and give the young lad a chance. . . . ."

I will conclude these extracts with a little word of
thanks, written in a mood of great depression about my
sister.

" Your letter was of great use to me, though I ought
" to be ashamed to acknowledge it.   I regret to say I
" am often very low-spirited, at my distressing and
" peculiar position ; but when I see the zeal with which
" my faithful band of officials discharge their duties,
" that fills me with pride, and with a sense of all that
" I owe to Providence."

CHAPTER V.

" I was not much over three years of age when I first
made the acquaintance of Mr. Bianconi. To him I
attribute my taste for horses, and the first thing that I
remember about him is his putting me astride on a
chair, and making me imagine I was on horseback.
From that time until his death I was on the most intimate terms of friendship with him. I never knew a
man change so little in all those years as Mr. Bianconi
did; almost to the last he was as active, as energetic,
and as impulsive as when I first knew him,—when
his black hair curled all over his head like the
ancient Roman statues. He was a handsome man with
a fine large head, very bright sparkling eyes, and a
deep florid complexion. His mouth was well formed,
he was always closely shaven, allowing no hair to grow
on his face. His peculiarity was always to wear frilled
shirts and large collars, which were invariably limp
and tossed in their appearance. In the daytime he
always wore a black frock-coat, and whenever I met
him of an evening in a swallow-tail coat, he seemed to

To face page 107.

me to be an altered man. I remember my father painting his portrait, about the year 1830, when he was as I have described him; the picture was subsequently exhibited in the Royal Hibernian Academy, and was considered an excellent likeness.

" At this time—in 1830—his car establishment was fully developed. He had then long retired from the gilding trade, and had disposed of his shop in Clonmel, of which I have often heard my father speak, as he knew Mr. Bianconi intimately many years before I was born. About 1830 the Massey Dawson cars were in the zenith of their prosperity.* They ran on two wheels, they held five persons on each side, and were drawn by one horse in the shafts, and another horse whose traces were fixed to a swinging bar running alongside. This swinging bar Mr. Bianconi used to call an outrigger. The weight placed on the back of one horse was very great: eleven persons, including the driver, a lot of luggage piled up on the centre or well of the car, and not infrequently a boy on the top of the luggage. They used, nevertheless, to travel at the rate of seven or eight miles an hour. Mr. Bianconi subsequently told me that one of the principal reasons that induced him to give up the long two-wheeled cars with shafts, and substitute for them four-wheeled cars, with a pole and traces, was the difficulty

---

* The largest and heaviest cars in Mr. Bianconi's establishment were known as the " Finn McCoul's," so called after Ossian's Giant; then came the " Massey Dawson's," named after a popular Tory Squire; and there were the cars called " faugh a ballagh,"—" clear the way," —a fast car, of a lighter build than the others.

be found in obtaining horses large and powerful enough
to stand the weight on the back of the shaft horse. At
the conclusion of the war, in 1815, large strong horses
were easily obtained; they were then bred for the
artillery, but at the time I speak of they were procured
with considerable difficulty and at a great cost.

"As a boy, both in Waterford and Clonmel, I have
often watched the starting of the Bianconi cars. It
was quite a sight in those towns, especially in Clonmel,
the head-quarters of the establishment. At Waterford,
I used to hurry away from Dr. Graham's school to see
the start of the three-o'clock cars, from Cummins's
Hotel. But on Saturdays, when we always had a half-
holiday, it was my greatest enjoyment to see the har-
nessing of the horses, the packing of the luggage on
the cars, and the final start, as the drivers blew their
horns, cracked their whips, and went off with a flourish.
Many a time in Clonmel have I seen Mr. Bianconi
relax from the dignity of proprietor, and when the
porters, from an unusually large quantity of passengers,
were in a difficulty about fitting on the luggage, he
would climb up on the top of the car and work
harder than any of them. I think he took a peculiar
pleasure in this packing when the opportunity offered
itself.

"The cars which went from Waterford to Kilkenny
and to Clonmel every day at three o'clock, Sundays
excepted, were driven by two cousins, Lorey and Larry
Hearn. These men were both queer fellows, especially
Larry, who drove the Kilkenny car. I well remember

the delight I used to feel when, about two miles outside
Waterford, the road to Kilkenny branched off from the
Clonmel road. Here there was a steep bit of a hill,
and Larry used to spring his horses up the slope in
true coachman style. It was extraordinary the speed at
which the horse in the shafts used to gallop up this
hill, considering the great weight there was on his back.
Accidents occurred very rarely, and I never remember
to have heard of a serious one where life was sacri-
ficed.

" After all, travelling on these cars was very pleasant,
though there were some who objected to going 'side-
ways through the world.' In wet weather there were
some inconveniences, it is true. The cars were provided
with large oil-cloth aprons, which protected the knees,
and came up almost as high as the chest, but these
aprons afforded no shelter from the drippings of an
umbrella. But worse still was the dreadful state of the
cushions in wet weather. At times the passengers used
literally to be sitting in a pool of water. Much trouble
was taken to prevent the accumulation of wet under
the cushions, and for a long time without much
effectual success. Mr. Bianconi told me how at length
he had solved the problem: he had read in Lover's
novel how Handy Andy was described as suffering
much discomfort on the top of a coach in rainy weather,
until he thought of taking a gridiron with him to sit
upon. Mr. Bianconi then felt that he had got the right
idea at last, and he had strips of wood placed length-
ways on the seats under the cushions, so that the water

remained in the interstices, and the cushions were kept fairly dry.

"Once, when I was on the car and Larry was driving, the car came to great grief. The wheel fell off and a spring was broken, and in fact there was a complete smash. Nobody seemed 'one penny the worse' for a roll on a very dusty road, and it was looked upon rather as an occasion for merriment. Larry said it was like the battle of Waterloo to see all his passengers spread out upon the ground. We were not far from where we had last changed horses, and another car was obtained after a short delay. But when Larry arrived at the next stage, the landlady of the little road-side inn came out and exclaimed, 'Oh dear! sure that isn't the usual car! What's become of the other car?' And Larry took some broken sticks out of his pocket, and said, 'There, ma'am, are some of the largest portions of it.'

"I remember once when travelling on one of the small cars, drawn by a single horse, which were for the most part used on the cross-country roads, between small towns, I had another experience. It was un- usually wet weather, and the low-lying country was flooded. On portions of the road the water was above the foot-board of the car, and up to the horse's girths; so it was thought advisable to get off the car, and the driver and the passengers walked along on the top of the wide bank at the side of the road, throwing stones at the unfortunate horse to make him go on.

"I have said that the head-quarters of Mr. Bianconi's

establishment was at Clonmel, and he lived in Clonmel for many years. There the largest number of horses were kept, and amongst them were to be found old screws that had come from all parts of the surrounding country; for when any animal was found to be un-manageable, broken down, or hopelessly vicious, he was forthwith offered to ' Bian,' who was sure to find a use for him. There was a large black stallion, who, if report be true, had eaten three men. He went daily under the Waterford car from Clonmel to Carrick-on-Suir, but there were only two men who dared to touch the brute; one man was in Carrick and the other in Clonmel. One evening, about half-way to Clonmel, the bridle, as luck would have it, slipped off this horse's head, and Lorey Hearn, who was then driving, pulled up with some difficulty, and got down to re-adjust the bridle; but the stallion gave a shriek, stood up on his hind legs, and attempted to bite so viciously, that no one dared lay a hand on him. At last Lorey mounted his box, resumed the reins, and managed to drive the remainder of the journey with the bridle round the horse's neck, depending altogether upon his manage-ment of the other horse.

"All the harness for the horses, and also all the cars and ironwork, were made at the factory in Clonmel. Every horse had a name, and every car had a number; and the names of the horses at every stage were (or ought to have been) as regularly put in the way-bills as the names of the passengers. Mr. Bianconi seemed to know every horse by name, when and how he had bought him, how much money he had given for him, and all his faults and peculiarities. I have often heard a conversation between himself and Dan Hearn, his factotum and general manager. 'Who says we must take Miss Moll off the Mitchelstown road? She'll do for the Fethard car. Tartar is on his legs again, and will be fit for work next week. Grey Tom is doing well in Sligo, and Tim Healy says he has no trouble at all now with Badger; he goes like a lamb, he says. Who has Dandy?' 'Oh! Pat Sullivan has him since Wednesday last. He's a good horse; but I don't know what we'll do with Stripper, that we bought from old Cassidy.'

" The way-bills were sent regularly to Mr. Bianconi, and he used to study them attentively. I have often heard him say that he had no time to read anything but way-bills, and indeed he never was a reading man, but very fond of getting people to read to him. When he was away from home, the way-bills were usually sent after him. I have met him travelling in his carriage on the Rock Road from Dublin to Kingstown, and I observed the bottom of the carriage and the cushions all covered with way-bills. He kept his accounts in a way of his own, and had a method of calculating intricate sums that was very rapid, but he was quite unable to explain to anybody how he brought out the result. His figures were like some unknown hieroglyphics, and his ordinary handwriting was at first sight almost illegible. I have heard my father say that Mr. Bianconi very often after writing a letter was unable to read it himself, that he used to call up Pat O'Neill, one of his assistants, and he read the letter without any difficulty. And my children used to say that they knew at once when I got a letter from Mr. Bianconi, because I first held it close up to my eyes, and then looked at it at arms' length, while endeavouring to read it. He told me one day that he thought it the luckiest thing possible that he had never seen a set of account books till late in life; adding that he felt convinced, if he had seen them, it would have been his ruin.

"By his own personal experience he had painfully realised the want of a cheap and rapid means of travelling from one town to another; many a weary mile had he walked with a box of engravings strapped on to his back. When he first came to Clonmel, the tradesmen and small shopkeepers, if they had business to transact, would walk to Waterford and back, about twenty-eight Irish, or thirty-three English, miles. Coaches were not so common then as they became afterwards, and their charges were too high to make them of general use to the ordinary traveller. Horse-hire also was dear; it was only the better class of tradesmen that could afford to ride on horseback, and they generally rode to Dublin, where they went once a year to make their purchases. Many went from Clonmel to Waterford by the long river boats which brought down bags of flower, corn, pigs, firkins of butter, &c., and brought back coal, hogsheads of sugar, chests of tea, and crates of merchandise. The boats usually took a day and a night to reach Water-

ford, for the tide had to be waited for from below
Carrick.　Coming back against the stream, the boats
were drawn by horses, and if the river was flooded, all
traffic was for a time suspended.　I have seen six
and even eight horses in a line slowly dragging a
heavily-laden boat when there was a flood, and I have
seen the animals swept off their legs, amid the shouts
and execrations of the boatmen who were helplessly
drifting down the stream.　To be conveyed the same
distance in a sixth part of the time upon a well-appointed
car was a wonderful change.　The effects it produced
among the people can hardly now be understood ; it was
in fact a small social revolution.　It has been acknowledged that Mr. Bianconi, by the establishment of his
cars, has contributed as much to the progress and prosperity of Ireland as any public man of this century ;
and because he made his fortune by the people, the
benefits to those among whom he made his home were
not less real, or looked upon by them in any ungenerous
spirit.　I have often sat with him in his carriage driving
along the roads through his own property, on which
very roads he had often walked in former years, when
all his worldly goods were carried on his back.　Surely
a feeling of pride and exultation was allowable in such
a man as he looked around upon his own fields, and
talked of his struggles of former times.

“ One day, when I was driving with him, he called
my attention to a particular place on the road from
Cashel to Thurles,—close to Boherlahan, where he built
the mortuary chapel in which his remains now rest,—

and he recounted to me, laughing heartily as he went on, how he had once on that spot met with a disaster, which at the time he thought was complete ruin to all his prospects. He had brought from his shop in Clonmel a large looking-glass with a gilt frame, on which he had bestowed over a fortnight's work. This was the most important job upon which he had ever been engaged, and he had bargained with a farmer to carry him and his glass into Thurles, where the purchaser of the glass resided. They had got on their way in the cart all very well as far as this particular spot, when he, in a fit of exuberant humour, began to tickle the horse under his tail with a straw. In an instant the animal reared and plunged, and then dashed off at full speed down the hill, and finally smashed the car into bits and the looking-glass into a thousand atoms against a stone wall at the corner of the road. The farmer overwhelmed him with reproaches for the destruction of his cart and for the loss of his horse, for the animal was nowhere to be seen. But worse still were his own feelings at witnessing the wreck of all his hopes, the absolute loss of his property, and the ruin that he foresaw impending over him: all this, he said, could not be imagined or described. A vein of humour and a turn for fun must have been strongly developed in his character. I have heard my father speak of this real love of humour in Mr. Bianconi, and I have myself observed it in the latter portion of his life, for it was then that I knew him best.

"There is another story about a looking-glass which

I may add as a companion to the foregoing. He was having a large-sized glass taken to a house near Cashel; it was carried on a man's back, but was such an odd-looking, unwieldy package, that the curiosity of an old woman on the way-side became excited, and she inquired eagerly what it was. Mr. Bianconi was close behind the man carrying the glass, and he immediately answered that it was the Repeal of the Union. The old woman's delight and astonishment knew no bounds. She knelt down on her knees, in the middle of the road, to thank God for having preserved her so long that at last in her old days she should have seen the Repeal of the Union.

"I had heard that the first car he started ran between Clonmel and the picturesque little town of Cahir, a distance of about eight miles, and I asked Mr. Bianconi why he selected that small town in preference to others that were larger,—instancing Cashel, Carrick-on-Suir, or Fethard. 'Well,' he said, 'that is a very natural question. The reason that most influenced me in selecting Cahir for my first venture was, that it was the only town to which I could make the journey there and back with one horse; the other towns were too far distant,—twelve miles and more.' And he also said, that although there was a good deal of intercourse and traffic between Clonmel and Cahir, there was no mode of public conveyance, such as the boats to Carrick by the river, or the mail coach to Dublin, which went through Cashel. His first attempt, he thought, was going to be a failure; scarcely anybody went by the

To face page 116.

car.   People were used to trudging along on foot, and they continued to do so, thus saving their money which was more valuable to them than their time.   Another man would have abandoned the speculation, but Mr. Bianconi did nothing of the kind. He started an opposition car, at a cheaper rate, which was not known to be his,—not even by the rival drivers who raced against each other for the foremost place. The excitement of the contest, the cheapness of the fare, the occasional free lifts given to passengers, soon began to attract a paying public, and before very long both the cars every day came in full. He had bought a great strong 'yellow horse,' as he called him, to run in the opposition car; he gave, he said, £20 for the animal. One evening his own recognised driver came to him in great pride and excitement: 'You know the great big yallah horse under the opposition car. Well, sir, he'll niver run another yard. I broke his heart this night. I raced him in from beyant Moore o' Barns, and he'll niver thravel agin.' Mr. Bianconi told me he was obliged to show the greatest gratification at the loss of his beast; but it gave him enough of the opposition car, which there and then came to an end like the poor horse. The habit of travelling on a car increased amongst the people when they had become alive to its advantage; the Cahir car became a success and the forerunner of many.

"In these early days Mr. Bianconi still carried on his gilding business, and the selling of prints; he used also to take in lodgers in his house. Alpenny, an English artist, occupied his drawing-room floor—it was from him

that my father first learnt to draw—and on the second
floor Purcell, a miniature painter, lodged. Pat O'Neill,
Mr. Bianconi's apprentice, slept in the attic along with a
numerous colony of rats, who infested the place to such an
extent that he always had a whip by him on his pillow to
beat them from off the counterpane. Pat O'Neill was
once sadly in want of some new shirts, but he hesitated to
let his master know of his need. 'Why don't you tell
him?' old Peggy, the housekeeper, would say to him.
' Sure you know the master has no idea of the state you're
in.' At length Pat got his opportunity. 'Pat, bring me
a glass-cloth,' said Mr. Bianconi one day in the shop.
' Yes, sir,' said Pat, and pushing down on one side the
waistband of his trousers he pulled out a handful of rags.
' If you want more, sir, I've got plenty more here,' he
said, pulling out a similar handful from the other side.
Mr. Bianconi was astounded. ' Oh, by gor ! Mrs. M——,
this boy is in a dreadful state,' he said, appealing to
old Peggy. ' Why was not I told of this before ?' By
this trick Pat O'Neill got a supply of new shirts.

" Alpenny was a landscape painter, and gave lessons
in drawing; and, probably incited by Purcell's minia-
tures on ivory, he took to painting portraits in oil, not,
however, I fancy, with much success. Old Peggy was
a connoisseur, and one day when Alpenny was away
giving a lesson, she came into the room in which my
father was working. She was standing opposite to
Alpenny's easel looking at the portrait he had been
painting. ' Sure that's not skin colour,' she said ; ' go
up-stairs and look at Mr. Purcell's ladies and gentle-

men. 'Tis there you'll see the rale skin colour. Sure them brown things isn't skin colour.'

" When the cars became definitely established on the different roads leading out of Clonmel, Mr. Bianconi took a fancy to have drab top-coats and glazed hats for his drivers, who, in truth, were often poorly clad. But the new clothes were not popular with the men; they considered it a sort of livery, and preferred the independence of their own ragged garments, so that it became difficult to get them to wear the coats. I have heard my father describe a dinner-party which Mr. Bianconi gave about this time.   Alpenny was at it, as was my father, and also the parish priest, Father Flannery. Father Flannery left early ; it was in the middle of summer, on a Sunday evening, and my father was deputed to see the old man to his house in the Irish town, as the upper part of Clonmel was called. The priest asked for the loan of a coat, and Mr. Bianconi produced one of the driver's top-coats, and held it open, winking at my father, while the poor old gentleman mechanically thrust his arms into the sleeves, thinking little as to the form or the cut of the coat he was putting on. But it was rather a trial to my father, who, as a young man reputed to show some talent for art, was well known in Clonmel, and those who only saw their backs thought it odd that young Hayes should be walking through the town arm-in-arm with one of Bianconi's drivers, whilst those who saw poor Father Flannery, enveloped in the drab overcoat, perceived at once that some joke was being played upon the worthy priest.

"It was about this time also that an occurrence took place in Carrick to which I have heard Mr. Bianconi frequently allude, as if to an old penal law at that time still in force, which would not permit any Roman Catholic to own a house of more than a certain value, and that he could be compelled to part with it at a nominal sum to any one professing Protestantism. I fancy, being a foreigner, he confounded the Alien Act with the penal laws, for the latter had been repealed by the Irish Parliament in 1780, long before Mr. Bianconi's time; but he used to say that he had then stables and a store in Carrick, that a scampish resident in the town took advantage of this law, and obliged him to give up the store. This proceeding was very much reprobated in Carrick, especially among the Protestant portion of the inhabitants, and a collection was immediately made in the town to indemnify Mr. Bianconi. In fact, the extreme stringency of the law only served to defeat its enactments; Protestants, in many instances, connived at and strove to nullify the unjust penal laws. This was specially the case with regard to landed property, which was often kept in the possession of the Catholic owners by the help and co-operation of their Protestant neighbours.

"I well remember my grandmother telling me of an incident very similar to that which Mr. Bianconi described. An old Catholic gentleman, one of the Power family, used to drive into Waterford with four fine horses, and on one occasion they were seized as being beyond the value a Catholic could by law possess. The old gentleman was very wrath, and on the Sunday following he drove in to mass at Waterford with four bullocks harnessed to the family coach. It was a strange state of society into which Mr. Bianconi fell when he first came to Ireland, so different from the Catholic Italy where he was born and passed his early boyhood. He told me that a great difference was made between him and his co-religionists on account of his being a foreigner. At that time he said Catholics were generally looked down upon as beings of an inferior race,—they were all classed together as being low, vulgar, and ignorant, even though their forefathers had been gentlefolk. The offspring of the cultured gentleman soon degenerates under the influence of poverty and oppression ; the wonder is that any kind of gentility, education, or property was left among them. It is difficult for us now, in the year 1877, to realise what the social state of Ireland then was, and through which young Bianconi fought his way to prosperity and wealth. I can recollect but little before the passing of the Catholic Emancipation Act in 1829 ; at that time the prevalent idea was that if you met a well-dressed and intelligent man, he must, as a matter of course, be a Protestant.

" I suppose it was from my father's profession as an artist that socially our family mixed so much amongst Protestants. There was neither the taste nor the means amongst the Catholic inhabitants of the small towns in Ireland for the cultivation of art ; many found it hard enough to make both ends meet, and of those who con-

trived to save money, very few possessed either refine-
ment or education. The division into Catholic and
Protestant society was very marked indeed, and to be
recognised as belonging to one was to be tabooed by the
other. A ridiculous aping of the manners and dress of
the better class prevailed ; the well-to-do shopkeepers'
wives and daughters turned out on Sundays in gaudy
finery that sat almost grotesquely upon them. The few
Catholic families who did belong to the gentry led comparatively isolated lives; they were too few and too
widely scattered to have much association amongst
themselves. Such was the state of society as I can
recollect it when I was a boy, but what must it have
been when Mr. Bianconi first came to Ireland? At the
time I speak of—about the year 1830—a rapid and
easy intercourse had been established between the
different towns by means of the Bianconi cars. Money
had become rather more plentiful, political equality had
been conceded, and a spirit of independence had grown
and spread with the progress of education.

"When my father subsequently became a resident
in Dublin, I found the same distinctions existing. I
remember about that time meeting a gentleman from
London, an accomplished musician, who came over to
perform at the concerts of the Philharmonic Society,
then newly formed, and he remarked that he was
unable to understand the social distinctions of Dublin.
About the year 1832 my father was painting the portrait of the Rev. Charles Boyton, a Fellow of Trinity
College. This gentleman took a prominent part in

politics, and he was very Orange in his tendencies. An old friend of my father's brought a relative of his to see this portrait of Mr. Boyton; it was generally held to be a good likeness, and so thought the visitor, who, turning round to my father's friend, said, 'Oh! Henry, don't you think he could eat a Papist?' My father's friend was considerably put out by this unexpected remark, but he promptly said, 'No; for he has not devoured our friend Hayes, as you may see.' Now this outspoken expression of feeling on the part of the friend of my father's friend would not have been made had he known that the painter was a Catholic; but it exemplified a feeling very prevalent at that time, and which happily is now nearly, if not altogether, extinct.

" These circumstances occurred long after the period I have been describing, when Bianconi carried on his business in Clonmel as shopkeeper and small car proprietor. It was in his shop that the first important picture painted by my father—then a boy of seventeen —was publicly exhibited. It was a view of Clonmel from the bridge over the Suir. Alpenny, my father's master, was very proud of the work of his pupil, and it had numerous admirers among the humbler classes, who formed a crowd around the window and criticized it freely, and, to my father's chagrin, they discovered that he had forgotten to put in the lamps upon the quay. Some twenty years after, while I was still a school-boy, a drawing of mine was exhibited in another window in the same street, of one of Bianconi's cars laden with passengers and luggage, and moving along at a fabulous pace. It was the wonder and admiration of my schoolfellows, who were unanimous in declaring it to be copperplate! that being the highest praise they could bestow upon a work of art. This drawing, together with some others, was subsequently engraved and published in London.

"Mr. Bianconi used to say that at this time he had in his establishment in Clonmel two Tommys, three Jimmys, one Patsey, three Larrys, four Paddys, two Mickeys, three Dickeys, four Johnnys, one Peter, three Jerrys, two Terrys, and one Mickeleen. One of the Jerrys was distinguished by the title of 'Jerry the Royal.' He was the porter specially attached to the cars, but he had a great many irregular competitors who skirmished around the passengers on the arrival of a car, and he—the Jerry—was in the habit of impressing upon the passengers that he was the 'rale porter,' which he pronounced like *royal*,—hence his cognomen. He had some defect in the palate of his mouth, that gave rather a nasal sound to his speech.

"During Mr. Bianconi's long residence in the south of Ireland he acquired a number of the idioms and peculiarities of pronunciation of the people among whom he lived. 'By gor! boys,' was a favourite phrase of his, and by several he was thought to be an Irishman. But he never lost his foreign accent in many words; nor could he quite rid himself of saying *dis* and *dat* for *this* and *that*; his English, however, was good, and he spoke it with perfect fluency. His manners were polished and agreeable, and it was impossible to be long in his company without seeing that he was a shrewd and an intelligent man. He was a hard and a keen man of business, but he was a very honourable and upright man ; he was a devout Catholic, and strict in the observances of his religion, though liberal in his views. He possessed great knowledge of character, and he had a singular faculty for picking out the men suited to the position he required them to fill. He took a country-house near Clonmel ; he became a director of the National Bank there, was elected a member of the corporation of the town, and subsequently he filled the office of mayor.

" At various times he encountered considerable opposition upon the roads over which his cars travelled, but at length he tired out and overcame his opponents. They always began by offering to take passengers at reduced fares ; but as he had arranged his prices at as low a sum as could be remunerative, he allowed his rivals to go on without lowering his charges, or he reduced them so as to be but a fraction over the opposition cars, which on every journey were overcrowded. The consequence was that though Mr. Bianconi's cars were not so full as those of his opponents, he continued to run them at a small profit, but his rivals broke down their horses under the extra weight in the daily struggle for the foremost place on the road. Mr. Bianconi, too, generally received the subsidy from the Government for carrying the mails, and the more respectable class were content to pay the extra trifle for the sake of avoiding the crowd on the opposition cars. On the backs of all his cars the names of the larger towns in the various parts of Ireland to which his lines extended were conspicuously set out in gold letters upon a red ground. The cars were well turned out, the manufacture was excellent, and they were handsomely painted and highly varnished; yellow and crimson were the preponderating colours, contrasting very strongly with the clumsy ill-painted vehicles that were started to oppose him. The only serious opposition he ever encountered was set up by a Mr. Gilliard, who started with a considerable capital, and put cars on to several of the best-paying roads. His cars were good, they were very like Bianconi's, and they had the names of the towns through which they ran painted on the backs. They lasted for a year and a half, and caused some loss to Mr. Bianconi, but at last brought disaster to their owner. There was also an opposition set up by Mr. Casey, of Clonmel, backed up by a Mr. Stokes, a wealthy tradesman in the town. This created a great deal of partisan feeling, especially amongst those employed on the cars; and the racing of one against the other was carried on to a rather dangerous extent, but Bianconi's car was generally in advance.

"About the year 1833 Mr. Bianconi began to substitute four-wheeled cars for the two-wheelers; he found that the weight on the shaft horse was too great. He also said that it became no longer possible to get a supply of horses similar to those he used formerly to buy,—a lighter description of horse was then mostly bred by the farmers. The four-wheeled cars were fitted with a pole instead of shafts, and held seven persons on each side; three horses were used, driven unicorn fashion, and sometimes when the roads were heavy and the load greater than usual an additional horse was put on. There were some four-wheeled cars holding only five on each side, and drawn by two horses; on the small cross roads the two-wheeled cars, holding three on each side, and drawn by one horse, were still used.

"I believe it was also about this time that he was over in London making arrangements with the authorities at the Post-office. He found some difficulty in describing his cars, and wrote to me asking me to make a few drawings of them, and send them over to him at once. I was only a boy at school at the time, but I complied with his request, and sent him the drawings. He told me afterwards that they answered his purpose admirably. I remember perfectly well that I was unable to make out from his letter where he was stopping in London,—he always wrote a most illegible hand, —and as no one could help me to read the address, I cut it off his letter and fastened it on to my envelope, very doubtful that it would ever reach him. I had heard that at the London Post-office experts were employed for this purpose, and when I knew that my letter had safely arrived at its destination I was convinced of their powers.

"I suppose it was the success of those little drawings that induced me to make some more ambitious attempts in the same line. Mr. Bianconi was so well pleased with my new productions that he conceived the idea of getting Ackerman to bring out a series of six aquatint coloured prints, entitled 'Car-Travelling in the South of Ireland.' One of the pictures showed the passengers sitting under their umbrellas on the car, the rain was pouring down in torrents, and the horses were dead beat and covered with mud. Mr. Bianconi looked at the picture for a moment. ' We won't have that,' said he; 'it's more like the real thing, though!' I was in Dublin with my father when a traveller from Ackerman's called to show me the prints. I felt very proud, I remember, especially when I saw in the corner, *M. A. Hayes, pinxt.* When I look now at these boyish sketches, I am surprised to see that they are so good.

"In after years, when I lived in Dublin with my father, I met Mr. Bianconi less frequently, but when he was in town he always came to see us. As he grew old he began to get fat, and his hair showed signs of greyness. He had purchased a house and property at Longfield, near Cashel, and became quite a country gentleman. He was made a J.P., and also a deputy-lieutenant. And he also became more of a politician; he was on intimate terms with Smith O'Brien, and joined the '82 Club. I remember seeing him in the green-and-gold club uniform, but it did not suit him so well as did that of the deputy-lieutenant which he wore at a later period."

CHAPTER VI.

My father used to glory in the fine set of men he had in his employment, and whom he had trained to his own uses. Worthiest of all was our good old friend, Daniel Hearn,—always called Dan Hearn. He has already been mentioned, and as his name will again frequently appear, I must try to describe him here at the head of this especial chapter. At home we were all so fond of him that what I can write seems to be very tame and colourless, and totally fails to bring back the man's fine genial presence and delightful heartiness. He was a splendid specimen of a Tipperary man, fully six feet high and broad in proportion, with the pleasantest smile and the whitest teeth, the rosiest coloured cheek, and the most delightfully mellow brogue possible. His natural fine health and good temper kept him full of vigour and fun even to the last. The constant exposure to every kind of weather, and the wear and tear of his life, had developed in him some natural tendency to heart disease, and he died, under seventy, after a year of failing health, just after my father was

beginning to get over the effects of his broken thigh.
I firmly believe that a winter tour of inspection in the
west, and the extra work my father's accident imposed
upon him, hastened his death. He sent a farewell
message to my father, begging him to sell the cars, for
after my brother died my father had willed them to
Dan Hearn, but he survived both the institution and
the man whom he wished to benefit.

I find a letter of Mr. Hearn's to my father's clerk
written from his sick-bed, asking who my mother had
to keep her company during my father's long con-
valescence ; and in another letter full of minute details
about the changes of horses consequent upon the out-
break of glanders, this pathetic passage occurs :—
" Your illness is no doubt most tedious, but you are
a healthy and a strong man, while in my case I can
see no chance. Nothing left undone, but yet no improvement, rather the reverse ; but welcome be the will
of God."

I do not suppose Mr. Hearn ever had much education given to him ; his handwriting was nearly as
illegible as my father's. His mother had tried to
make an apothecary of him, but after a six weeks'
trial he quitted his master. Dan Hearn was one of
nature's gentlemen ; he knew all my father's most
private affairs, still he never overstepped a certain
invisible social line in the most familiar intimacy. I
might fancy that I over-estimated my old friend's
good qualities, but my husband, who certainly had
a pretty fair experience of life, concurred in all my

opinions, and always professed the greatest regard and esteem for him.

Dan Hearn was the head man over all the traffic of the establishment; he was the chief buyer of horses and of stores, with the fullest power of changing men and horses, subject only to my father's all-pervading sway. He had even power to draw cheques. Under him were three principal travelling agents, with similar though lesser powers—Messrs. Carrigan, Peter Mullaly, and Phil Sullivan; the two latter had risen from being drivers. Mr. Carrigan I remember distinctly, because he was frequently summoned to the congress, and my father took a special interest in him. He became an agent very young, and he had a mother who was also an agent. His wife, too, was agent at Galway even during her husband's lifetime, and only resigned her post when that line was sold after my father had retired from business. Her husband was a particularly lively, merry, active man. I remember having seen him vault over two horses. Mrs. Carrigan was also a great favourite of my father's, and he used to delight in telling her how he turned off her husband for marrying without his consent, and then forgave him when he met his wife, he having called upon them purposely in order to carry out his rule of dismissal.

At that time there prevailed a very horrible practice which I hardly know how to describe. Girls, and particularly those of the lower classes who dwelt in the towns, were encouraged by the state of the law to trump up scandalous charges against any young man who had been frequently seen in their company, and more than one young fellow had to choose between the gallows and a perjured bride. To protect his men from this state of things, my father made a law that any bachelor in his establishment who married without his leave should be dismissed. He used to say that the best results followed from this law, that it kept the men out of the clutches of these harpies, and that it checked too early and imprudent marriages. Though my father was at no time an admirer of the female sex, and possessed a dread mingled with antipathy towards young and good-looking widows—whom he declared ought to be choked by the girls in whose way they stood—yet he frequently employed women as agents. As I have already said, he had at one time over twenty female agents; but there were many difficulties in the way of women at these posts which would seem almost to unfit them for the undertaking. They had to maintain a strict supervision over the stable-yard, and to see that the ostlers did their work properly, that the horses got their proper amount of corn, and that they were properly groomed after they had come in heated from their journey. The wonder is, indeed, that they should have done their work so well; and my father used to take a great interest in his female officers, as he grandiloquently called them. One prosperous lady, who was not an agent in her own name, but who used to help her uncle, was a Miss Bragg, and my father persistently kept asking her why she did not change her ugly name, until he was silenced by the rejoinder that she might not have so much to boast of if she did.

As a child I remember being often fetched into the office, and told to shake hands with sundry weather-beaten drivers, almost enveloped in their capes and great-coats. Glasses of whisky used to be put into my little hands to give to them, which they would take with a profound bow, and wish good luck to Miss Minnie. Occasionally it would happen that some extraordinary drivers were teetotallers; they were sent down to get their dinners in the kitchen, and they did not omit to give me their blessings as they went. I hear that as a rule the drivers were men fat and red in the face,—two facts easily accounted for by a sedentary life passed in the open air, and with plenty of means of getting good food. Many of them were well-to-do in the world, and showed by their general appearance that their families were honest and respectable. There were the three Mullalys, the sons of a prospering yeoman, whose fine farm had to be sold after his death. These were the sort of men my father was always anxious to secure. The three brothers all went into his service, where they stayed and prospered. Then there was Phil Sullivan, whose letters, written in a neat, old-fashioned, copper-plate hand, were such a relief to me when I had to act as secretary. On one occasion Phil was offered a couple of half-crowns to delay the car a few minutes, the briber saying that he would take all the blame upon his own shoulders. Honest Phil indignantly refused the money, and showed that he was considerably astonished at the offer being made.

Tim Haly was a paragon driver. He was always known on the road as Lord Gort, though how he got his nickname I have never been able to ascertain. He was sober as a judge, and a parish clerk could not have been more assiduous than he in saying his prayers. Tim was a prime favourite with all the ladies, and especially with the Quaker ladies, who travelled on his car. His line was from Clonmel to Cork, and one day as he was going along, driving his three horses at a good swinging pace, a donkey-cart was in the middle of the road, full in the way of the long Bian. Tim shouted out, "Keep your own side." The donkey-driver made frantic efforts to pull his beast anywhere, and triumphantly drew him up in the very middle of the wrong side of the road, straight in the way of Tim Haly's car. Tim had to perform prodigies of skill to avoid absolute destruction to the humbler equipage, and, instead of using strong language, which might naturally be expected, he simply exclaimed, with the most perfect good-humour, " Shure, you did it as well as you could ! "

One reason why my father was fond of Tim Haly was that Tim Haly was fond of his work. I will now let my father tell his own story about him.

" Tim Haly," he said, " was an old and valued " servant. I had him for many years driving a long " Bian from Cork to Clonmel."——A long Bian was a long car carrying nineteen passengers—eight on each

To face page 134

side, two on the well, and one on the high seat next to
the driver. It was drawn by three horses, two wheelers
and a leader, to which another horse was added when
the roads were heavy.——"Tim was very popular along
" the road, being a good-natured fellow and full of
" stories. He always kept the passengers amused, and
" generally contrived to avoid a row with the cart-
" drivers, who were more frequent on the road before
" the days of railways than they are now. Tim's
" manner of clearing the way was an exception to the
" general rule. Instead of using abusive language to a
" man who was driving right in the middle of the
" road, or, worse still, who was on his wrong side, he
" would call out, 'Wake up, my boy, wake up!' or,
" 'Do, like a good fellow, give me a little bit of the
" 'road, if you please!' And the result was, that Tim
" at all times got a clear stage and a 'God speed you!'
" One day he came to me, and seemed very uneasy. I
" asked him what was on his mind. He said that the
" boys below there in Clonmel were very much troubled
" at seeing the priest being so much up and down with
" the parson. It appeared that the two clergymen
" were both of them very sociable good fellows, who
" frequently partook of each other's hospitality, and did
" not allow the fact of their being pastors of different
" flocks to interfere with their friendship. Tim, not
" quite comprehending this ideal state of things, said to
" me—'We had a meeting last night, you know, and
" 'determined to send a deputation to his reverence to
" 'ask him not to be so great with the parson.' On the

" following morning Tim accordingly introduced the
" deputation to the priest, and made known their
" wishes to him. His reverence told them not to be
" uneasy, as he was trying to convert the parson,
" and he thought he would succeed, as he was going to
" dine at the rectory on the following day; and he
" added that, if Tim would come up to him on the
" morning after, he would let him know of his success.
" So the deputation expressed their thanks and went
" away. Now, his reverence always took his tumbler
" of punch after dinner, to which he added a second
" when he dined with his good friend the parson. And
" having recently received a present of a few gallons of
" 'the real old stuff,' that had never paid duty, a happy
" thought struck him that a gallon of it might be
" acceptable at the rectory. At the appointed hour
" he arrived at his friend's house with the potheen,
" and a jolly good evening they had over it. By eleven
" o'clock it was evident that the staying powers of the
" parson were not equal to those of his guest, and after
" many efforts to preserve his equilibrium he fairly gave
" way. The good nature of the priest would not let
" him depart without first providing for the comfort of
" his host, so he called in the man-servant, and with
" his assistance he put the parson into bed. The next
" morning Tim and his deputation, who had been
" totally forgotten by the priest, called to know the
" result of the previous evening, and anxiously inquired
" whether his reverence had succeeded in converting
" the parson. 'Not quite,' was the reply; 'but I

" 'staggered him amazingly!'—'Good!' says Tim, 'I
" told the boys he could never stand before you!'"

Jim Halloran used to drive upon the same line from
Clonmel to Cork. He was an oddity in his way, though
a different man from Tim Haly. He was a sturdy,
witty, insolent fellow, and a great politician. Like
most Irish "characters," he was not always able to
resist the attractions of the whisky bottle; he did not
lay up a store for his old age, and I am sorry to say
that he finished his career as a helper in the stable.
Many a time he was seen driving his long car into
Hearn's hotel-yard in Clonmel with a pocket-handker-
chief tied round his head, his hat having been left behind
on the way. Once he had been racing an opposition
car, and arrived without any passengers at all, and no
cushions on the seats. My father was in the office when
he came in, and had him up for punishment. Jim
swore that he started with two Quaker ladies, and in
about an hour's time the two ladies arrived in a
common cart. They were not seriously hurt, but their
dresses were torn and considerably damaged. My father
was all sympathetic suavity : he repaid them their fare,
and offered to buy each of them a new gown. Jim was
often threatened with dismissal; but he was far too
conscious of his own value to take the threat at more
than it was worth. The moment that either my father
or Dan Hearn reproached him too severely, he would
turn on them and dismiss them. No one knows how
often he did not give warning to his employers.

Guards were, of course, attached to all the coaches,—

in some cases there were two or three. One was the official mail guard, put on by the Post-office ; the others were supplied by my father to attend to parcels and to the passengers. At one time, however, during a fit of official economy, the coach proprietors had to supply the mail guards—an ingenious arrangement, by which some saving was effected to the department. Most famous of all guards was M'Cluskie, whom I recognised in one of Mr. Anthony Trollope's novels—" The Macdermots of Ballycloran," and from him I got the following letter about the old guard :—

" I remember M'Cluskie well. He was guard on the Dublin and Boyle coach. I did not know that he had ever been one of your father's folk. But he and I were great friends. ' A fellow-feeling makes us wondrous kind,' he said to me once on the top of the coach, when I had been vindicating the character of donkeys.

" One day I was going down the streets of Lucan, and I was proselytizing him, telling him how wrong were the Papists and how right were the Protestants ! We were then passing just between the church and the chapel. ' Yes,' said he, ' I see it all. While we raise on high the blessed emblem of our redemption, you believe in the cock.' There was an old-fashioned weathercock on the spire of the church.

" When he was guard on one of the coaches which then went from Dublin to Kingstown he had to go down in plain clothes to come up with his coach, and on such occasions he would always be very spruce. He went down on a car with an officer from the barracks, and the two men quarrelled on the way. The officer demanded his card—preparing for a duel. M'Cluskie brought out a card with a picture of a coach upon it, showing a man blowing a long horn, and pointing with his finger to the picture he said, 'That's me.' 'I knew you were some low fellow,' said the officer. 'I am a low fellow,' said M'Cluskie, 'but you *didn't* know it.'

"He shot a man once in a drinking-house, and killed him,—he suspecting that the man had murdered his father. He had twitted the man with the murder, and told him that he would shoot him if he crossed a certain bench. The man rushed to attack M'Cluskie, and M'Cluskie shot him dead. He was tried and acquitted.

"He drank, and then for years he became a teetotaller. He was a man of great courage, of much reading, and of a most ready wit."

A lady tells me that her sisters used frequently to travel under his charge; and one of them remarked that he was not playing on his key-bugle, as usual, "The girl I left behind me," and he at once replied, "Why should I play it when all the pretty ones are with me."

Dan Hearn had many stories about M'Cluskie, mostly relating to the gullibility of the British tourist. M'Cluskie, travelling all day, generally brought some eatable provisions with him, and these he used to put into the top of the boot. A cockney tourist discovered this small store, and when the guard had alighted at a

stage to deliver his mails, he quietly purloined and ate
the packet of sandwiches. Something of a suppressed
grin on his countenance aroused M'Cluskie's suspicions.
He opened the boot, and called out in a tragic voice,
" Where are the sandwiches ? " The cockney could not
prevent himself from smiling. The guard then called
out in a louder tone, " Can any one tell me about the
poisoned sandwiches for the keeper of —— to poison
the cur dogs ? " This was too much for the Londoner.
At once he began to feel ill. M'Cluskie was very kind
to him, and recommended his stopping at the next stage
and taking a strong emetic, with which recommendation he complied. Later on in his journey, when he
had partly recovered from his dose, M'Cluskie further
punished him by setting all the passengers into roars of
laughter, declaring that he had brought the sandwiches
for his own luncheon.

Good old M'Cluskie ! He left the breezy coach-top
for the close guard's van in a railway train ; but he did
not live long after he quitted my father's service. All
his fun and drollery, his reckless pluck, his staunch
theology, the wide and varied knowledge of books which
he contrived to pick up, besides his unconscious studies
of men and women, deserve a better record than what
can be written of him here.

Then there was John O'Mahony, another famous
guard, whose life is like a romance, not without its
tragic side. He seems the very antithesis of Dame
Comedy's well-beloved son M'Cluskie. Not but what
John O'Mahony, Esquire, now her Majesty's Collector

of Customs at Natal, has as keen a sense of humour as any one. He was the son of a most respectable and intelligent man, rich, too, for his station in life, who had a large business as a smith and farrier in Clonmel. He had the shoeing of all the Bian horses, and he naturally wished that his son should succeed him. But John's mind was then more ambitious. His father's great-grand-uncle had been a captain in James II.'s army; "and when"—I quote John O'Mahony's words, in a letter written from Natal—"when that worthless poltroon's (James II.) hope was gone, this Captain O'Mahony went with the Irish brigade to the French service. He so distinguished himself at the siege of Cremona as to win the esteem of King Louis, and in the course of time was a great favourite with that king, who created him Count."

All this stirred up the mind of John, and in spite of all persuasion he would be a soldier. My father used to maintain that it was over-education that made him so obstinate. He was for some time in the army, but found that he could not stand the changes of climate. He then came home and entered my father's service, where he remained for some years. The exposure to wind and weather on the top of the coach was too much for him, and he afterwards got a situation in the Post-office. My father was willing to try and promote his old servant, and exerted himself with the late Duke of Newcastle, who appointed John O'Mahony to his present responsible post in South Africa.

I give here a letter of the Duke's to my father about the old Bian worthy.

"Downing Street, Nov. 20th, 1863.

"Dear Mr. Bianconi,—I return to you Mr. J. O'Mahony's letter, which I have read with very great interest. It is full of sensible remarks, and is written in so good a spirit that it is impossible not to be impressed with a regard for the writer.

"I am glad that it was my good fortune to be able on your recommendation to send out so good a colonist to Natal.

"I am yours very truly,
"Newcastle."

In a letter written from Natal he says, "All my affections were centred in Clonmel while my father lived; since his death I could not bear to go there. There are a few lines in Horace, in the sixth Satire, Book I., about the 89th line,

"'Nil me pœniteat sanum patris hujus,' etc.

"In all Horace, where there is so much to admire, there is nothing that I love him for so sincerely. He expresses your sentiments and mine. But he felt them about a score of years before Christ was born, and they will ever be proudly echoed by souls not yet created."

Many years after John O'Mahony had been out in Africa, when he heard of my father's death, he had a solemn requiem mass said for him. He used to call my father the Rajah of Longfield,—and not a bad title either for a benevolent and somewhat despotic patriarchal ruler.

My father used to tell the two following stories, which were also told me by Mr. William Barry, of Bally Adam. I will give them as Mr. Barry gave them to me. I can vouch for the accuracy of the first one, except that I thought that the scene was laid in Kilmallock. However, that matters little.

"About the year 1836," Mr. Bianconi said to me, "Dan Hearn and I were at the fair in Thurles, and "remaining there late, we had to put up at a carman's "stage on the road home to Clonmel. On inquiring "for beds and supper, we were told to step in, and have "a bit to eat, though it might be doubtful whether we "could get a bed. So we went in, glad to find our- "selves under any shelter, as the night was wet and "stormy. In a few minutes some bacon and potatoes "were put before us, to which we did ample justice. "Then, after a little delay, we were shown upstairs into "the only spare room in the house, and in the corner "of the room there was a bed. We both got into it, "but found that we could not sleep. We became "very restless, and we each said that the bed was "very cold. At last Dan exclaimed, 'By Jove, I "think there must be an iceberg under the bed.' "And he put his hand under the bed as though to "satisfy himself. He suddenly withdrew his hand, "and with one bound he was in the middle of the

" room. He never waited to exchange a syllable with
" me, but darted down the narrow stairs into the kitchen,
" where a lot of carmen were drinking and smoking.
" Dan stood there with only his night-shirt on, and
" called out to me:

" ' Bloody wars! Mr. B., come down out of
" ' that!'

" I immediately jumped out of bed, and followed
" Dan downstairs.

" ' Did you see it?' said he.

" ' See what?' said I.

" ' The Divil,' said Dan.

" ' Where?'

" ' Under the bed.'

" At this time Dan and I were standing in the
" middle of the kitchen, quite unconscious of our want
" of clothing. Biddy Minehan, the hostess, came
" forward, and said to me:

" ' I had nowhere else to put it, yer honour.'

" ' Put what?' I replied.

" ' The corpse, yer honour.'

" ' Good heavens! Do you mean there is a corpse
" ' under our bed?'

" ' Oh, yer honour, a wake was going on when you
" ' came into the house and asked for a night's lodg-
" ' ing; and I thought it would be hard to lose the
" ' chance of a few shillings, and having no spare place
" ' in the house, I just slipped the corpse under the
" ' bed.'

" I need scarcely add that Dan and I lost no time

" in getting on our clothes, and departing as quickly
" as we could from Biddy Minchan and her corpse."

Mr. Bianconi also told me the following story :—

"I once had a horse named Bobby,—the best, I
" believe, that I ever had, and I worked him for a good
" many years. He was a dark chestnut, and had a
" white spot in the middle of his forehead. Poor
" Bobby was at length used up, and I had to part with
" him. Some months afterwards I was at the fair in
" Thurles, and I saw a horse so like my old Bobby,
" that I thought it was he, until going close up to him
" I observed that there was no white star on his fore-
" head. I asked his price, and, after a little huckster-
" ing, I bought him for about three times as much as I
" had got for Bobby two months before. I sent him
" home to Longfield, and the next day Dan Hearn
" came to see the horse.

"'I never saw two horses so much alike in all
" ' my life,' said Dan, with a grin on his face. 'In
" ' fact, sir, if you were to travel all Ireland you
" ' could not get anywhere such a perfect copy of
" ' Bobby.'

"'Ah, Dan! you're out this time. I know what
" ' you are thinking of. It is impossible the horse can
" ' be Bobby, for Bobby had a white star on his fore-
" ' head, and this fellow has none.'

" Dan made no reply, but walked into the stable and
" returned with a sponge in his hand. He began to
" rub the horse's forehead, and to my surprise the old
" white star showed itself as large as ever. I took

" care for the future never to buy a horse upon my own
" judgment."

It used to be as good as a play to hear my father
and Dan Hearn lamenting how the horses had de-
generated. Of course they agreed that the undefinable
animal, the real old Irish horse, had long since been
improved off the face of the earth. At one time, they
said, a short-legged, wide-chested beast, capable of
drawing any weight for any number of miles and hours,
and during any number of years, could be had for £6 or
for £10. But in an evil hour English stud-horses and
English gold had superseded. Broken-down hunters,
or blind carriage-horses, or great coarse brutes from
the cart, had to take the place of the ideal Irish horse
with legs of iron and a heart of steel. Within my
recollection, they secured one animal who might be
considered as a specimen of an ideal Irish horse. He
was sold at an auction because he had killed the wife
of his former owner. Dan Hearn, who bought him,
said that five afflicted husbands were very eager in
their bidding. But the brute was so incurably vicious,
that Dan sold him to an Englishman for £50 before
he had kept him a week.

Dan Hearn used gravely to say that one of his life's
troubles was the naming of the horses. They were,
when possible, called after their owners, unless there
happened to be too many of a name, or unless there
was some special quality in the seller or in the animal
that suggested a name. There was one beast called
Miser, because his late owner was known always to drive

a hard bargain; and there was one raw-boned brute who was called Rampike. As a child, I remember hearing fabulous tales about a certain horse named Lion. He was a very fine and gigantic black horse, but so wicked, that he was very difficult to manage. Before he came to my father, he had killed and partly devoured one man, and then his owner sold him to Dan Hearn for a mere trifle. He always used to run under a coach, as one of the wheelers, and while he was in harness he was very willing, and acted as a sort of trainer to the other horses. On one occasion, a sulky, idle beast was put in beside him in the shafts, who would not do his share of the work. So Lion seized hold of him by the neck, and worried him as a dog would worry a cat, and made him move his legs along a little faster. But it was in the stable that Lion was the most troublesome. There were very few men that he would let approach him. He disliked my father, and he disliked Dan Hearn still more. When Hearn was making his visits of inspection in the stables, the horse would dart forward, and sniff like a dog—for he was nearly blind. He would put back his ears and show his teeth, and strike out wildly with his fore legs, making such unearthly screeches that Hearn was glad to get out of the stable as soon as he could. Lion, however, took a remarkable fancy to one of the helpers, and with him he was as quiet as a child. This man had a little grand-daughter whom he actually used to bring into Lion's stall, and encourage to play with him. Dan Hearn has told me how once, when the old man was ill, he saw the pretty fair-haired child lead out the huge black horse, and desire him to stand still. The animal obeyed her, and stood stock still while she mounted on a stool, and put the harness on his head and on his back,—no man daring to approach him. Lion lived to be a great age, always running as shaft-horse in the coach, and never losing his ungovernable temper. It was a puzzle with my father to know what to do with him when the old helper should become incapable. Happily, however, in course of time, the fair-haired little girl got married to a young helper, and he, through her introduction, succeeded to the grand old horse's affections.

I think I recognise Lion as the large black horse mentioned in Mr. Hayes' Narrative, though Mr. Hayes makes him run in the car from Clonmel to Carrick-on-Suir.

CHAPTER VII.

CATHOLIC Emancipation in Ireland was soon followed
by the repeal of the old iniquitous tithe-laws that
pressed with such hateful severity upon the poor man's
tillage. Happily, the tithe rent-charge that succeeded
it is quite impartial in its operations. Municipal reform,
though designed in England in an unsectarian spirit,
had in Ireland the effect of throwing open the corporations to Catholics. It was only when these two
measures had become law that the lower and middle
classes felt that they were truly emancipated.

The two important elections in Clare and Waterford
were the direct precursors of the Emancipation Act.
The Waterford election, in 1826, may be considered the
turning point in my father's fortunes. The thousand
pounds he then made really enabled him to command
the market and establish his business on the solid
foundation of capital. I think it must have been about
that time that he shut up his shop and threw all his
energies into the car traffic. It is singular how utterly
I have failed in finding out when and how he retired

from his gilding business. I rather think that as he contemplated marriage, many of his wares found their way into his own house, and others he gave to friends, or put them up in the hotels connected with his cars. Very probably he allowed the looking-glass trade to slacken as his car traffic increased; but I cannot satisfactorily find out how he got out of the trade. Had he sold his stock by auction I should have found some trace of it in the local papers.

Everybody in Ireland knows the great difference between a shop and an office. The distinction between classes is, in some ways, stronger in Ireland than in England, and the man who owns an office considers himself superior to the man who keeps a shop. It was my father's intention not to marry until he had attained a respectable position,—until he had got out of the shop and come away from behind the counter.

Years before he had received great kindness from old Signor del Vecchio, the patron and patriarch of the Irish-Italian colony, as fine old Paolo Colnaghi was the father of the London Italians. Now, Mr. Del Vecchio rented from my mother's father a pretty villa, to which he gave the Italian name Campobello. It adjoined my grandfather's own villa, and the two men used often to stroll into each other's grounds on summer evenings. Del Vecchio introduced his young country-man, Charles Bianconi, who soon became a great favourite in my grandfather's family. He there saw my mother, a little girl in a pinafore, and he has told me that he then made up his mind that she should some day be his wife. Meanwhile he tossed the children about in the haycocks, and was a regular visitor at the house whenever he went to Dublin.

My grandfather, Patrick Hayes—no relation, as I have said before, to Mr. Michael Angelo Hayes, whose narrative forms the fifth chapter of this book—was a stockbroker and a notary public. He was one of the first Catholics who became a notary, and, owing to the penal laws then in force, he had to serve a double apprenticeship, fourteen years in all. He married during his second apprenticeship, just before the rebellion, Henrietta Burton, second daughter of an English half-pay officer, Captain John Burton, who had married an Irish wife, Mary Ann de Burgh, of an ancient Connaught family. My grandmother, Henrietta Burton, and all her family were Protestants, but at that time mixed marriages were much more frequent than now, and her connections proved of great use during the rebellion, when Catholics were much exposed to suspicion. I remember seeing her, a tall stately old dame. I have heard that when she married at sixteen she was a fine blooming girl with a lovely voice. Of her many children only four grew up. She was a woman of strong common sense, and my father had the highest opinion of her judgment, to which he frequently deferred in family matters. Rather than have two religions among her children she had them all brought up in their father's faith. She was an upright, pureminded, open-handed woman, but I do not think that

she ever troubled herself much about points of dogma
or that she sought much after abstract truth. My
father admired the regularity and plentifulness of her
household, and he was very sensible to the advantages
of the maternal training of so thorough a gentlewoman.
My mother, I have always heard, was pretty, small, and
dark-haired, with straight features, dark grey eyes, and
a fair skin, and, what my father much vaunted, beautiful
feet. She was a grave, gentle girl, refined and accomplished. The early death of an elder sister threw a
shadow over all her household, and deepened her
natural gravity.

When my father had got rid of his shop, and when
he had two thousand pounds to make a settlement, he
then proceeded to his deliberate wooing, and though he
was by no means a sentimental man, or at all capable
of tumbling, Irish-wise, over head and ears in love, he
was really actuated by soft feelings, as he afterwards
proved. My grandfather, though a rich man, rather
suited his daughter's fortune to the settlement her
husband could make on her than to his own means. I
suspect my father felt a little disappointed, but he
boasted that he would not lose a wife for a few hundred
pounds. He told me once, "It was your mother I
wanted and not your grandfather's money." My
grandfather, though his business was prosperous, and
he had at that time landed property and houses both
in and near Dublin, only gave my mother £1,200, and
my father made a settlement of £2,000 upon his wife
and children. I record this with some pride because

it shows that my father was not actuated by mercenary motives, though I am quite willing to admit he was frequently actuated by them on other occasions. I rather think he felt a little aggrieved at not receiving a larger portion, and at the same time he was proud that a rich man's daughter should have been freely intrusted to him, and doubly proud to be able to show it was the girl and not the wealth he wanted. My mother, Eliza Hayes, was rather more than twenty years younger than my father. They were married on 14th February, 1827, in the front drawing-room of my grandfather's town-house, by the late Archbishop Murray, who had also christened my mother. These church ceremonies in private houses were another relic of the penal times when the danger attending the public offices of our Church led to the custom of administering sacraments in private houses instead of in the public places of worship.

My father was accompanied by his intimate friend, Mr. John Luther, who then and there lost his heart to my aunt, though some little time elapsed before the bridesmaid and groomsman went through the same ceremony they were then witnessing.

After the marriage, the pair went home to my father's house in Clonmel. This house opened into the main street in front, and into the great yard at the back. My mother was agreeably surprised at seeing the fine pictures that hung on the walls in her new house. She also found a profusion of that beautiful cut-glass that was formerly made in Waterford, of the finest damask linen, and silver. Glass, linen, and silver are found in larger quantities in foreign households than in similar Irish homes. My father had, too, books of fine old engravings, to which he constantly kept adding. When he had been alone, engravings and musical boxes had been his great resources of amusement, and I think he learnt more from prints than from any regular books of reading. Hobracken's heads had certainly taught him more than any books of history.

The only thing that was wanting to his house was a garden. My father had failed to secure a certain pretty house on the Mall,—the only thing that he ever set his heart upon in vain. Every summer he used to take his wife to the sea, and on their way to Tramore they always stopped a short time with his old friends the Flemings, before both the families rejoined each other at the sea-side. There was a life-long friendship began between my mother and Miss Maria Fleming, whose son, many years afterwards, married her niece.

My grand-parents also came down to see them at Tramore. My father did not regard his wife's family, British fashion, as his natural enemies ; on the contrary, he seemed to look upon them as his own kindred. When my grandmother was a widow, he used often to regret that she would not make his house her home, and he was always delighted when she came to stay any time with him.

My sister Kate was born on the 4th of June, 1828. According to the Irish custom, she should have borne her maternal grandmother's name, but my grandmother herself interposed, and declared that the little baby should bear the name of her dead Italian grandmother, —a little trait that deeply touched my father. She was a fine strong child, and the parents had little reason to apprehend her early death. As my mother was not able to nurse her herself, she engaged the services of a young widow, whose husband had been a sergeant in the militia. Mrs. Catherine Curtain, or "Nurse," as she was generally called, brought up all my mother's children, continued on in her service as upper housemaid and general care-taker in our absence. She lived to see my brother's children and my boy, and died only in 1872, having been in our family for more than forty years.

About six years after his marriage my father converted his Clonmel house into Hearn's Hotel, and moved to the old Charter School,—a quaint old Georgian house with a nice farm attached to it. He changed its name to Silver Spring. There he lived until he bought Longfield. He tried his hand at farming; he made a pretty garden, pond, and terrace; and during the famine times set up a sort of private relief kitchen, and, according to the Lombard fashion, he gave the people macaroni and polenta. He got a Frenchman who lived near the place to learn them how to boil these messes. The Frenchman's directions for cooking the polenta were not altogether bad. He said: "You put him in a pot, you stir him about, and when he say, 'Puff, puff, puff,' you take him out and eat him."

Though I chanced to be born at Queenstown, near Cork, Silver Spring was my first home.

After his marriage my father's car business prospered rapidly. He felt the " land hunger " strong on him, and was nearly purchasing a nice property; but speaking to the Liberator about his plans, Daniel O'Connell in a friendly way pointed out to him that he could not purchase land, as he was yet an alien in the country. His marriage with a natural-born subject, the birth of his child, his increasing business, and his avowed intention of always living in Ireland, were all excellent reasons for his application being successful. The late Sir Robert Peel offered to procure his naturalisation, and to have a private Act of Parliament brought in for that purpose; but the course that was afterwards adopted saved this expense.

My father had a long memorial drawn out, bearing date 8th of June, 1831, and addressed to the Marquis of Anglesey, then Lord-Lieutenant of Ireland, showing how he came to Ireland, his early occupation and profession there, how he became a car proprietor, how the establishment had prospered, and the moral and material good it did to the country, and that he had thereby honestly acquired some personal fortune which he was desirous of investing in the purchase of land, provided that he should be naturalised and enabled to make such purchases in the same manner as Her Majesty's natural-born subjects, and he prayed that he might be admitted to the benefit and privileges of naturalisation under the Act of Parliament 36 Geo. III.

cap. 48. In answer to this memorial, Mr. Ebbs, Clerk of the Council, wrote to my father that he must transmit testimonials from the principal magistrates of the town or place where he resided of the facts set forth in his memorial, as far as they may have knowledge thereof, with any recommendations they might think proper to add thereto, and that he should also annex a certificate from at least one member of the Privy Council, recommending the application, and expressing an opinion that he was a fit person to whom the license should be granted. My father got all the necessary testimonials, and more than enough, with which I need not trouble the reader, and finally became naturalised a British subject on the 31st of August, 1831.

My mother's recollections of her early married life were full of political excitement,—elections, patriots, and all such kindred matters. My father rejoiced in having people about him, and he had quite imbibed the Irish notions of a proper hospitality. My mother never knew what kind of people would turn in, or for how many to provide food. The clergy were of course her frequent visitors, and I have been much amused at her impressions of famous old Father Morrissy—that prince of sportsmen, who used to make his sick calls when he was riding across country, and whom I well remember was permitted as a special privilege to retain a partly sporting style of apparel, when all the other priests in the diocese were made to don the Roman collar and single-breasted coat. Father Cuddehy was also one of her friends, and he never passed by without paying her a visit.   My husband has told me that his father, John O'Connell, of Grenagh, was often at my father's house, and how he used to say at home, "What a nice young wife Bian has got."   The favourable impression was mutual.   My father-in-law (that would have been, had he lived) was a remarkably tall, fine man, not so well favoured as his famous brother, but very agreeable in company, though at times apt to be pugnacious.   His face was rather disfigured on account of a bullet having passed through his cheek in one of the duels that he had fought for the Cause.   Mr. Fitz-Simon, of Glancullen, M.P. for Dublin, who married the Liberator's eldest daughter, was another guest, and his daughter afterwards married my brother.   It has always struck me that for my father's disappointment in the failure of male issue,—for my brother had no son,—it was some compensation to him that his race should merge into that of his great leader, by the marriages of his children with the grand-daughter and the favourite nephew of the Liberator.   Priests, politicians, and patriots, who were not actually either in orders or in Parliament, overran my father's house in those days.   He used to speak kindly of some of these adventurers, whose minds he did not doubt were sincere; but he could not refrain from drawing a moral of the melancholy results consequent upon not staying at home and minding one's own business.

My father still kept up the acquaintance of some of his art friends of former days.   His young lodger friend, Edward Hayes, had married before him, and was frequently in Clonmel. And there was a young artist, James O'Neil, a protégé of my father's, who had only one hand, but who showed a remarkable aptitude in his profession. He was painting a picture of my brother and sister, but the poor fellow died before he had quite finished it. My father wished to have portraits of his family in his house. There was another picture of my sister, done when she was a child, one of my mother, and two of himself. One of these latter was so hideous that my mother would not have it in the house. We have also a daguerreotype, which represents him between forty and fifty years of age, just as he was beginning to get stout. The face is full of power, and the keen eyes seem to throw out a challenge to fortune. The full lips are well set, the nose is finely cut, and the chin shows all the firmness of his character.

My brother, who was named Charles after his father, was born on the 14th October, 1832. My father used often to say what a pretty boy he was, and what a pleasure it was to see him in his mother's arms. My father had now almost everything that his heart could desire,—it is true that I was not then born,—he had a fond wife, a son, a pretty little daughter, he had a fine business that gave him ample means, and all that had clogged the youth of the alien Papist was now removed. He was a free man,—and was a British subject.

The year after my brother was born my grandfather Bianconi died. Indeed, I fear that my father had lost all recollections of his family. From when he first landed in Ireland he had never seen them or had had any concerns with them. Doubtless had he been brought up at home instead of by his grandfather and uncle, the family tie would have been stronger. It was through the British consul in Milan that my father was traced. The foreign custom ordered a division of the dead person's property, and his few acres could not be divided among his children until the fate of the missing Carlo was ascertained. The English consul at Milan had heard of Bianconi's cars, and it struck him that this man must be the long lost Carlo Bianconi. My father at once responded, but he had so lost all trace of his home that he had to make many inquiries as to his family. Since then he kept up a good deal of correspondence with them. He did not in the least avow any shame for having so long forgotten his people, but instead he proceeded to enact the part of a benevolent rich uncle. He left his small property to an orphan niece, he sent money for the education of all the children, he bought substitutes for all the boys in the conscription for the army, and when any one of the girls got married he sent her £50.

I think his early married life was divided between his cars, electioneering, Repeal agitations, and getting into the corporation of Clonmel. Very little of his time was passed at home, as he was rushing about at least four days out of the six, and very busy in his office and in the town when at home. He took great pride in his children, and was very fond of my mother, though perhaps in a peculiar way. He

was a very good husband to her in all material points,
—good-tempered, liberal, anxious that his wife and
children should have comforts and luxuries, and still I
do not think he ever realised the perfection of married
happiness,—the perfect community of thoughts, hopes,
and wishes. He never had time for anything but business, and he seemed to care for no recreation but men's
society. He was very fond of us all, and very good to
us; he and I were more thoroughly friends than parents
and children often are; still the peculiarities of his
foreign nature, and total absence of early domestic
habits, often made him less pleasant than he really
meant to be. My father had little need of sympathy
himself, and he lacked the power of helping one on
with the little burdens of everyday life. His head was
too full of his own affairs for it ever to cross his mind
that a woman wanted anything more than she asked for;
he had no conceptions of the strain of the daily petty
cares, or of the dull monotony of a domestic woman's
life. For a man of such excellent common sense in
most things, he was not a judicious father. He suffered
my handsome brother to grow up without a profession,
he over-stimulated my brain in a delicate and precarious
childhood, until it was purely owing to the goodness of
God, and lots of fresh air and cold water, that I grew
up into a strong healthy woman, able to take care of
myself. I do not say this disrespectfully, but I must
tell the truth, and I think that men of my father's type
do not understand sentiment nor the good that a little
of it may do.

M

I was the third and last child of my parents. I was
born eight years after my brother, on the 16th of September, 1840, and I find my birth entered on the credit
side of my father's private ledger. I was to have been
christened Henrietta, after my grandmother, but at
her express wish I was called Mary Anne, which
had been the name of her dead daughter and of her
mother.

Once when the Liberator was staying in my father's
house, my father asked his advice about sending my
sister to school. " No, no, no," he replied. " Never
take her away from her mother. Get a governess to
assist the mother in little Kate's education, but never
take the child from her mother's care. The tender
affection of the parent educates the daughter's heart."
My father then made some apology to O'Connell for
bringing in his children. " Your time is so limited,"
he said, " I fear they must tease you." " Your apology," returned O'Connell, " reminds me of my friend,
Peter Hussey, who was not remarkable for his politeness. ' Dan,' he said to me once, ' you should not bring
in your children after dinner, it is a heavy tax upon the
admiration of the company.' ' Never mind, Peter,' I
said to him, ' I admire them so much myself that
I do not require any one to help me.' My eldest
daughter told me she was afraid I should spoil her
Mary. ' I don't think I shall,' I said to her. ' I know
I did my best to spoil you, my love, and I could not
succeed.' "

I have heard much about the snow-storm in 1834;

in fact, "the big snow" and "the big cholera" are favourite reckoning dates with the poor people. The snow-storm set in one day after my father had gone into town, and it was so heavy by dinner-time that my mother sent in the close carriage for him. He brought home a gentleman who stayed and dined with us, and who refused to be driven to his house after dinner. In less than half an hour he was brought back insensible, and seemingly dead; but by the aid of restoratives and much rubbing, he soon came round again. Less fortunate was a lovely country girl, a rich farmer's daughter, whose cart was upset against a milestone. She was much hurt in the head, and was carried into one of our labourer's cottages, and there carefully tended. But unfortunately, in spite of my father's advice, she was removed too soon, and died within a day after getting home. Our kitchen in those days was full of people engaged in clearing the road to Clonmel,—it was lucky that there was also food for them to eat. While the snow lasted my father used to send out great fatigue parties to make a passage on the road, and as Jim Halloran, one of the drivers, went with them provided with a keg of whisky, by the time they had triumphantly worked their way into Carrick, none of them were very well able to describe their adventures. My father saved a whole family, whose hut in a little dell was completely hidden by the drifting of the snow. Their cries were heard through the chimney, and it was only by stripping off a portion of the roof that the unfortunate people escaped.

I have already spoken of Father Cuddehy, an old friend of my father's, and whom he helped to shake off the robe of St. Francis, and to start on a useful career as a missionary priest in America. He is now the parish priest of Milford, in Massachusetts. I received not long ago a letter from him which I will here reproduce. I think it will sufficiently explain itself.

"DEAR MRS. O'CONNELL,—I received your most welcome letter of 17th July, and was delighted to hear that your mother, yourself, and your young son were all well. I am glad to find that you are working on the life of the Governor, as we all used to call your father. I am sure you will find abundance of material in his multitudinous and useful correspondence to make his biography most interesting and instructive. The first time I ever remember seeing him was about fifty-four years ago, when I was called on as a little boy to serve mass in his house at five o'clock on a fine Christmas morning, though he did most of the 'serving' himself. I always remember the crowd that assembled there, and the circumstance that first made me acquainted with him, and which was such a source of pleasure to me in after life. It was under his hospitable roof that I had more than one meeting with the Liberator— the great O'Connell, Richard Lalor Shiel, General Sir de Lacy Evans, of the British Legion in Spain, who came to help Otway Cave, the Liberal member for Tipperary, to fight any Tory that dare insult Cave.

There I also met Dr. Madden, the historian of the *United Irishmen;* Tom Steel; Barrett, of the *Pilot;* Dominick Romayne, M.P.; Judges Ball and Pigot, and a host of other brilliant celebrities, who have all, with the exception of Dr. Madden, long since passed away from us. In fact, it was at your father's house and at his hospitable board that whatever was brave and liberal in politics, bold and enterprising in business, was discussed, and often carried into execution, both as regarding Clonmel and the county at large. It was well that it was in Clonmel he took up his early residence, for in no other town in Ireland could there be found at that time such an independent and daring spirit of freedom as in the capital of Tipperary, and which harmonized so well with your father's own position; for had Ireland had anything like a legislature of its own, as we have here in Massachusetts, to develop her resources, Clonmel would have been one of the most enterprising, active manufacturing places in the land. And I always remember what I heard O'Connell say at a meeting for the Repeal: 'What better Chancellor of the Exchequer could we require than my friend Charles Bianconi?' It would be easy to show from the Liberator's correspondence what a high opinion he had of your father's abilities, and the work he did in his time for the comfort and convenience of the people of Ireland, in running cars everywhere through the land. This alone would show him to have performed a service to the country, second only to O'Connell himself.

"I cannot close this letter without calling to mind the

many social hours when we used to play whist with your grandmother, that grand old woman, so ladylike and genial, of whom I have often been reminded by the strong-minded women of Massachusetts, but to whom she was superior by her good sense and wisdom. We who have often been at your father's house have no reason to complain, for Providence has been very kind to us all, and has assisted us to do our duty in our several spheres,—your father especially, in his long and useful career, also your husband Morgan John, in his brilliant parliamentary course, and your honoured mother in works of charity and bringing up children and grand-children. May you all long enjoy the fruits of your worthy father's labours in the land he loved and served so long. For myself, although I love Ireland as I ever did, I thank God for sending me to a land literally flowing with milk and honey. The finest, freest, and most fruitful country on earth. Oh, how I wish we had more of America and less of England and Ireland!"

CHAPTER VIII.

THE MAYOR OF CLONMEL.

KING SOLOMON in all his glory never felt more proudly happy in giving laws to the Children of Israel than did Charles Bianconi when he ruled the little community where the "Alien Papist" had once found it so hard to gain a footing. The Municipal Reform Act had virtually thrown open the borough to Catholics, and they hastened to profit by the opportunity. The Liberator himself had not disdained to accept the civic chair in Dublin, and his faithful follower, Charles Bianconi, gloried in his Clonmel mayoralty. I can barely remember him in his chain and red robe. I think a benevolent policeman once held me up in his arms to see him on the bench. I have some recollections of him walking about with his white wand, I suppose inspecting the markets, and I remember being puzzled and half afraid as to whether the police had not some sinister designs on his person.

In March last year, just thirty-three years after his mayoralty, I visited Clonmel, and I there became acquainted with Mr. Thomas Dorney, my father's clerk

during his term of office. Mr. Dorney kindly made out
for me a report of some of the proceedings that had taken
place, of which I will extract portions, and place them
before the reader somewhat in the form of a narrative.

My father had taken a prominent part in the local
doings after the Corporate Reform Act in 1842, and then
Mr. Dorney was directed to attend every day during
the month of July, when two barristers, sent down by
the Lord-Lieutenant, were busy revising the burgess
roll.   I here quote Mr. Dorney :—

" Like every other Act passed by the British Parliament for Ireland, this contained a penal clause, to the
effect that no person could be enrolled as a burgess
unless he had paid that most obnoxious impost, 'Minister's Money,' up to the previous 31st of August. The
majority of the Roman Catholics refused to pay it, and
the wealthy members of the prescribed creed, after a
consultation, got up a subscription, headed by Mr.
Bianconi, and called upon the Protestant rector of the
parish, requesting him to open an office as required by
the Act, and to have his collector present. The clergyman was only too glad to do so. The people were then
directed by the leaders of the Liberal party to call at
the office, when I was appointed to pay the minister's
tax due from each person out of the funds given to me
for that purpose. Then each in their turn received the
collector's receipt, and at the revision the barristers
placed them on. the burgess roll. The result was that
at the election the Liberals had a large majority."

The Tories were furious; they thought they could hit my father, and, through him, the whole of the Liberal party. On the following Sunday the new reformed corporation were to ballot for their Mayor, and on the previous Friday the Tories had served my father with a notice stating that as he was an alien he was thereby disqualified from being a burgess. That evening Mr. Dorney was sent off to Dublin by the night mail coach to bring back an attested copy of the Letters of Naturalisation granted to my father in 1831. Mr. Dorney had a letter to Mr. Simon Creagh, a well-known solicitor, who escorted him to the Castle, where the attested copy was happily procured. By another night journey Mr. Dorney arrived in Clonmel on the Sunday morning; he attended the meeting and produced the document that showed Charles Bianconi to be as good a townsman as his fellows. My father was placed high on the list of candidates for the mayoralty, but was not actually Mayor until 1845.

On the 1st December, 1844, Charles Bianconi was unanimously elected Mayor of Clonmel for the ensuing year amid loud and continuous cheering. That was the third time that a Catholic had filled the office. He at once wrote to the Liberator for general advice, and for instructions as to what law books he should study, and received the following characteristic letter :—

"MY DEAR MAYOR,—If you wish to discharge the duties of the mayoralty with perfect satisfaction, act

upon your own sound common sense and do not look
into any law book.

" Faithfully yours,
"DANIEL O'CONNELL."

I have heard many a good story of my father, after
he had given a decision, saying to his secretary, " Tom,
is that English ? " or, when he was more grandiloquently disposed, he would talk of his ignorance of
the English language when some one said that he had
put a wrong construction upon the wording of the Act,
or twisted the technicalities of phrase so as to suit his
own views.

The old corporation had made off with all the para-
phernalia, and the new Mayor, besides having to
purchase his own chain, provided a handsome stand for
sword and mace ; the sword was carried by Mr. Dorney,
who acted as sword-bearer, pursuivant, and as city
marshal. When other Mayors, after my father's term
of office had expired, had not their own chains, he
would *hire* out his to them on the condition that they
paid £3 to the Sisters of Charity. On the day of
installation the late Mayor, our good old friend Dr.
Phelan, alluded gracefully to my father's rise among
the people of Clonmel, his charity, and his love of
justice. Town-Councillor Bianconi was then duly
introduced as Dr. Phelan's successor. He got up to
make his speech, and when the cheering was silenced
he said :—" Gentlemen of the Corporation, and Bur-
gesses of Clonmel, I feel exceedingly the burden you

have placed upon me, nevertheless I have great confidence, from the morality and great public virtue of the people here, that the duties of my office will not be onerous. That the people of Clonmel will continue in their hitherto good conduct I entertain no doubt, and that they will enable me to discharge those duties for their benefit and advantage (hear, hear). I shall want your assistance, for we are partly in the dark. We are one of the most respectable corporations in the county, but our predecessors, I regret to say, did not feel satisfied at our getting our turn of the office they so long occupied, for when they went out of office they took with them the legal books that of right belonged to their successors. But I hope they will take the hint and return to us those books, which are of no value to them now, but would be of good service to us (hear, hear). Gentlemen, I pledge myself to you that the interests of the town shall have my most anxious and serious attention (hear, hear). First, I shall endeavour to have re-elected a market jury (cheers). Secondly, it is my intention, and I give this public notice of it, to weigh the bread of every baker in the town (loud cheers), and I won't tell either you or the bakers when or how I'll do it (laughter). Therefore, I give the hint to my friends the bakers not to be too fond of high profits, but to be content with small profits and a large business (cheers). I shall attend to the shambles also, which must be kept clean, and washed out at least once a-week. My friends the victuallers will, I trust, save the necessity of my adopting measures on this head, which otherwise it is my intention, as it will be my imperative duty, to have recourse to for the benefit of the inhabitants at large (hear, hear). The corporation have made a code of byelaws for the government of the borough ; I shall have copies of these extensively posted through the town, and any person offending against them it will be my duty to punish (hear, hear). To every person aggrieved by the misconduct of the inhabitants, or the officers under me, I shall give every redress in my power, as I have accepted the office of the chief magistrate not for my own sake but for yours (cheers), for in all conscience I had enough already on my hands (laughter). But now that I am in office my best endeavours shall be used to discharge the important duties faithfully, honestly, and impartially (cheers). I have frequently asserted that I have great confidence in the morality and virtue of the people ;—let the truth of that assertion be carried out by you (hear, and cheers). Having said so much as to what I will do, I will now tell you what I will not do, and those unfortunate persons who have deserted the banner of my friend Father Mathew would do well to mind what I am about to state. I am afraid our worthy friends, Alderman Hackett and your late Mayor, allowed their kindness of heart frequently to get the better of their duty in respect of punishing those persons who were brought before them charged with drunkenness. Now, I do not intend to go to the police office at all on Sundays, therefore I strongly advise you to keep sober on Saturdays unless you want to lose mass on Sunday (laughter). I will, in fact, do everything in my power to put down drunkenness, notwithstanding that I see many of you looking so *rum* at me (laughter). I pledge myself also that I shall use my best exertions to establish National schools for the education of the youth of the borough; that important subject shall have my first and paramount attention. In conclusion, I shall follow in the footsteps of two worthy predecessors, and I fervently and anxiously hope to discharge the important duties conferred upon me to the satisfaction of the public." (Loud and continued cheering.)

On his inauguration night the new Mayor took the chair at an annual meeting of the Mechanics' Institute. He was a warm supporter of the institution, and was a firmer believer in its powers and virtues than many modern sceptics are disposed to be. At his banquet in Hearn's Hotel, he entertained the Corporation, the clergy, the official townspeople, and many of the gentry of the place. There were eighty guests in all. My father's good-humour kept harmony amongst the somewhat discordant elements, for the "true blue" respectability were there in only a small proportion.

Mr. Thomas Meagher, the then Member for Waterford, and formerly Mayor of that town (Mr. Meagher was the first Catholic Mayor of the Reformed Corporation, and this fact is recorded on a mural tablet in the Waterford Town Hall) about this time wrote to my father, touching his new office of Mayor of Clonmel.

"I am glad to find that you are making your office so truly useful as you appear to be doing. There is hardly anything more essential to health and comfort than well-regulated markets. You seem to have more to do than I had in that respect, and also to have more power. This probably is from some local Act or some general Act applied to your town. The oath, I suppose, is so authorised. In other respects my plan was much the same as yours, to appeal to the good sense and good feeling of the people to remedy any complaint detrimental to the public, and to show them how far it lies in their power to do this. Besides, I used to visit the markets constantly, and this, I think, also contributed to keep things in order. I shall be most happy at any time to give you the best opinion I can upon any matter if you wish to consult me."

I will also insert here a letter of Lord Glengall's to my father :—

"The more I consider the subject on which we conversed lately, viz., the establishment of exchanges for the public buying and selling of all species of agricultural produce, the more I am satisfied of its utility and practicability. I have lately seen the new Corn Exchange in the city of Cork, and I thus learned that the buying and selling in that public market gives the greatest satisfaction to the merchant as well as to the farmer. I am convinced that the establishment of such a market for the sale of wheat, oats, and butter in Clonmel, and indeed in other towns, would be of great advantage to the agricultural interests as well as to the interests of the merchants. This system is adopted in almost all the large towns in England, and I see no reason why the same should not be the case in Ireland. To enter into the details of the Cork Exchange would be beyond the limits of a letter, but I am convinced that the formation of railways will lead to a complete change in the present system of purchase and selling of all agricultural produce.

"Allow me to call your attention to the present state of the burial-grounds in Clonmel, and the positive necessity that exists for forming a cemetery outside the town. I am in hopes of inducing the Government to bring in a bill to enable parishes to take ground for constructing cemeteries, and for repairing the enclosures of churchyards both in towns and in the rural districts by grand jury presentments.

"I remain, dear sir, yours truly,

"GLENGALL.

"The Mayor of Clonmel."

Shortly after his election my father sent out circulars to the Town Council to attend him in state to mass upon a certain Sunday that he had fixed upon with Dr. Burke. At that time it was a misdemeanour for a Catholic Mayor to wear his robes at mass. Even the Liberator used in Dublin to drive to Marlborough Street in his robes, and then leave them in the carriage. Mr. Dorney was very uneasy in his mind, and armed with this great precedent, he went to my father and inquired what was to be done with the robes and chain during mass.

" I'll take care of them myself, Tom," replied his worship.

Mr. Dorney then respectfully urged that such a proceeding would be illegal.

" Illegal or not, I'll wear them during mass. I've bought them and paid for them, and if the Government wish to prosecute me for wearing my own property, let them do so. I cannot discover any treason in wearing my own gold chain, the scarlet robe, or holding the innocent wand."

And he fully acted up to his word.

The government authorities thought it prudent to pass the matter over and say nothing about it, though it was two hundred years since a mayor had gone to mass wearing his robes.

On the 8th January, 1845, Charles Bianconi first took his seat as Chairman at the Borough Petty Sessions, assisted by two Justices of the Peace. James Ryan was brought up and convicted of being drunk, and tearing a constable's waist-belt.

Mayor: " Well, Ryan, what have you to say ?"

Ryan: " Nothing, your worship; only I wasn't drunk."

Mayor: " Who tore the constable's belt ?"

Ryan: " He was bloated after his Christmas dinner, your worship, and the belt burst."

Mayor : " You are so pleasant, that you will have to spend forty-eight hours in gaol."

Michael Breen was convicted of an assault upon a night watch, and ordered to pay a penalty of 7*s.* 6*d.*, or to be imprisoned for a fortnight.

Prisoner : " Will I get a week to pay it ?"

Mayor : " No. When any of the authorities are assaulted whilst in the execution of their duties, I will not allow an offender any indulgence. The peace of the town must be preserved, and drunkenness must be checked," &c.

Mary Cooney was convicted of drunkenness on New Year's night.

Mayor : " I have made up my mind to clear the town of characters of your description. There is not one of you who is brought before me for improper conduct, that I will not commit to gaol unless you provide securities to be of good behaviour for the future. The town must be protected from the annoyance of bad characters."

On that same day the Mayor gave a short homily on petty thefts. He said : " I take this opportunity of stating that I am determined, as far as I possibly can, to put the law in force against those persons who are in the habit of plundering straw and other property from the farmers who attend our markets. I shall endeavour to abate that disgraceful nuisance."

The sitting was concluded before three o'clock, and at that hour the Bians used to leave Clonmel for Waterford, for Kilkenny, for Fethard, and for Dungarvan.

As quickly as possible the chief magistrate doffed his
civic robes, and in a very few minutes he was engaged,
both by his example and by his commands, in assisting
his porters in the packing of the luggage on the cars.

My father was indefatigable in his exertions to
induce the bakers to make a uniform-sized loaf, and at
one of the meetings of the corporation he thus addressed
the court :—

"Gentlemen,—Since my appointment to the office
of Mayor, I have taken great pains to persuade the
bakers of this borough to make a uniform penny loaf.
All my efforts failed. The penny loaf averaged from
eight to ten ounces. I then issued a proclamation,
and called upon the bakers to have scales and weights
in their shops agreeable to the provisions of the Act of
Parliament, and for the public to insist upon having
their bread weighed. I had 500 of those proclamations posted through the town, and being of opinion
that the posting of those proclamations would not
be of sufficient pressure, I directed the inspector of
weights and measures to get 1,000 copies of that proclamation printed in quarto, and distributed among the
inhabitants generally (hear, hear). I am very proud
to have to tell you that since then the weight of the
penny loaf has increased from $8\frac{1}{2}$ ounces to 11 ounces
the minimum, and $12\frac{1}{2}$ the maximum (hear, hear).
With one exception I succeeded in coaxing them when
I had failed in coercing them by law (laughter). The
exception I allude to is a baker who, under the
specious pretence of selling two loaves for $1\frac{1}{2}d$., sells

those small loaves to retailers, who charge the public a penny, and thus in a manner defraud the public of their just right" (hear).

Alderman Hearn: "It is very difficult to make the bakers have a uniform-sized loaf, there being no assize of bread in this town. There has been a great deal of good effected by your worship, I admit; I find the benefit in my own establishment."

My father had a very great dislike to all pawnbrokers and their business, and had a strong idea that they were a curse to the country. "Don't you see," he would say, "that wherever one of those *traps* is placed, public-houses are always close by." He spared no pains to keep the pawnbrokers strictly to the hours of business allowed to them by the Pawnbroking Acts. His well-meant exertions brought down upon him the anger of those traders, but he invariably used to say, when this fact was spoken of, "Don't you know the story of water falling off the duck's back?"

Mr. Dorney told me that although there were certain men with whom my father was strict and severe, yet, on the whole, he ruled the little community with equit-able leniency. On one occasion he was obliged to be absent from Clonmel when the court was sitting, and he deputed one of the justices of the peace, an old Indian officer, to take his place, saying to him, "Now recollect you are to be me and not Colonel, during my absence; what I mean is, that you are not to be more severe than I would be myself on offenders brought before you." The colonel promised obedience; but when my father returned he asked his secretary how the colonel had treated the offenders. Mr. Dorney replied that there was many a poor prisoner who much regretted the absence of the Mayor, and that they did not at all relish the colonel. "Oh! Tom," said my father, "he's the devil!"

My father's avowed determination to support National education exposed him to sundry private innuendoes and open admonitions. To the last he always used to say, "There is no fear of our people when the priests do their duty." Not even grand old John of Tuam's anathemas could shake his fidelity to national education. Still he had no notion of deserting his old friends the Christian Brothers. A letter containing the following paragraph appeared in the *Free Press* newspaper at the time :—

"The laudable anxiety you feel for the education of the poor is well known and duly appreciated. It seems from private report that you are engaged in certain proceedings with regard to the establishment of National schools on an extensive scale in Clonmel. National schools are very good things in their way, and become partial blessings when no better can be had. . . . Let us then, by all means, have our Catholic youth, the Christian Brothers, with their admirable system of education. This education is the only sure basis of human improvement, and from such alone can you expect to make truly good men and worthy citizens."

In answer to this letter, my father sent to the Christian Brothers a present of £50, and also twenty suits of clothing for the most deserving of their pupils. These twenty suits of clothes he continued to give them every year until his death.

While I am on the subject of charities, I will quote the following from Mr. Dorney's report:—"During the time that Mr. Bianconi was in office he was entitled to certain fees, which amounted annually to about £60; and on the evening of his inauguration he sent for me and said, 'Tom, am I not entitled to some fees?' 'Yes, sir,' I replied. 'Well,' said he, 'I will not put one shilling of them into my pocket, but as the guardians of the poor refuse to provide coffins for the destitute who die outside the workhouse, it is my desire that you hand over every week the amount to which I am entitled to my former agent, Mr. Patrick O'Neill, and whenever a coffin is wanted, on your getting a certificate that the applicant cannot afford to purchase one —this must be signed by a clergyman, no matter of what religious denomination, or by a doctor—you will then give an order on Marks English, a respectable old mechanic, and at the end of every month get his account and audit it, and then give an order on Mr. O'Neill for the amount. For, as far as it lies in my power, the poor of the town without difference of creed shall receive a decent burial.'"

And upon another occasion the following conversation took place in the court :—

Town Clerk : "There are some money accounts to be passed to-day."

Mr. O'Brien : "What are they?"

Town Clerk: "There is a claim by the Mayor for half a year's salary up to the 1st of July" (laughter).

Mr. Kenny: "Oh! the Mayor won't accept any salary."

Mayor: "I would not take the office at all, only I thought there were some pickings in it" (laughter).

Town Clerk: "I am directed by his worship to hand in the amount of his salary to Dr. Burke in aid of the school for the poor that is being erected in Blind Street."

Mayor: "Although I do not intend to put a shilling of the salary or of the fees into my pocket, it does not follow that I should be deprived of the pleasure of bestowing it for useful purposes; and I know of none more useful than contributing to diffuse the blessings of education amongst the children of the poor."

One incident occurred that considerably worried my father, and ruffled the prosperous smoothness of his career as Mayor. The revision of the burgess roll came before his court in November. His assessors were Mr. Graham, a high Conservative, and Mr. Hearn, a staunch O'Connellite, and a faithful follower of Charles Bianconi. My father ruled that the premises described as "yard" did not give a qualification for a vote; and after much discussion the Mayor and his fellow-assessors struck off the roll sundry candidates, who happened to be mainly Tories. My father was therefore accused of doing it for party purposes, though a high Tory had joined with him in his

decision. Two Tory shoemakers appealed, and the
Court of Queen's Bench decided that the Mayor had
given a wrong decision, and directed that he and his
assessors should be mulcted in costs. The costs, however, my father paid, as his colleagues had been led by
his misinterpretation of the Act, which he persisted in
setting down to his ignorance of the English language.
At the next meeting of the court, he made the following
statement :—

" Gentlemen, since last we met, a very painful duty
devolved upon me in the revision of the burgess roll.
Next to trial by jury, I consider the principle of allowing every subject who pays taxes to participate in the
administration of public affairs as the most important ;
nothing therefore could give me more pain than to be
coerced, from the defective state of the law, to disfranchise many respectable and useful citizens (hear,
hear, hear). I repeat that nothing could be more painful to me than to be compelled by the wording of the
Municipal Act, to disfranchise those gentlemen, and
deprive them of having a voice in the administration of
the municipal affairs of this borough (hear, hear). You
must be aware that if premises are not described on the
poor-rate book, singly by the name of house, warehouse,
counting-house, or shop, that the persons presiding in
the Revision Court are not in a position, from the
wording of the Act, to give the persons so rated the
benefit which, I am certain, was intended by the legislature, and dictated by common sense (hear) ; and if
both parties engaged in the contest at the late revision

were equally within the law in the proceedings, the
result would have been that the majority of the bur-
gesses of Clonmel, without any guilt on their parts,
would have been disfranchised by the absurd technicalities of the law (hear). . . . I allude to this most
important matter with a view that the legislature may
have the opportunity, during the ensuing sitting of
Parliament, of adopting such remedies as will correct
the admitted evil (hear, hear). I entertain a hope that
every man rated at five pounds and upwards, who pays
his taxes and performs the duties of a citizen, will have
the privilege of voting at the municipal election, the
same as in England, unless it be intended to govern us
again under the old rule of *divide et impera*, which
God forbid (hear, and cheers). Gentlemen, if I had no
other reasons for retiring from the honourable position
which you placed me in, and the duties of which I have
discharged so feebly (no, no), the defective state of this
law would be a sufficient reason for my refusal of the
honour which public report says you intend to confer a
second time on me (hear, hear). The same feeling on
this subject actuate the assessors who presided with me,
and I am bound to say that it would be impossible to
find men possessed of more sterling honour, integrity,
or impartiality (hear). . . . I witnessed with delight
an amalgamation of the good men of Clonmel of opposite religious and political feelings, merging those feelings into one of local and national good (hear, hear).
It would afford me much pleasure to see all men—the
children of the same Deity—subjects of the same sove-

reign — fellow - Christians and fellow - citizens amalgamate together for the public local good, and the advancement of the interests of the country (cheers). I refuse, therefore, to continue longer than this year in office, as I could not again consent to administer a law so defective,—a law which has a tendency to divide society, and to prevent the good so much to be desired."

About this time my father joined the '82 Club, got up in memory of the Volunteers of 1782, and invested in the green-and-gold uniform of the Club. This, indeed, was at the Liberator's request, for Mr. Ray, his secretary, wrote to my father, "The Liberator says he expects to see you at the dinner on the 16th April— that we cannot spare any one to be away. You will have to give an order for the suit, a grand affair, green with gold for an embroidery, &c.; it will cost about £15. Köhler, of Sackville Street, is making the Liberator's and Mr. O'Connell's suits." My husband, Morgan John O'Connell, then M.P. for Kerry, was also one of the Members of Parliament who attended the great demonstration and dinner in Thurles, where the old Liberator had literally "raised" Tipperary, having got much help from his Worship of Clonmel, whom he had ordered to produce a few thousand Tipperary boys.

My father had taken a most active part during the Liberator's previous imprisonment; and on his release he attended what Mr. Dorney terms "The Martyr's Levée." "The great and imposing levée," says Mr. Dorney, "was held by the Liberator and his fellow-martyrs in the Rotunda, May 30th, 1845. Mr. Bianconi headed the Clonmel Corporation, and wore the splendid green-and-gold uniform of the '82 Club under his civic robes. He was warmly greeted by his friend the great O'Connell, and he signed the parchment-roll, pledging himself never to desist from constitutional agitation until the ill-fated Union should be repealed."

At a meeting of the Corporation of Clonmel on the 1st December, 1845, Dr. Phelan proposed and Alderman Keily seconded the re-election as Mayor of Town Councillor Bianconi; and their addresses were received with unanimous applause.

Alderman Hackett : " We are threatened with a dreadful visitation, and the re-election of my worthy friend will meet with our heartiest approbation."

Mayor : " Gentlemen, it is extremely distressing to me at all times not to have it in my power to comply with the wishes of my fellow-citizens. Your kindness in my regard is most flattering to my feelings" (cheers); " but it is impossible for me to comply with your wishes " (loud cries of " No, no ! ")

Councillor Thomas Prendergast (Conservative) : " We are determined, sir, to re-elect you."

Mayor : " It would be impossible for me to reconcile to my feelings the acceptance of the mayoralty for another year. I must in candour tell you, gentlemen, that if you persevere in your intentions I shall retire from the Council."

The entire body rose, and simultaneously cried, " No, no, no ! "

Alderman Hackett: "I call upon your Worship to put the resolution."

The Mayor hesitated.

Alderman Kenny: "You are bound to put the resolution."

Mayor: "I do not like to put that resolution" (laughter).

Alderman Keily: "You have no alternative."

Mayor: "There is a regular conspiracy against me" (laughter).

The resolution after a brief interval was put, and carried amidst loud cheers, which were repeated lustily by the people outside.

The Corporation were quite unanimous in their wishes; and I do not think that my father's first refusal was merely a *nolo episcopari.* I think that, as his mind was then set upon the purchase of land, he did not want to take the year's duty until it was actually forced upon him. However, when he did undertake it, so far as it lay in his power, he did his duty by the starving people.

In the first month of his second mayoralty, my father had to go to Dublin, and he deputed Mr. Ryan, R.M., to act for him in his absence. Mr. Ryan went to the office one morning before Mr. Dorney had arrived there, and carried off all the official documents to the office of the county magistrate's clerk, alleging that the Mayor was not a magistrate. My father at once took an opinion from Mr. Pigot, afterwards Chief Baron Pigot, and put himself in communication with Mr. R. Pennefather, the Under-Secretary of State.　I here give Mr. Pigot's opinion on the matter:—

" MERRION SQUARE, 10th January, 1846.

"MY DEAR SIR,—I have read the documents which you sent to me, relating to the jurisdiction of the Mayor of Clonmel.　I find that the matter is now under the consideration of Government.　I presume you will be made acquainted with the opinion of the law-advisers of the Crown.　My advice to you is, that you should be governed in your official conduct by that opinion, whatever it may be.

"But I can by no means advise that you, or the inhabitants of Clonmel, shall rest satisfied with any opinion or determination of the Executive of which the result shall be to deprive you and them of those weekly sittings for the borough, *under the presidency of the Mayor as its chief magistrate*, which it has now enjoyed, I believe, for a period beyond the reach of living memory.

"The Mayor is, unquestionably, a justice of the peace, within the new municipal boundaries.

"It is competent to him, and any one or more magistrates having jurisdiction within the borough (as all county magistrates of the county of Tipperary have), to hold petty sessions for the borough.　It is a mistake to suppose that such petty sessions cannot be held, because Clonmel is not within a petty sessions district prescribed or defined under the statute 7 & 8 Geo. IV. chap. 67, or 6 & 7 Wm. IV. chap. 34.　Petty sessions might have been lawfully held, and were in fact held, before those statutes were passed. They were so held, as I am informed, according to a usage of very long standing in the borough of Clonmel.

"It is, indeed, quite plain that the borough petty sessions not only were held prior to the passing of the earliest of those statutes, but were purposely left unaffected by the arrangements made in 1828, under 7 & 8 Geo. IV. chap. 67, for the district adjoining Clonmel. A petty sessions district was then assigned by the county magistrates, comprising portions of the county contiguous to the borough, but including no place within the borough, save only the county courthouse, in which the county petty sessions were held; and it was expressly declared, in the order or resolution appearing in the book of the clerk of the peace, 'that the jurisdiction of the Mayor of Clonmel shall continue upon the same basis as heretofore.'

"The arrangement then made has, I understand, been ever since uniformly acted on, until those proceedings were adopted within the last fortnight, of which you have complained. The practice, I understand, has been, that a sitting of petty sessions has been held at the county court-house, for the county petty sessions district, on one day of the week; and that on another day a sitting of the petty sessions for the borough has been held, at which the Mayor has presided.

"It is, in my opinion, perfectly clear that the Municipal Act made no change whatever in reference to the

Mayor's jurisdiction, as justice of the peace, or to his competence to hold, with one or more other magistrates, petty sessions for the borough, save that his jurisdiction, as such justice, is now derived from the Act of Parliament and not from the Crown's Charter, and that it is confined to the new municipal boundaries.

" I anticipate that the view of this subject which I have here stated will be taken by those charged with the duty of counselling the Executive.

" If, however, the Government shall be differently advised, or if the course recently pursued in Clonmel shall be persevered in, then I think immediate steps should be taken by a public remonstrance from the inhabitants to the Government, and by petitions to Parliament, to impose upon the Executive the responsibility, either of adopting promptly such measures, whether administrative or legislative, as shall replace the borough in the possession of that local jurisdiction which it has so long enjoyed, or of distinctly declaring that Government decline to do so. And if (which I am very far from anticipating, from what I assume to be the intentions and desires of those now at the head of the Executive in Ireland) such remonstrance be unavailing, I shall be ready to bring the whole matter before Parliament; to call upon the responsible advisers of the Crown in the House of Commons to introduce, if necessary, an amendment of the law; to propose myself to Parliament a measure for that purpose, if the Government shall decline to do so; and (if it be deemed expedient to do so) to seek an inquiry into the circumstances which have led to the recent proceedings.

"I think the documents now before me should be forwarded to the authorities at the Castle. They should receive all the information which it is in your power to afford. Copies of these documents should be kept; as it may be convenient to be prepared with them in the event of a motion being made in either House of Parliament for the production of the correspondence.

"Believe me to be, dear sir, very faithfully yours,

"D. R. PIGOT.

"To Charles Bianconi, Esq.,
    Mayor of Clonmel."

The result was that the Mayor's authority was confirmed; and the Clonmel and Carrick resident magistrates were ordered to assist him on the bench. In fact, it was a complete triumph of borough over county.

About this time the line of railway running from Waterford to Limerick was being planned, and the promoters of it met with considerable opposition. Mr. Thomas Meagher writes to my father from Waterford, under date 16th September, 1844 :—

"MY DEAR SIR,—Mr. Billing and Mr. Thomson have been with us on the subject of the railway from Waterford to Limerick; they are now about to visit Cork, and they will take Clonmel on their way. The line they propose from Waterford to Limerick, through Carrick and Clonmel, has met with the unanimous approbation of

our local committee. I hope you will exert yourselves
and unite with us in promoting it. These gentlemen
will explain matters to you as far as they are con-
cerned, and I trust you will give them every information in your power.

"Believe me, my dear sir, yours faithfully,

"THOMAS MEAGHER.

"To Charles Bianconi, Esq., Clonmel."

And a few days later, Mr. Meagher writes :—

"WATERFORD, 26th October, 1844.

"MY DEAR SIR,—I was pleased to observe by the
Mercantile Advertiser, of yesterday, that you had become a shareholder in our Waterford and Limerick
line. I regard your accession to our company as an
important evidence of its utility and safety, and at the
same time I am satisfied that you have consulted your
best interests. When I was at Clonmel addressing
your townsmen upon the subject, I took the liberty of
making an allusion to you. I do not suppose that I
was mistaken, and that although the result of a line of
railway from Limerick to Waterford may be to lessen
your car traffic on the main lines, yet I think that the
railway will give a stimulus to your cars, and that the
benefits will be mutual.

"As you are, therefore, embarked with us, I trust
you will give us the benefit of your valuable experience
and active co-operation, and that you will take your
proper share in the management of a line which must

serve your future interests as much as it will be benefited by your future individual operations. . . . . I hope
that those who have taken an active part in the work
may hereafter see the benefits they have conferred
upon the country, and especially upon the poor.

"I remain, &c.,

"THOMAS MEAGHER."

The opposition to the undertaking came from the
Dublin and Cashel Railway Company and from the
Suir Navigation Company, both, of course, trying to
prevent further competition against themselves. It would
be useless to relate that struggle here : it has now long
since passed and gone, and there is nothing in it that
calls for special comment. I will merely publish a
letter from Lord Glengall to my father, and the memo-
randum of agreement between the two rival railway
companies.

"DUBLIN, 16*th* *March*, 1845.

"DEAR SIR,—Many thanks for your enclosures. Mr.
Meagher's letter is very satisfactory. Though absent,
I have friends working for us in a particular quarter
which will serve us when the day of difficulty comes.
I think we shall succeed after much trouble; but trouble
is a thing upon which I always calculated and laid out
to overcome long ago. The standing orders is the
great danger; there our opponents worry us at small
cost.

"The river Suir from Clonmel to Carrick is only fit

for mills and for fish; and this will be seen after the railway from Clonmel to Waterford has been open a year. The export trade will break down on the river as the import trade must naturally come up by the railway, we lowering our tolls and charges so as to smash the horse line. I see no reason to make a secret of a plain fact.

"Yours truly,

"GLENGALL."

"GREAT SOUTHERN AND WESTERN RAILWAY COMPANY,
"COLLEGE GREEN, DUBLIN, 29*th March*, 1845.

"WATERFORD AND LIMERICK RAILWAY COMPANY,
AND
GREAT SOUTHERN AND WESTERN RAILWAY COMPANY.

"At a meeting between a Deputation of the Waterford and Limerick Railway Company and the Directors of the Great Southern and Western Railway Company, it was agreed that all the terms as proposed by the Great Southern and Western Railway Company to Mr. Hunt in London, on the 15th day of March last, shall be consented to by the Waterford and Limerick Railway Company, and that every straightforward and honest support shall be given by each company for the purpose of supporting the bills of the other as recommended by the Board of Trade.

"Signed, THOMAS MEAGHER,
WILLIAM MONSELL,
JOS. W. STRANGMAN,
CHARLES BIANCONI."

The line was made, but it did not prosper. For many years it was a bad speculation for its shareholders, though I believe it is now in a better condition. It was not merely to get an interest for his money that my father took an interest in the new railway ; he was thoroughly imbued with the notion that traffic, traffic, and more traffic must be good for the welfare of a country. Never was there a man who had a greater horror of inactivity and want of energy, or who had a greater idea of the value of the means of locomotion. He well recollected the tedious journeys on Tom Morrissy's boat between Clonmel and Waterford, and he also recollected, perhaps still better, his shoulders aching with the weight of his pedler's pack as he had slowly trudged along the road. He used to say sometimes that the Bians grew out of his shoulders. He was, I think, one of the first to perceive the advantages from railway traffic, and he at once gave way to what he saw was inevitable. As the railways broke up his great lines, he would run cars to meet them at the stations where the trains stopped.

My old friend Dean Kenny, of Ennis, frequently met my father at the Imperial Hotel in Dublin, and he has told me that on one occasion, when sundry coach and canal-boat proprietors met together in the Imperial Hotel, they were discussing and laying plans as to how they could oppose Mr. Drummond's great central railway scheme. My father, who sat still all the while listening to their ideas and their plans, said at last : " I think I know as much of the country as any gentleman in this room, and I look upon it to be as foolish to try to prevent the establishment of railways as to try to stem the Liffey. My own loss by the establishment of railways would be greater than that of any gentleman here present, I may almost say greater than the combined losses of all the gentlemen here present. Still I see that railways must be made, and I not only do not oppose them, but I have taken shares in the undertakings."

My father was a great apostle of traffic, and it was his constant wish to procure the means to the poorer classes of travelling themselves, and of getting their goods home to them as cheaply as possible. He was a man sometimes hard in business matters, exacting an eye for an eye, and therefore not likely to allow false philanthropy to run away with him; but whatever his faults may have been, he was sincere in his desires to assist those who were willing to assist themselves.

I will conclude this chapter by a humorous letter from the Liberator to my father; I cannot say, however, whether the application was successful.

"To

"THE RIGHT WORSHIPFUL THE MAYOR OF CLONMEL.

"Mr. John O'Farrell, who is already most favourably known to many of the directors of the Waterford and Limerick Railway, and who possesses every quality that renders a man respectable in character and trustworthy in conduct, seeks for the professional appointment of engineer to the company. He will be strongly supported by the Mayors of Waterford and Limerick; and, I, the late Lord Mayor of Dublin, *command* you, foreign carman, and worthy Mayor of the central town of Clonmel, to give him your support, vote, and interest, and by your so doing you will much oblige your sincere and affectionate friend,

"DANIEL O'CONNELL."

CHAPTER IX.

In 1835 Daniel O'Connell founded and established the National Bank in Ireland, and of that bank he was the founder, the patron, and the governor. It was intended to be especially a poor man's bank, got up for the purpose of enabling the lower classes to invest their small savings, and thus get a small interest for their money, instead of trusting their pound-notes to the fortunes of an old stocking, a cracked teapot, or even a hole in the thatch. These expedients for saving money were not uncommon, and those who were a little more enlightened used frequently to hand over their money to a friend to "keep safe" for them. Even I, born five years after the National Bank was first established, have been asked by people to take charge of their little hoards. And in the old days there were many traders, like my father's old friend Mary Kirwan, who used to gain considerably by the small sums intrusted to them,—of which they were allowed to keep the interest.

The few banks that were then in the country were mostly private speculations of old Protestant families of position, and the gentlemen who managed these banks only too often used their influence in political and in religious matters. However, I must say that the fine old Tory gentlemen, the Messrs. Ryall, stood most nobly by my father in his early struggles, as he himself has recorded.

I will here quote a short passage from Fagan's "Life of O'Connell": "O'Connell's reason for thus connecting himself with the banking system of the country was because of the monopoly—the religious monopoly—carried out in the management of the Bank of Ireland, and because of the political influence exercised by that establishment." Men's motives in establishing a bank, as in other undertakings, are generally mixed, and I think Mr. Fagan is wrong in only attributing to the Liberator the desire to establish a counter leverage to the Conservative banking interest in the country. And I must more directly contradict Mr. Fagan, for I do not believe that such was the Liberator's main reason. My father was so deeply in the Liberator's confidence that I may almost style him his financial father confessor, and he has frequently told me that O'Connell's object was to induce the people to put up their savings in a rational manner, and to enjoy the advantages of access to ready money. To get Irish rural capital out of the old stockings, or the holes in the thatch, and to have it circulated through the country instead of lying dormant, was what he always believed to have been the great man's chief aim. Doubtless, not to let his opponents, the Tories, have the battle all their own way

was an argument with him, but it was no more than an
argument.　Daniel O'Connell knew the people of Ireland thoroughly ; he had that intense sympathy with
them which is not uncommon, though in a lesser degree,
with other Celtic landlords.　My father firmly believed
that to benefit the actual tiller of the soil was the Liberator's chief motive in establishing the National Bank
of Ireland.　Any one who saw how he allowed his
tenants to split up their farms to enable their children
to marry and settle at home, and how he allowed unfortunate evicted creatures to squat on his land at Beg
Darrynane, would have perceived how the man's large
heart was moved to endeavour to benefit materially the
people that were around him.　Those who did not know
him intimately were apt not to consider his great sympathy for his suffering fellow-creatures, and to over-
look how this sympathy influenced all his views and his
actions.

When the Liberator got his charter and started the
Poor Man's Bank, patriots, lay and clerical, hastened
to take shares, and in some instances to set up sister
institutions.　Clonmel was an intensely patriotic town,
and a rich town, too, before the railway came and left
it in a corner, to be approached only by cross lines.
Some enterprising Catholics availed themselves of the
National Bank Charter to set up affiliated, though
practically independent, branches.　Charles Bianconi,
an O'Connellite, and beginning to be a rich man, was
naturally a prime mover in the scheme.　Never, perhaps, was there a man who thought more of turning

his money. He would sooner lose a lump sum than lose the two or three days' interest upon an investment. Truly, he was a worthy scion of that Lombard race who invented bills of exchange, for financing was a positive passion with him.   A peculiarity of the new institution, and certainly one calculated to test its staying powers, was that most of its early managers were chosen because they were respectable and patriotic Catholics, merchants, gentlemen-farmers,—men who knew nothing about banking as a business, but who managed to combine it with their every-day pursuits, and who had to be supplied with a sort of dry-nurse in the person of a skilled assistant, in whose hands undue powers became practically vested.   Some of these gentlemen certainly got on admirably;—perhaps it is peculiar to Irish people to possess a general adaptability for doing work that they are not intended to do.   However, after a time the Clonmel Bank, with the Cashel and Thurles branches, gave up its separate existence, and became incorporated with the original National Bank.

The following letter is from my father to the late Dr. Leahy, who afterwards became our revered archbishop.

"KINGSTOWN, 23rd *September*, 1843.

"MY DEAR SIR,—To show you that I am not an " idle spectator of the position of our country, I will " give you the statistics of the stock of the National " Bank of Ireland, of which I have been a Director of " the Clonmel branch since its opening. . . . .

" The National Bank commenced in 1835, and has a
" capital of 20,000 shares of £50 each, on which
" £17 10s. has been paid. Its paid-up capital is,
" therefore, £350,000. Its constitution is that all
" persons having five shares have one vote, twenty
" shares two votes, sixty shares three votes, a hundred
" shares four votes.

" In 1836 there were 246 shareholders having votes,
" of which only 43 were Irish. Now in 1843 there are
" 481 shareholders having votes, of which only 106
" are English. Clonmel alone possesses between
" £20,000 and £30,000 of the capital of this bank.
" This is correct, and if necessary, I can give you
" further particulars.

"I am yours very truly,
" CHARLES BIANCONI."

I will now give in full the Liberator's Address to
the People of Ireland, made on the occasion of the run
on the bank in 1836. I quote this at length because
it so exactly confirms my father's theory about his
great leader's object in founding the bank. There
breathes through every line of it the man's intense
desire to see our people a steady and a prosperous race.
Lavishly generous as he was, almost despising money for
its own sake (and let me say here that few things vexed
my father more than to hear people insinuate that
Daniel O'Connell was actuated by mercenary motives),
he could see how our people lacked all the steady virtues
which are exemplified in having a balance at one's

banker,—the first step towards which is to have the banker.

"TO THE PEOPLE OF IRELAND.

" NATIONAL BANK OF IRELAND,
" Office, DAME STREET.

" DUBLIN, 22nd November, 1836.

" Whilst the run for gold continued on the National Bank, of which I am Governor, I was often asked by friendly persons, unconnected in interest with our establishment, to use the influence which the people of Ireland allowed me to possess, to put a stop to the unusual demand for gold in lieu of National notes.   I refused to do so.   I refused to interfere until the demand should have ceased, and until the National Bank had practically proved its readiness and punctuality by paying every demand made upon it.

" I did, indeed, think that the people of Ireland ought of themselves to have shown that confidence in me, and to have testified their conviction that I would not be one to circulate amongst them any paper which could cause any loss or injury to anybody.   But I would not complain, nor do I now complain;—I am only grieved that the people should injure themselves by striking down prices, and should deprive the farmers of good markets, and take away from almost everybody the means of giving employment to the labourer and to the poor.

" The three last years have been years of low prices,

and of great difficulty for the industrious classes to pay their rents, and to sustain the heavy burdens which have pressed upon them. This season, on the contrary, opened well, there was a remunerating price for everything, when a foolish panic seized a number of persons, and they, most senselessly and culpably, made a run on the banks. It did, indeed, afflict me much to see people thus injure themselves. It also grieved me to see that the Irish people, intelligent though they be, did not understand the security against any ultimate loss which arises from the constitution of a joint-stock bank, where every shareholder is liable to the full extent of all his property. Every bank-note is in the nature of a judgment debt, and binds all the real property of the shareholder. This I tell you as a lawyer, and I pledge my professional credit thereupon.

" For example,—the Agricultural Bank has ceased to pay its notes with banking regularity. I am sincerely sorry for it, for it was a kind and a useful bank to the farmers and traders.

" I have no sort of connection whatsoever with that bank, or with the respectable class of persons who are its shareholders. But I am bound to tell the people that I am perfectly convinced that every single note of that establishment will be ultimately paid in full, and I declare it my opinion that no man should part with an Agricultural note for less than its full value.

" I have, I repeat, no connection with the Agricultural Bank, neither have I with the Provincial Bank ;

but I know that the Provincial Bank is a very wealthy establishment. I know that its shareholders in London are extremely opulent. I know that the people are perfectly safe in taking and in keeping Provincial notes, and that it is folly, and in fact great wickedness, to make any run on that bank, because it would interfere with its directors in their readiness to accommodate farmers, merchants, and traders, and thus keep down prices and prevent trade and employment.

" I say these things of the Provincial Bank without having had, directly or indirectly, any communication with any person connected with that establishment. It really is so solvent an establishment that its shareholders may perhaps smile at my seeming to uphold their credit. They mistake me ; it is not for their sakes, it is for the sake of the people of Ireland that I write. It is to warn the people against being their own enemies by preventing the Provincial Bank from discounting bills, and advancing money to the industrious classes of society.

" With respect to the Bank of Ireland—the Government bank—I beg leave respectfully to thank their directors for the liberality with which they have come forward to sustain public credit.

" I do not know of greater madness than that of the people who made a run for gold on some of the branches of the National Bank ; it was sheer insanity, again striking down the prices of their own commodities and taking away the means of employment. It is not merely as Governor of the National Bank of Ireland, it

is as one, alas! of the oldest and steadiest friends of
Ireland that I address you ; as the friend of the people
I call on them to allow the banks to do them good.

"I instituted the National Bank merely to do good
to the people of Ireland.   I call on them to assist me to
serve themselves.   Every shilling of property I have in
the world, all the property of my eldest son and of his
family, all the property of my son-in-law, is involved
as security for the notes of the National Bank, together
with the property of all other shareholders.   The run
has now ceased and the demand is over ; I only ask the
people to return to the tranquil enjoyment of those
advantages which I sought to secure to them by establishing the National Bank.

"I cannot conclude without candidly confessing
that several Conservative landlords have come forward
to sustain public credit, and have sunk all considerations
of angry politics in order to do public good.   This is a
kind and right feeling which ought to be cultivated
and encouraged at every side and by everybody.

"I think I deserve the confidence of the people.   I
call on them to confide in me and to follow my advice.
No man can be injured by doing so, every man will be
the better for taking the advice, in this instance, of

"Your devoted friend,

"DANIEL O'CONNELL,

"Governor of the National Bank of Ireland."

During these years my father was obliged to make
periodical visits to London, and I will here give

an anecdote which shows very truly one of his peculiarities.

One day, in Fleet Street, just after he had engaged a four-wheeled cab, my father saw a stout gentleman walking very quickly towards him who was evidently in distress at not being able to find a conveyance. The spirit of Charles Bianconi, carman, woke up within him too strongly to be suddenly quelled. "I have a cab, sir," he said. "If you will give me your fare I will set you down where you like." The stout gentleman was profuse with thanks, and said he wanted to go to the Exchange. When they were in the cab he begged to be allowed to know to whom he was indebted. "My name is Bianconi," said my father. "The great Bianconi?" replied the gentleman. "And what is your name, sir?" replied my father, without half the politeness of his companion. "My name, sir, is Rothschild." My father, in telling me the story, admitted that he was so much overawed by the presence and by the affability of so famous a man that he had not the presence of mind to return his compliment and say, "The great Rothschild?"

This was by no means a singular instance of my father's eccentricities in this way; often at home, in Ireland, when he was driving in his own carriage along the high road, he would take in a traveller who would otherwise have gone by the car, provided that he paid the car fare.

Man is often a strange creature, and some of my father's oddities were assuredly of the strangest kind.

That he was a good and charitable man nobody who knew him will, I think, deny. He was the most helpful man, but his help was too often given in a very disagreeable manner. He did not mind having his own corns trodden on, if, indeed, in the metaphorical sense, he had any, but never was there a man more certain to stamp upon his neighbour's toes. He took a positive delight in trying to set people's affairs straight for them, but his remedies were of so violent a nature that any one who had force of will to submit to them would never himself have got into trouble. His assistance was very frequently in the form of a bill at three months, or a credit for so much at the National Bank. Even after he had ceased to be a shareholder in the bank, he regarded it with a sort of paternal fondness, and I suppose he considered that interest for cash was a sacred rite of which Mammon should not be defrauded by any favoured worshipper. Otherwise I cannot imagine why he exposed people of limited, though of certain income, in whose integrity he firmly believed, and whom he respected and was fond of, to the annoyance and the expense of bills and renewals.

My father was perpetually getting situations for people. To my own knowledge three managers of National Banks have owed their appointments to him. One was the son of a car agent, and another the son of an old friend who had been kind to him in former days. I find their letters to him telling him of their successive promotion carefully put away, and plainly bearing traces of having been carried about in his pocket. And other letters of his, written by people to whom he had rendered some service, show evident signs of having been long kept in his pocket. I suppose he cherished them in some sort of way, and liked to keep them close to him for a certain time, until he stowed them away into his cupboard. He procured matronships for at least two ladies; he used to get appointments for the head boys from the Christian Brothers' schools into warehouses and railway offices. Two or three times he heard from the Jesuits of clever boys without means to begin a profession, and to them he advanced money, or opened a credit for them in a bank. As to the girls that he got cheaply into convent schools, the boys into shops, offices, banks, and model schools, their number would be legion. And he never forgot anybody whom he had once befriended. At different times he helped to get deserving young men into the Catholic priesthood. He partly paid for the education of one clever young lad of good parentage who remembered no home but the workhouse, and who told me, only last summer, that he was going abroad to complete his studies for the church. My father, too, had a sort of genius for worrying people in authority into assisting young people to make their start in life. But his helping hand never went so far as when he worried that most excellent and kind-hearted nobleman, Lord Carlisle, into giving a good living to a clergyman of the Church of England. My father used to take a great interest in his protégés, and would be very vexed if they did not do him credit. Two letters of Cardinal

P

Cullen's to him relate to grumblings of my father's about a boy who spelt badly; and this from Charles Bianconi who could hardly be taught how to spell "money"! His finger was in every man's pie, and in many a woman's pie, too, for the old man was not averse to a bit of match-making. He gave £1,000 to a young relative who married the descendant of one of his early benefactors.

The bullion trade in which my father was engaged in his early days, and of which I have already spoken, opened out to him chances for other money transactions. He used to lend money at interest, and of this he made no secret. He never charged usurious interest, or laid himself out specially for money dealings as a trade, but when he began to realise capital during the years that he was yet an alien, and could not accomplish his cherished hope of buying land, he used to lend out his money on the security of land, and, from what I have discovered in looking over his papers, usually at five per cent. interest. He never was a professional bill discounter, but, like most tradesmen at that time, he was always ready to "do" a bill for a solvent customer; and if he had not taken stamped paper in exchange for goods he would, indeed, have made sorry bargains with the Irish gentry of sixty years ago. I repeat that my father made no secret of his money dealings. He was not a professional money lender, though he lent a good deal of money in a fair and honest manner and at an equitable rate of interest; and I am bound to add, with all the love and respect that I had for him, that the instinct of turning his money was so strong in him that he has charged me, his own daughter, his special confidante and friend, five per cent. interest for money lent. My husband once said to him in joke, though with a mock earnestness as though he believed it, " Well, Governor, did you really make the Liberator's acquaintance upon a bit of stamped paper ? "

The veneration and the love that my father had for Daniel O'Connell was almost unbounded, and this was the more singular as the natures of the two men were so wholly opposite. Permeated to the core as my father was with all Poor Richard's axioms and wise saws, it is astonishing that he could ever have respected a man for allowing his liabilities to get beyond his immediate control. Yet the Liberator's too open-handed generosity, that once left him in galling, though only temporary, difficulties, sank deeply into my father's naturally warm heart. He and two other gentlemen undertook to set O'Connell's affairs straight for him. They saw that his income was large enough to meet the demands without sacrificing even a single farm. My father cross-questioned O'Connell about the details of his property, and about his liabilities to the bank, and, unlike most men in difficulties, O'Connell concealed nothing nor left any secret untold. My father put his questions as delicately as he could, but he has said that he never suffered more acutely than in seeing the Liberator wince and so plainly show his sorrow. He, however, made a bargain, and a very wise one, too, in dealing with my father, that he was not to be bothered about the matter until it was all settled. At length the happy day arrived. My father called upon his friend and found him standing writing at his high desk. He did not at once begin to talk about the matter, but held the bank-book in his hands, and he could see O'Connell occasionally looking askance at the little vellum-bound volume, pretty much as a child eyes his spelling-book.

" Well, Liberator," my father said, " won't you take a look at your bank-book ?"

The question did not make a pleasant impression, and my father was obliged to open the book and point with his finger to the sum total, showing a fair balance to the credit of Daniel O'Connell, Esquire. My father has said that he never would forget the expression that was then upon his friend's face. After a moment's bewilderment, O'Connell lifted up his eyes to the big crucifix that hung over his desk, took off his cap, and said in a low and reverent tone, " Thanks be to God !" Never was my father so much astonished as he was then at seeing O'Connell thus raise his thoughts to heaven before he had verified the accuracy of the figures. No man ever recognised more heartily than my father, that though he had toiled and planted, it was God who had given him his good things, yet he must have worked out the account for himself, and seen that it was correct before he could thus reverentially express his gratitude.

I will conclude this chapter by a letter of my father's, that I may call Dick Whittington's advice. It was written to the son of one of his early benefactors :—

"DEAR ———, I am obliged for your letter, and I
" am delighted at your arrangements, particularly at
" your determination not to change, and the more so as
" you will now have a first-class school for your boys.
" For means you are all right, and as long as you are
" living, you will want nothing.

" I remember when I was earning a shilling a day
" in Clonmel, I used to live upon eightpence, and that
" did not prevent the people from twice making me
" their Mayor. I did the same at Cashel and at
" Thurles, and that does not prevent me from at
" present living between the two towns on a property
" of seven miles' circumference, and on which I pay
" her Majesty £7 2s. 6d. per year, or from being a
" J.P. or a D.L.

" It gives me sincere pleasure in seeing you follow
" the sound principle of having your wants within your
" means. Don't be fond of changes. It is better for
" you to be at the head of a small republic than at the
" foot of a great one.

" I shall always be happy to hear of your welfare,
" and with best wishes,

" I am, yours faithfully,

" CHARLES BIANCONI."

I may add as a postscript what my father once said
to a young Yorkshireman : " Keep before the wheels,
young man, or they will run over you. Always keep
before the wheels."

CHAPTER X.

ELECTIONEERING.

THIS chapter, that was to have been written by my late husband, Morgan John O'Connell, would, had death spared him, been one of the best in this poor book, but now, undertaken by me, it will, I fear, be one of the worst. It was to have been my husband's special and chosen task. The wide experience that he had gained from forty years of Irish politics—and during nearly half that time he sat in the House of Commons—his intimate knowledge of men and measures, the genial wit and playful humour that ran along so pleasantly through all his speech and in his letters, which pleasantness now makes my eyes wet, would have made this chapter far more interesting than I can hope to make it, and would have given it a force such as I cannot expect to achieve. As a young man my husband had, nearly every year, spent many pleasant weeks in County Tipperary. There was hardly a political house of our faction in the county where the handsome, gay member for Kerry was not a welcome and a frequent guest, so that he had direct and personal knowledge of parliamentary electioneering in Ireland. I fear that I am powerless to do justice to the points in my father's career that I had most set my heart upon making worthy of the man; to show how, in the prime of his life, he gradually grew into an Irishman, and to explain the working of his heart and soul in Irish politics. I have already mentioned how he would playfully allude to his early days, —" While the big and the little were fighting together, I grew up amongst them."

Unfortunately, I have never seen an Irish election. I should have liked, above all things, to have been an eye-witness to one of those exciting scenes which have now, perhaps happily, become more peaceable since the introduction of the Ballot. My mother had a horror and a dread of contested elections, and she objected very strongly to any woman going near the hustings, so I had to curb my desires, and trust to my father and to my husband for their second-hand reports. My father came home one day with a great gash on his forehead, and remarked very coolly that had the stone hit him an inch higher, he would, instead of walking, have been carried home on a shutter. My mother was probably quite right in not allowing me to go outside the gates while these scenes were going on. To her a contested election meant mobs of excited patriots, secret conclaves everywhere, great piles of food in gentlemen's houses ready for any one who would come in and eat; loud and eager voices over the post-prandial punch, priests rushing about in all directions amid the screaming, the stick brandishing, and the stone-throwing of a furious crowd, which every hour became more frantic by additional glasses of whisky. Irish elections certainly have not been without violent angry riots on the part of the mob against the Ascendancy party, and perhaps in Tipperary the contest has usually been fiercer than elsewhere. Still, my father unquestionably enjoyed the battle. I rather think that the many years he passed as a voteless man tended to make him doubly prize the acquired privilege. In Ireland, before the days of the Emancipation Act, religion and politics were very closely allied, and it was only by means of the Catholic Association that he was brought into the charmed circle of Irish political life.

Then later on, by means of his cars, he became an electioneering agent on a large scale. I have already told how, in the great Waterford election of 1826, he had let his cars to the Tory party, and then when he found them overturned in the streets, and made use of as barricades to prevent the Liberal party, then really beginning to rise and have a power of their own, from coming to the poll—how he then broke off his engagement with the Tories, and went over to the Liberal cause. He never again lent his aid to the Tories. I rather think my father's sense of humour must, even at the time, have been pleasantly tickled by the events that took place. He had no sympathies with the Tories, though he had let his cars to them; and then having vainly tried to carry out his contract—for he did start the cars that afterwards got smashed—he went over to the opposite side, to the side on which all his wishes were engaged, feeling tolerably sure also that he would get a compensation for the destruction of his property.

It was delightful to me to hear my father speak of those palmy days when Dan O'Connell and Sheil, and many other now half-forgotten celebrities, were guests at his house. He would speak of the Liberator and Sheil together, and make comparisons between the two men. He loved to speak of O'Connell, and to recall the many traits of real kindliness of heart that he unconsciously showed.

Once in the middle of a contested election, when the Liberator was staying at my father's house, and there was a long day's work in hand, he was late for breakfast, and my father rushed up into his bedroom to hasten him down-stairs. He found the big man standing in the middle of the room with a razor in his hand, his face half smeared over with soap, listening to my pretty little sister tell him of her joy at getting a new doll, and of her perplexity that "Dolly wouldn't drink." And after the day's work was done, no one was so charming in company as Dan O'Connell. His conversation was so amusing, and his manner to women and to children was so pleasing, that he exercised a sort of fascination over people wherever he went. His nature was like that of a fine diamond throwing out its fire and light on every side. His mind was very quick to catch the impressions of the moment, he had some feeling in common with every class and grade of Irishmen. He was very susceptible to sudden emotions, con-

sequently he was impulsive, and his adversaries spoke
of him as a humbug, or a play-actor. It was simply
that they who did not know him failed to see the man's
many-sided nature, and how a dozen thoughts, all iu
different directions, would be working in his mind at
the same time.

The following story will, I think, tell in the
Liberator's favour in the eyes of all fair-minded
people. One Sunday morning he and my father both
communicated at early mass in the Clonmel Friary,
and my father noticed that at the altar O'Connell wore
a white glove on his right hand. Now, my father was
a curious and rather inquisitive man, and he rarely
failed to gratify his curiosity. He had a demure,
matter-of-fact way of asking questions that invariably
elicited a reply without betraying indiscretion on his
part or giving offence. So, after service, he blurted
out in his usual manner, " Liberator, what makes you
wear a white glove at communion ? "   O'Connell
turned round and looked at my father ; he raised his
hat slightly and said, in a tone of voice that my father
never forgot, " That hand once took a fellow-creature's
life ; I never bare it in the presence of my Redeemer."
My father has told me that he then wished that the
earth had opened her mouth and swallowed him up,
or that O'Connell would have scolded him severely for
asking such an impertinent question—anything rather
than his calm and simple allusion to the duel in which
he had killed a fellow-creature.

That Dan O'Connell could rate a man soundly and

give him a piece of his mind in very plain language is
so well known, that I need hardly do more than make
allusion to it here.   My father used to tell a story that
at a meeting Dan had fallen foul of the press, and had
styled certain Orange reporters who had used every
petty means to clip and twist his speeches by the name
of mice.   One of them instantly jumped up and said,
" Do you dare, sir, to call me a mouse?"   " No, sir,"
replied Dan, " I don't call you a mouse; I call you
a great big rat."

My father wished two more facts to be recorded of
his dealings with the Liberator.   Though he had himself joined the Repeal movement vigorously, his sympathies were not with it; he preferred Imperial to Home
Rule.   Some one once taunted him with this, and he
coolly replied, " Any man would have followed Dan
when he was in the right ;—it is my boast to have followed him right and wrong."   My father justified this
course by alleging that the Repeal Agitation got many
good things for Ireland, especially judgeships.   A due
proportion of Liberal Catholic judges was one of his
ideals.   When he went to take leave of the dying
Liberator he followed him to mass.   Dan's last words
were, when they parted at the church door, " I should
die happy if I saw an impartial Bench and pure administration of justice."

My father had plenty of stories, too, of Sheil, whose
genius he much respected, but whose fine and sometimes caustic wit he did not admire as he loved the
Liberator's genial fun and pleasant humour.   Sheil's

angular gestures, the shrill tones of his voice, his
sparkling eyes, and the deep pathos that he would
throw into the defence of a condemned prisoner, interested my father very much. It happened once that
Sheil was lodging just opposite to my father in the
same street, and a poor old woman came to my father
in his room, and begged him to ask Sheil's landlady to
have an eye to the poor crazy gentleman over the way.
My father rushed to the window, thinking to see a
man in a fit of madness, but instead he discovered
Sheil standing before a great looking-glass, rehearsing
to himself the speech for the defence of a criminal that
he was about to make on the following day.

I have not concealed that my father was, to a certain
extent, fond of popularity, and that he was not without
vanity, which he did not endeavour to hide as a Briton
would perhaps more artistically have done. I have no
doubt that he was prejudiced against the Ascendancy
party, but I have also no doubt that the state of things
into which the Italian boy dropped, as though out of
the sky, was specially calculated to engender and foster
his natural inclinations. I have lately been looking over
old law reports, over O'Connell's and Sheil's speeches
at agrarian trials, and I find on comparing these with
my father's stories, that what I was once half inclined to
ascribe to intolerance on his part is fully borne out by
facts. In political matters my father thought strongly
and he spoke strongly, but the plain and matter-of-fact
way that he looked at things in the face enabled him
generally to see the right and wrong of a case without

suffering his judgment to be warped by sentimental or party feeling.

When the bulk of the administration of the lands of Munster was in the hands of venal agents and grinding middlemen, when Drummond's famous dictum, " Property has its duties as well as its rights," was received with a storm of landlord indignation, it seems only too natural that there should have been a system of organized resistance on the part of the poor peasantry. Then came the Tithe system, the worst and the hardest to bear of all the grievances under which the Catholics then laboured. This fell with peculiar severity upon the poor man, for he was compelled to pay from his small substance towards the support of a Church that was not his, and towards men whose object was to keep him in a state of servitude.

In my father's mind the house of Beresford was the most perfect type of the Ascendancy party. They were undoubtedly a clever race, and tradition loves to dwell on their great size and manly beauty, their lordly manners and the love of sport which has run through their family. The Beresford who broke his neck in the hunting-field is still affectionately spoken of as " The Marquis," though there have been two marquises since his day. They were mostly personally popular, generally good landlords, and given to spending their time and money in manly sports among the people. Even the Liberator freely admitted that he had been their advocate in ordinary lawsuits, and had every reason to think well personally of his clients. But this masterful race so personified Ascendancy, that when their power was broken by the election in 1826, when Villiers Stuart got in for Waterford in opposition to one of their house, it was a matter of public rejoicing.

So far as I can gather, my father was perpetually at work on behalf of one or more Liberal candidates. He never himself sought for parliamentary honours; I do not think that he ever felt that longing to pass beyond the big policeman into the sacred precincts of St. Stephen's, that his friend Mr. Anthony Trollope has so graphically described. But even to the last he would bristle up at the sound of a contest. He has gone to the poll and recorded his vote with the weight of eighty summers upon him, and a broken leg into the bargain—ay, and been fresh and lively after it, too. Perhaps there was nothing that interested him more than a general election, he was always busy on behalf of some Liberal candidate; the leaders of the party were always his friends, and frequently guests at his house; and I have a notion that half of their campaigns were planned and partially worked out in his dining-room. By degrees as his cars spread, the man of thirty votes became an important political power; and I break no trust in saying that, before a general election, my father invariably informed himself who were the candidates most agreeable to the Liberal Government. Of the Liberal Government, he was an avowed partisan; he considered their administration to be all that was right and good for our country, and in Lord Carlisle's lifetime, when a general election was at hand, he always went to him to offer his vote where it was most needed. Of the many Government men for whom he voted some he liked and others he disliked. There were two, however, for whom he entertained a peculiar regard, whom he used specially to designate as being pure men, and in his mind political purity was a rare virtue. These two men were the late Chief Baron Pigot, and the present Lord O'Hagan.

I will now give a few letters touching upon the events of the time, and it will be better perhaps to let them speak for themselves. In some of these there are little traits that go beyond the region of politics, and show the character of the writers. I will not attempt to put them chronologically, but those of the Liberator's I keep together and place them first.

This letter I found among my father's papers; it was evidently sent on to him by Mr. Maher, who was for a long time M.P. for Tipperary :—

"Derrynane Abbey, 13th *Sept.*, 1829.

"My dear Maher,—I got your letter so late that I fear my reply will not reach you before the dinner to Mr. Otway Cave has been actually given. I regret extremely that the shortness of the notice prevents me from being able to pay him that compliment which I am quite certain he merits. I think I know him well, and I am convinced the House of Commons does not contain a man of more pure, honourable, and patriotic mind. He is one of the most unaffectedly honest public men in the British dominions; and I trust I shall live to see him,

and that shortly, fill the station of representative of your
county [Tipperary]—a county which has been so long
misrepresented by scions of a very worthless aristocracy.
Indeed, my indignation against the great men of your
county is at this moment at its height, because I learn
from the newspapers that they are so totally regardless of
constitutional feeling and common humanity as to seek
to have the infamous measure of the Insurrection Act introduced. But their vile speculation will, I trust, be disappointed by the firmness of the Government, and the
better sense of Parliament. The people, too, should be
thoroughly aware that the way to defeat their enemies is
to observe the law, to avoid all riots and outrages, and
not strengthen the hands of their enemies by committing
crimes. Crimes must and will be punished. The crimes
against the people are for the present less likely to meet
punishment. But the scenes that are gone by will
never be repeated, and the people will themselves learn
that the way to triumph over their malignant enemies
is to abstain from secret societies, illegal oaths, and
Whiteboy outrages. If Mr. Otway Cave were the representative of your county he would cause the magistracy to be purged, or he would at least expose the delin-
quencies which the improper part of them may commit.

"Express, I beg of you, to Mr. Otway Cave my very
sincere regret that I cannot be at this dinner, and tell
him that nobody can more desire to show him every mark
of respect and esteem than I do.—Very faithfully yours,
"DANIEL O'CONNELL.

"To Nicholas Maher, Esq., Thurles."

[Most private, most confidential.]

"Limerick, 6*th May*, 1831.

"My dear Bianconi,—You will hear with indignation as well as surprise that Lord Kenmare has turned against me in Kerry, having given up Waterford, and being now doubtful in Kerry. Many friends of mine have turned their longing eyes to Tipperary. I write to you for an answer to these two questions.

"1st. Could you get for me a requisition to stand respectably signed?

"2nd. Could you return me beyond any doubt?

"Write to me here, and do not show this letter to anybody, unless in the strictest confidence.

"Believe me always yours, very sincerely,

"Daniel O'Connell.

"Charles Bianconi, Esq."

"Merrion Square, 24*th March*, 1843.

"My dear Friend,—What the deuce is Tipperary doing? What the double deuce is Clonmel doing? And especially what is its valiant Corporation doing? Sligo, Drogheda, Limerick, Cork, Waterford, Dublin— all the Liberal Corporations except Clonmel—have either given proofs of Irish patriotism, or else have shown themselves alive to it. What is Charles Bianconi doing? A vivacious animal in himself, but now seemingly as torpid as a flea in a wet blanket. So much for scolding you all. And now, my good friend, is it not a crying shame that your noble county

should remain in such apathy and torpor when all the
rest of Ireland is rousing itself into a combined effort
for the Repeal. I want a Repeal meeting either at
Clonmel, or Cashel, or Thurles. I want to see from
60,000 to 100,000 Tipperary men meeting peacefully,
and returning home quietly, to adopt the Petition, and
to organise the Repeal Rent. Now you know you
must get into motion, there's no use at all in hanging
back any longer when you set about it. I know you
will do the thing right well. I am to be at Rathkeale
on Tuesday, the 18th of April, and I could be at either
of the three towns I have mentioned upon Thursday,
the 20th April; so now put these things together and
set about working. Do nothing without the co-operation of the clergy. I need give you no further advice
or instructions. Though you are a foreigner you have
brains in your noddle, and are able to perceive, even
amidst the levity of my phrases, the intensity of my
anxiety to bring forward Tipperary speedily and
energetically, but peaceably. What will you do for
the cause ? You should answer me that. With
sincerest regards to your family, believe me always,

" Yours most faithfully,

" DANIEL O'CONNELL.

" Charles Bianconi, Esq."

[Confidential.]

" DUBLIN : MERRION SQUARE, 1st September, 1846.

" MY DEAR FRIEND,—Are you humbugging about
standing for Clonmel ? You are quite aware that you

are not eligible, and that you could not continue to sit. You are also aware that there is no man living I would be more anxious to serve and oblige than yourself; and if you were capable of sitting for Clonmel, it would delight me to have you returned, but, I repeat, my opinion in point of law is that you may be turned out of the seat without the expense of a petition, but on a mere motion, and at any time after you have once taken the seat. I have a notion, too, that you would be liable to a penalty of £500 for each day you sat in the House. I do not say this positively, because I have not had time fully to investigate the law.

"If you are serious as to standing for Clonmel, consult some eminent counsel before you do anything. What I am afraid of is that we should be laughed at if you were returned.

"I venture, therefore, to entreat of you to give up the idea, if you seriously entertain it. But at all events, and in every event, believe me to be your attached friend,

"DANIEL O'CONNELL.

"Charles Bianconi, Esq., Mayor of Clonmel."

"THE COLLEGE, THURLES, 4th *June*, 1847.

"MY DEAR FRIEND,—I have an idea of the loss we have sustained in the death of our beloved Liberator. It is irreparable.—I trust in God his great spirit will continue to guide us. We must, however, be men, we must be united; every honest man in the kingdom must now act an honest part. Unless we stand together the county is inevitably thrown back half a century. The Orange party are now quite sure of regaining their former ascendancy. They are in this county making active preparations already to recover their lost ground. We had a meeting here to-day to confer about testifying publicly our sorrow for our beloved Liberator. Mention was made of the Attorney-General intending to stand for the county, when all to a man at once scouted the idea indignantly, especially the priests. This between ourselves. Now what is to be done? Whatever is to be done should be done quickly. The enemy is already preparing to take the field. There should be county meetings at as early a day as possible. Not a day, not an hour to be lost. I'll tell you what would be the best of all: you yourself standing. Run over and get the necessary Act passed with as little delay as you can. The Government will be anxious to do it, that the county may not pass into the hands of the Tories. I know the feelings of the priests, and I am positive, as I am of my own existence, that they would not merely support you, but support you with all their hearts, and carry you through triumphantly.

"Believe me, my dear Mr. Bianconi, yours truly,

"PATRICK LEAHY. ✠"

"*Thursday.*

"DEAR SIR,—You ought to know that 'old birds, like horses, are not to be caught with chaff.'

"You showed me yesterday an ancient constituency return that was four years old. It was not quite convenient, I guess, to show the state of the votes for 1845. I can, with more candour, give you the present state of affairs. Our last reports state there are not, *bonâ fide*, 1,300 men who could vote on the 1st February, 1845, deducting, of course, changes of farms, deaths, &c. Now if a few Catholic tenants stay away, or vote with their landlords, I should imagine we should have some sort of chance.

"I remain, dear sir, yours, not quite in the dark,

"GLENGALL.

"C. Bianconi, Esq."

"REFORM CLUB, DAWSON STREET,
"30*th August*, 1846.

"MY DEAR BIANCONI,—In a few days now, I dare say, the new Chief Baron will be glad to get his appointment, which will cause an election in your town. The fate of our county and borough will be greatly influenced by your acts. This is the time for men to show not only their common sense, but their love of old Ireland, and also of justice. I really never before entertained such strong hopes as at present; such a Government Ireland never had before. If your town acts under your advice, and I sincerely hope and believe it will, as one of your old road-companions, I will say in the language of my own trade, give Lord John a good wheeler, and, believe me, the coach will work steady. The only law-prop they had will be removed to the bench ere long; supply his place with another, and continue the honour to Clonmel of always assisting the Liberal Government. The idea of a split now amongst the Liberals is too monstrous to entertain. For my own part I will not give it a thought. I feel certain, however, that there may be some mad rogues everywhere, but our friends in Clonmel will act as thinking, steady men when headed by such men as yourself and your admirable clergy. I have every hope, you will ask why I am so solicitous, but on consideration you will not do so. I will simply reply, because I love my country, I love my religion, I wish to see the people well governed and happy, and I believe the present Government have these objects at heart. I threw up J.P. and D.L., and would have done the same if I had situations of emolument, sooner than serve under such an Irish Government as the last. But I am proud of being restored to my former rank, which they have done in the handsomest manner, by classing me with such men as the Liberator and Lord French. Were the vacancy to have been in county Wexford, or its borough, I would have expected a similar hint from you. So excuse my entreating you to assist by every means in your power such a Government as we are now blessed with.

"Ever, my dear friend, yours most sincerely,

"JOHN H. TALBOT."

The following is an extract of a letter written by my father to his secretary, Mr. O'Leary :—

" Many thanks for all the interesting news you give me, particularly about the elections ; but I fear our present material to fight the great Cromwellian county of Tipperary is as hopeless as could be expected. However, I hope the virtues of our people and their reconstitution, as a unanimous principle of moral and political activity, will get us our rights.

" What a pity that the few good men we have amongst us cannot be put in motion. Your account of Mr. Lawless and Clonmel was most cheering. He is, with all his faults, a first-class M.P. I greatly regret the demoralisation at Cashel, but good will come from it. I fear —— will be returned for Limerick. What a shame ! I regret the two last men for that city. I hope we are safe in county Dublin, and that my friend Reynolds was returned by a great majority for the City of Dublin. I should like very much to see Green returned for Dungarvan. What a pity that Connemara has not had a separate and local sale. I fear our poor people there are going from the frying-pan into the fire. Who bought New Park ? And tell me all about the late sales. Be sure Lisheen is not sold unknown to us. What a pity I had no one to assist me in getting Price's place instead of Grubb. To get it such a bargain under my nose ! How is Father Kirwan, and how are all our reverend friends ?

I hope he will take a run to us and give himself some recreation.   Tell him this world will be after him.

"Yours truly,

"C. BIANCONI.

"D. F. O'Leary, Esq."

"DUBLIN CASTLE, *March* 31, 1857.

"MY DEAR SIR,—I received your letters late yesterday evening, for which many thanks.   I have seen the Attorney-General on the subject, and find he has written to you to Athlone, requesting you to go to Galway to vote for Blake and Dunkillen, and to-morrow to Cashel for Sir J. O'Brien.   Thursday, as you intended ; I trust you may be able to do so.

"Yours very faithfully,

"FRED. HOWARD.

"C. Bianconi, Esq."

The first election that I remember taking any interest in was for the county Tipperary in 1857. There was then what my father called an unnatural contest between two Liberals, The O'Donoghue and Mr. Waldron.   The following letter from the Archbishop of Cashel to my father will show how the matter stood :—

"THURLES, 9*th March*, 1857.

"MY DEAR SIR,—This unnatural contest is most afflicting.   Is there no possibility of inducing The O'Donoghue to retire ?   If he did retire, he and Mr.

Waldron would be returned without a contest at the general election. There can be no doubt that the present supporters of The O'Donoghue would be his supporters then too; and there would, I think, be no disposition to oppose him. He can retire with a certain prospect of being returned at the general election. It is not so with Mr. Waldron. His retiring now would not ensure his return at the general election, for the Club are, I understand, pledged to Major Massey, and it is to be presumed that the supporters in general of The O'Donoghue will go with the Club. If The O'Donoghue retires now, he is sure to be returned at the general election. If Mr. Waldron retires now he is not sure of being returned then. This ought to induce the former to retire.

"I remain, my dear sir, yours very sincerely,

"P. LEAHY. ✠

"C. Bianconi, Esq.,
&c. &c. &c."

As a general election was near at hand my father staunchly supported Mr. Waldron, and did all he could to dissuade The O'Donoghue from coming forward to contest the single seat, as his return would be morally certain a few months later. He took, then, a rather singular step, and one that would have been considered very impertinent had anybody else so interfered, but as he was well known to have peculiar ways of his own of doing things, it passed off without any special remark. He went to Cork to a wise and

old friend of his, whom he knew to have business
relations with the young candidate, and whom he suspected of being his purse-bearer, in the fond hope of
stopping the supplies, and thus averting a split in the
Liberal camp, and also of saving the Liberator's kins-
man the large sums of money that were sure to be
spent in the contest. But all to no purpose. My
father returned only to tell the story against himself,
and to see the lavish expenditure he had endeavoured
to save. The end of it all was that The O'Donoghue
got his seat; and at the general election he was again
returned together with Mr. Waldron.

My father always continued to vote for Mr. Waldron
until that excellent gentleman crossed what seemed to
my father the bounds between Whiggism and common
sense. "What the d—l is he at," my father would
emphatically exclaim, till at last he found that he
could vote for Mr. Waldron no longer. The two men,
however, kept up their good feeling for each other in
spite of their political differences.

In February, 1865, The O'Donoghue retired from
county Tipperary, and transferred his services to Tralee.
Many in our county were indignant, but my father
thought it was natural and prudent for him to sit for a
borough in his own county, where the expenses of
renewed contests would probably be not so great.

I do not wish to be considered responsible for all
my father's prejudices, but there was one which I fear
was only too well founded; and few people will deny
that the same sort of thing has not happened else-

where. He always maintained that when the Tory landlords saw that they would fail to get one of their own party into Parliament, they encouraged their tenants to vote for the Fenian nominee, in the hope of baulking the steady-going Liberal, who could, as my father loved to express it, "afford to be honest." And I have known a great Protestant landowner boast of having given tacit support to the ultra-Liberal candidate in the pious hope that he would thereby cause mischief in the Liberal benches.

Just before the general election of 1865 my father broke his thigh, from which he never completely recovered, though even in his crippled state he managed to get about marvellously. After his accident he was laid up for six months, quite incapable of stirring, and this inactivity worried him beyond measure. Two days before his mishap he had attended a county meeting in Thurles, and my mother has told me that he never was better or more lively than he was then. Then, in his seventy-eighth year, he came down the steps and jumped up on the car as though he had been a young man. And later, when the fracture was partially mended, he would have himself driven to the polling booth, then be helped on to his crutches, and so go and record his vote amid the stones, the mud, the dead cats, and other missiles not uncommon at elections in Tipperary.

At length the general election of 1868 came on, and my father had then got used to his infirmity. He was moved about in various ways; on the level ground he walked a little with the help of his crutches, but he had to be lifted into his carriage, and at railway stations he was frequently wheeled along sitting upon his portmanteau on the luggage truck. His butler, James Sweetman, whose care I think prolonged his life, always accompanied him, and showed great ingenuity in getting him about; and Sweetman was probably inclined to doubt my father when he said that he was "as fresh as ever he was." He certainly was "very fit" at that time, if I may be allowed the slang phrase. His interest about the elections was intensely keen, and I never lived in such an atmosphere of politics as I did then. What he could not do himself he deputed to my husband, and he assuredly was not slow in responding to the call. It used to amuse me beyond measure to see Morgan John O'Connell, who had let his brilliant prospects slip away from him through a sort of indolent carelessness, work at the elections as three other men would have done. Thoroughly as he enjoyed the pleasures of canvassing, my husband was in truth guided and kept in bounds by strong conscientious feelings, and it would be well if all men were actuated by the same plain notions of political honesty as he always showed. He went to Cork and to Clare, he ran down to Kerry, his old county, to rally round his nephew, The O'Donoghue, at Tralee, where his election was threatened. My husband had no vote there, but the people liked to see their old county member; and 'if there was one thing on which he prided himself it was his electioneering for other people.

In the autumn of 1869 my father indulged in a fit

of manœuvring which was incomprehensible to me, and I believe, if he were alive now to speak the truth, he would say incomprehensible to himself also. Whether he was actuated by his natural love for a bit of scheming, or by a fit of economy, I cannot say; any way, his plans failed, and I should add, deservedly failed, for they were about the worst that any sane man ever adopted. There was at this time, consequent upon Mr. Moore's death, a vacancy for the county of Tipperary. No Catholic squire was disposed to put himself forward, the Fenians and the Tories were pretty busy each on their side, and were prepared to coalesce up to a certain point, and there was no man of our party round whom the people would rally and to whom they would give their support. Some of the Catholic gentry, and the elder and more staid men among the clergy, wished that my husband would offer himself as the parliamentary candidate. Had he done so and come forward at once, I think he would have been a very desirable man. The magic name of O'Connell, his political antecedents, his personal popularity, and his rich and influential father-in-law, were all good qualifications in his favour. He had represented Kerry for seventeen years, and when the "bad times" had compelled him to retire, he carried with him the goodwill of all parties. For a man who was neither rich nor great, "Morgan John," as he was everywhere called, was about the most popular man of his time.

Now, my father had not been at first much dis-

posed to help my husband to a seat in the House of
Commons, but after four years' close intimacy, when
he had seen that his son-in-law was not disposed to
repeat the extravagancies of his youth, he became
anxious that he should re-enter public life. At this
time my father had made his will, but neither I nor
my husband had any notion of what he intended to do
with his property. Between my father and myself the
warmest friendship and the closest confidence had long
existed. I constantly acted as his secretary in important private matters, but to no living soul—perhaps to me less than to anybody else—would he ever
reveal a word of how he intended to leave his property after his death. Our friends and the people about
us of course knew nothing about our family matters;
and I suspect that some imagined that my husband
would have my father's money after his death.

I really think that my husband would have been
returned at the cost of a few hundred pounds for legi-
timate expenses but for a little extra caution on his
part, and but for a certain tacit suspicion of something
with which "the wily Italian" never failed to inspire
his friends the clergy. After Dr. Leahy, the Archbishop
of Cashel, my father and my husband were all dead, I
accidentally heard that His Grace had said to a popular
priest who was known to wish for my husband's candidature, "Take care of old Bian! don't stir unless he
lodges £4,000 in a National Bank." Now this was
just what my father would not do. He offered to open
a credit, to advance the money at five per cent.,—to do

anything but risk it; but my husband was too cautious. He felt how a burnt child dreads the fire, and he plainly refused to put himself forward as a candidate upon his own responsibility. I am far from saying that my dear father was wrong in refusing to advance any money to my husband to enable him to get into Parliament, but I think he was very injudicious in wishing that my husband should come forward, and yet not say whether or not he would assist him pecuniarily if he made the attempt. My father began to scold me roundly, saying that I had prevented my husband from a public life. I could not altogether deny this. I replied that I had told my husband that I could not advocate such a step, though I would not for a moment oppose him if he thought it right. What were my father's motives all this time, what was working in his mind, I am at a loss to conceive, unless it be, as I have said, his innate love of dodging, joined to a desire not to spend his money upon an object of which he did not see the practical utility. Could he have rendered to my husband a service adequate to the money to be expended, he would, I believe, not have hesitated; but he did not like to risk his money on the chance that his son-in-law might gain a temporary distinction that was more honourable than lucrative.

Had my father been as plain and frank in the matter towards my husband as my husband had been towards him, much trouble would have been saved. As it was, my husband's candidature dwindled away, and he found himself at last canvassing for Mr. Caulfield

Heron, who polled a smaller number of votes than the Fenian candidate, O'Donovan Rossa.

My father's election correspondence would of itself form a small curiosity shop. There are letters from viceroys and from car-agents, from archbishops and from poor curates, from Daniel O'Connell and from William Smith O'Brien. There are letters from lord chancellors of Ireland, from judges who had sat for some years on the Liberal benches in the House of Commons, from lord-lieutenants of counties, from patriotic editors, and from recalcitrant tenants,—all of which would throw some light on the political history of Ireland during the last forty years. Some of these letters are interesting, and some of them are now very amusing. They form a record of honest ambition duly gratified, of disappointed hopes, broken vows, empty threats, bribes, donations, and false compliments. Happily for one's faith in man, there are also letters from a few politicians, such as Lord O'Hagan and the late Chief Baron Pigot,—men who never forgot their religion, their honour, nor their country.

In all these letters my father's sagacity and his indomitable pluck come out very strongly. The old man faced the temporal threats of tenants and the spiritual thunders of patriotic parish priests, and after a time, when the heated passions had become cool, he and his adversaries again became excellent friends. Interesting as this correspondence is, I have neither the wish nor the ability to write a history; I cannot do more than mention it at the close of this electioneering chapter.

CHAPTER XI.

LONGFIELD.

LONGFIELD is a pretty, small property in county Tipperary of six hundred Irish, or a thousand English, acres, and situated within a mile and a half from Goold's Cross Station, from whence you may reach Dublin by the train in rather less than five hours. It is the last estate in the parish of Boherlahan, and in the south riding of the county. The large cheerful house is beautifully situated, overlooking the river Suir, and the well-wooded pleasure-grounds slope gradually down towards the banks of the river. From our windows the Galtee Mountains and the far-famed Rock of Cashel may be seen; and from the top of the Hill of Ring, within five miles of Longfield, you get a fine view of a flat and well-cultivated country, stretching for twenty miles to the foot of Slieve-namore; the Galtee Mountains, and Knockmealdown being farther in the distance.

This was my father's first and principal acquisition

of property, and indeed his home ever since 1846. He bought it from Captain Long by private contract shortly before the days of the Encumbered Estates Court. Captain Long told my father that, though he differed very much from him in religion, he sold his property to him because he knew he would be a just and generous master to his tenants. The purchase was made in March, but we did not come to live here until the 16th of September following.

This was my sixth birthday, and I have still a lively recollection of the crowd of people, the popular enthusiasm, and the hearty reception that was given to my father, all the more pleasant, perhaps, as he was totally ignorant of it till he found the people ready to greet him and bid him welcome. Large bonfires were made on the roads near the house, a triumphal arch was erected over the avenue gate, and the grounds were thronged with the tenants and the labourers, and with their wives, their sons, and their daughters. An amateur band from Cashel, dressed in their uniform, had come out to greet my father; and the band of course made an occasion for a little dancing. The lads and lassies were

> "Tripping on the light fantastic toe,
> Whilst the merry pipes kept tune
> With violin and tabor."

It was a pleasant and joyous scene, showing some of the good traits in the Irish character. After the dance there was an interval of some twenty minutes, and then a deputation from the tenantry came forward and presented an address to my father. I take these details from an account of the proceedings written for a local newspaper by Mr. Thomas Dorney, my father's clerk during the two years that he was Mayor of Clonmel. Mr. Dorney describes the address as being "an eloquent composition." I have not the slightest doubt of this fact, but perhaps my readers will excuse me for not giving them any further proof. I will, however, with their leave, give my father's reply, as it shows how he was actuated towards his tenants, and it shows also some of his strong common sense;—though it was by no means an "eloquent composition," such as the deputation had presented to him, but rather a collection of Poor Richard's wise-saws. He said:—"Friends and neighbours,—I thank you for the honour you have done me, and I accept your address with great pleasure. It affords me much satisfaction to meet my tenants and neighbours, who latterly have become proverbial for morality, good conduct, and temperance (cheers). I am delighted to be so intimately connected with so deserving a class. I have always recognised the ever-memorable saying of my lamented friend, Mr. Drummond: 'Property has its duties as well as its rights.' We should all, according to our state in society, have our rights (cheers). The landlord should have his, the mechanic and the labourer should also have theirs (cheers). I think the poor man who earns by his labour a shilling a day has as good a right to enjoyment and to his cabin as the Queen has to her throne (cheers). The citizen,

and the farmer also, have their peculiar rights, and it
shall ever be my duty to see those rights vindicated
(cheers). These men also have their duties. The labourer
cannot expect to be paid unless he works in return.
If the landlord does his duty to you, he will expect of
you to do the same to him. You must understand
your duties as well as your rights. I am determined
to do everything a man ought to do to those whom
Providence has placed under me. The rich and the
poor are God's creatures (cheers), and, as a landlord, my duty is to see that my tenants shall have
proper time and facilities to cultivate their land; and I,
in return for giving them the land for its value, expect
to be properly paid. I have no idea that one man more
than another should not be bound to discharge the
respective duties which he owes to the great human
family; therefore I feel great pleasure in receiving
your address. It gives me too much pleasure to find
that I have to do with a peaceful, moral, and industrious class of men, and I regret that I was not aware
of your kindness in time to have refreshments prepared
for you, particularly after the delightful scene which I
have had the pleasure of witnessing. The merry dance,
continued with such truly Irish spirit by the young
men and really handsome girls among whom I am
surrounded (cheers), was a sight that did me good, for
I love to see young people enjoy themselves in a whole-
some and honest manner. It is my wish that when you
want anything which is in my power to grant you, that
you should not be thinking about it. Whenever you

want any improvement to be made, either in your land or farming implements, ask me; it will always afford me much pleasure to assist you by every means in my power in everything that can tend to ameliorate your condition (cheers). Before I conclude these hasty observations, allow me to impress upon you the great importance of respecting the laws. The laws are made for the good and benefit of society and for the punishment of the wicked. You cannot offend the laws with impunity. No one but an enemy would counsel you to outrage the laws. Look around you, and will you not see the face of society improved? Much of that improvement is owing to the temperate habits of the people,—to the mission of my respected friend, Father Mathew (loud cheers), and to the advice of the Liberator (cheers). Above all things avoid secret and unlawful societies. There has been much blood shed in this country through their means; but I am bound to state that the advice of the Liberator is now generally followed (cheers). There are, however, still a few lurking vagabonds in this country. But their 'occupation is nearly gone.' Therefore, if any man ask you to violate the law, seize him, grapple with him, drag him before a magistrate, or your clergyman; for depend upon it he is your enemy, and an enemy to your country. Follow the advice of O'Connell, be temperate, moral, peaceable, and you will advance your country, ameliorate your condition, and the blessing of God will attend you (loud cheers)."

It was a fortunate thing for the poor that my father

purchased Longfield, for he made the best use of his means to give them employment during the times of the famine. Such of the old gentry as could manage to hold on were terribly crippled in their means by the falling off of the rents, and consequently they had no money to spare for labour that was not immediately remunerative. My father was not only a landowner, he was also a man of business, and with the money that came in to him daily from his car establishment he righteously and honestly laboured to relieve the suffering poor.

I cannot do better than here give the substance of what I took down from the dictation of Jemmy Ryan, one of my father's small tenants. He had evidently prepared his statements, and I have the fullest belief in his trustworthiness.

"When 'The hunger' came among the people, the small tenants came to my father and said that they would surrender, that they could hold on no longer. He told them to keep where they were and that he would assist them. They told him then that it was impossible, that they could hold no longer. He then sent them to America, and put money into their pockets. Since then he has received letters from them thanking him for his kindness, and blessing the day he sent them away." Perhaps a stranger may not realise the terrible meaning of "The hunger," as applied to the famine times, or all that is conveyed to an Irish ear by the phrase, "they could hold no longer." "Holding on" to a farm during the famine meant such a terrible struggle with want, misery, and wretchedness as would now be difficult to conceive. It was in the years 1848, 1849 that the ten or twelve small tenants surrendered their holdings and went to America.

My father was very fond of ship-shaping his land, as he used to call it: that is, when one tenant from any cause went away he would try and divide the land into symmetrical portions. He had long been wanting to acquire for his own use the small holding of Jemmy Ryan, one of his small tenants. He had asked Jemmy four times to sell his bit of land, and four times Jemmy had refused to accede. At last Jemmy consented to take £20 for his small holding, thinking that with the money he could emigrate to America. He himself is my informant of my father's proceedings, and he told me how when he had nearly made up his mind to go abroad my father came one day into his cottage to pay a visit to his wife. "Mrs. Ryan," said Charles Bianconi, "I have agreed with your husband for £20. You are a delicate woman, and it will kill you to cross the sea. Take a friend's advice, and if he goes away do not you go with him." Here was a nice announcement for Master Jemmy. He thought that my father might have minded his own business without coming to interfere with his. However, my father finished by saying that he would give Mrs. Ryan the cottage and haggard rent free for her life, and that he strongly counselled her husband to stop where he was and do his work at home. The offer was too good a one to be refused lightly, and Jemmy consented to stay;

but he told me that while the £20 was still burning in his pocket he often set off to go to my father to tell him that he must go away, and that when he got up to the door of the house his courage failed him, and he always returned leaving his word unsaid. Jemmy Ryan still dwells on the estate. His known honesty of purpose, his power of endurance and of resistance to the wiles of the weaker sex commended him to my father during the famine weeks; and it certainly required some skill and considerable firmness of temper to manage forty-four Tipperary women, as not unfrequently fell to his lot.

In 1848 my father began his drainage works when he saw the hunger setting in through the land. At that time a labouring man would only earn 8*d*. a day; but the drainage works were mostly paid piece-work; so that a diligent ablebodied man would earn nine shillings a week, and there were few who earned less than six,—a fourth more than could be got by ordinary day labour. It is true that the work was severe, and that many of the men had to be standing in the water for several hours in the day. But big strong men came flocking in from all parts of the neighbouring country. The steward remonstrated at this, wishing to confine the work to the men of the parish, but my father turned round upon him and said sternly, "I don't care where a hungry man comes from, I'll employ him." Jemmy Ryan tells me now that he is certain that for a considerable time there were more than a hundred men employed. Thank God no one died from want at Longfield, but there were some poor old people who died in the workhouse.

One day my father said, " All the men are employed to be sure, but I want to do something for the women." So he broke up his good grass land and set flax and potatoes on it. Though the potatoes were then being sold in the market at 8*d*. or 10*d*. a stone, he sold them to his people for 4*d*.; and he so continued to sell them up to the date of his death, no matter what the market price for them might be.

From March to November in that year Jemmy Ryan was appointed commander-in-chief over forty Amazons who were employed in preparing the ground for flax. This lasted until the month of May, when it was set. Once set, the place was nearly left alone till August, when, as the pretty little blue flowers began to wane, the flax was pulled, dried, and prepared for the market. It was usually sold in Clonmel. The people, however, clung to the potatoes; but even at first there was a very large proportion of black ones among them, the number of black potatoes increasing by degrees till there was only a small fraction of them fit for human food. My husband has told that during these times he has seen the crows on the hill-side in Kerry staggering from want of food.

Building, draining, striving to grow potatoes, and other attempts, some of them strange enough, to relieve the distress of the poor, all went on together. Grievous as the misery was, I think my father liked the fact of having a dozen irons in the fire all red hot at once. In

these bad times Ned Myers, one of the smaller tenants,
much amused my father by his ingenuity in walking to
Cashel in time for early mass, and then afterwards officiating as clerk in the Protestant church, taking care
not to say *Amen* when he did not approve of the doctrine.
My father could not resist telling the story to the son of
an English bishop; it then got abroad, and rather
against his will the excellent parson of the village, who
was too deaf to know whether his clerk had responded or
not, was obliged to dismiss him and replace him by a
Protestant. My father felt some remorse for having
peached upon poor Ned Myers, but he made it up to
him afterwards in some other way.

Jemmy Ryan has told me that once he was going
with some cattle to a farm of my father's in county
Galway, and he stopped very early in the morning to
redden his pipe at a cabin on the roadside. The good
woman had not yet lit her fire, but begged Jemmy to
wait a bit, adding that he would go along the road for
five miles before he came to another cabin that had a
roof to it. Jemmy stayed and lit his pipe, and found
it to be a long five Irish miles before he came to a
cabin that was covered over at the top. This does not
in the least surprise me, for many and many were the
roofless houses that I saw in those days in Munster. The
horrible famine, with its want, misery, and desolation,
cast a gloom over my childhood. I have witnessed
scenes which then took place that I shall never forget;
and there are no doubt others who could tell tales of
horror quite as heartrending as mine.

I will now insert a short narrative of Mr. Michael
Angelo Hayes, saying something about Longfield, and
about my father's dealings with his tenants.

"The first time I saw Longfield Bianconi had been
there for some years. It was on his birthday, which
he always celebrated by a large dinner-party, and I
think it was in the year 1853. I met his son, then
just of age, outside the avenue-gate, driving a well-
appointed drag and four horses. He at once offered me
a seat by him on the box, and drove me all round the
estate. I noticed that Bianconi had built substantial
two-storied houses with slated roofs for some of his
tenants, and that he had made many improvements
in fencing and in draining. He had, consequently,
rather offended the susceptibilities of the landed gentry
whose property surrounded his. They did not like the
idea that a new and self-made man should make such
innovations, and seemingly instruct them in their
duties to their tenants. For though well-built houses
with slated roofs are common enough in farms in
England, it was comparatively rare to see then in
Ireland a comfortable farmhouse with any other roof
but a thatch. It is possible that Bianconi may have
been a little ostentatious in his improvements, and that
if he had taken a little more time about them, and used
a little more tact, he would have followed a more prudent
course. As it was, the gentry were apt to look coldly
on him, and to hold themselves aloof; but he had a
great independence of character, and he cared little for
their antagonism, or at all events he appeared to be

callous to it. He followed his own way, and in the end he achieved his purpose, and as he became known he was always esteemed and respected.

" The father of the late owner of Longfield had been shot dead close to the house, and when Bianconi bought the property he found the house defended and barricaded like a fortress. He never disturbed the thick-plated iron that was on the doors, nor did he meddle with the ponderous bars and bolts. He rather took a pleasure in showing them to visitors, and glorying in the fact that he did not require such defences. It certainly was a strange state of society in Ireland when Bianconi was there as a young man. The landed gentry lived like conquerors in a county surrounded by a people who were openly hostile to them, who both hated and feared them, who were slavishly subservient and bitterly antagonistic. And Bianconi, as a landed proprietor, did not wholly escape from falling under the common ban. There was much in his character that would cause misunderstanding and ill-feeling. In principle he was inexorable, he would lose a ship for a halfpenny-worth of tar, and although a most honourable and upright man, he was hard, and in a bargain he was exacting. It is said that he was marked out to be shot; it was even thought that the deed had been planned and attempted, and frustrated only by the parish priest, who asked him to take a seat in his gig on his way home from Cashel. Bianconi had driven in from Longfield in his own carriage, but he accepted the priest's invitation, and went back with him. Now there are two roads leading from Cashel towards Longfield House, and the priest chose the longer of the two. 'Why do you take this road?' said Bianconi. 'I prefer it,' replied the priest, and nothing more was said then about it, but it was suspected that the old priest had heard something, or got some warning, for it afterwards became known that a party of men had that night been watching on the other road. Whatever cause for dissatisfaction existed, or was supposed to exist, was only temporary. Bianconi was a popular man, and was undoubtedly a good landlord; but his strict sense of justice as between man and man may not always have accorded with the illogical and one-sided views of a shrewd, suspicious, and ill-educated class of men. I believe, however, and hope that the Irish peasantry are improving. Let us recollect that until the suppression of the penal laws there was very much against which they had to contend.

"Bianconi had a great fancy for acquiring landed property, and he made purchases in several districts. The last act of his life was the buying of a small property near Clonmel. The purchase was completed, or just about to be completed, when death at last overtook him. His own account of a purchase he had made some years before in the Landed Estates Court amused me much. He had been watching the sale of a property near the mountain called the 'Devil's Bit,' in county Tipperary, and after he was declared the purchaser, a well-known land-agent and solicitor of Clonmel said to him, 'Do you know the kind of property you are just after buying?' Bianconi replied that he knew little or nothing about it. 'Well, they are there the most lawless set of ruffians in the whole county; there's no getting a farthing of rent out of any one of the tenants.' 'Oh murder!' cried Bianconi, 'I'm ruined entirely; what will I do?' However, there was no help for it; the property was his. He told me that when he made his first visit to the estate, he called together all the tenants, and said to them that he made it a rule not to have any tenants on any estate of his who would not take a lease. 'A lease, your honour!' they answered, 'what would the like of us do with a lease?' At the same time, Bianconi told me, they were all dying to have leases. 'Every man,' he said, 'must have a lease on my property. I will give you all leases upon Griffiths' valuation.' The valuations were ascertained and put at greater rents than they had hitherto paid, and the result was that he had no tenants on any property who were more punctual in paying their rents; and they afterwards became orderly, industrious, and thriving.

"I have spent many pleasant days at Longfield House. 'The old Governor,' as he was generally called in the family circle, was very hospitable. He was a most kind and genial host, and he loved to see his old friends round his table, especially upon his birthday. Men of note, either in politics, or literature, or art, were well received at Longfield; and strangers visiting that part of Ireland usually managed to get an introduction to Charles Bianconi, and were always hospitably welcomed. He was fond of art, and had collected some good pictures,—together with some bad ones. He once came across an ancient-looking oil-painting, which he thought was especially good, but wishing to have another man's opinion, he sent the picture down by the Clonmel car to a Mr. Anthony, of Piltown, who was known to be a man of taste and judgment. With the picture Bianconi also sent a short note :—

"'MY DEAR ANTHONY,—I send you a Saint Aloyosious. I think it a good thing.
"'Yours truly,
"'C. BIANCONI.'

"The next car from Clonmel brought back the picture, together with the following reply :—

"'MY DEAR BIANCONI,—Your picture is more like a devil than a saint.
"'Yours truly,
"'T. ANTHONY.'

"Bianconi was not long settled in Longfield when he took the fancy to build a mortuary chapel on his estate, as a last resting-place for himself and his family. It was almost the only hobby of his life. And he set to work, unaided by any architect, or even a builder, but with the help of a few artisans in his neighbourhood he constructed a wonderful little chapel. It was very substantially built of limestone and grey sandstone.

He joined a flat-roofed Italian campanile, or bell-tower, to a Gothic steep-roofed chapel. And on my pointing out the incongruity to him, he said, 'Well, what matter; does it not look very handsome?' He must have spent over a thousand pounds on the building. Yet it was small, and practically useless. He had a very fine bell hung in the campanile, and it surprised me that, without any advice, he hung the bell in the only proper way that it could be hung,—from a wooden platform or framework resting upon a projection of the wall. Most men would probably have built the supports into the wall, and the vibration thus caused by the ringing of the bell would have been ruinous to the structure."

I here interrupt Mr. Hayes to say a few words about the mortuary chapel. I forget the exact date when it was consecrated, but I know it was a bright clear day in the autumn. The chapel was filled with priests chanting the service, and outside the people were collected in great numbers in the little cemetery outside. The Rev. Dr. Leahy presided, and he sang his part of the ceremony in a beautifully clear high-pitched voice. He then went round the graveyard, followed by the priests and the people in procession.

A short time afterwards, my sister's remains were brought over from Italy, where she had died. She was the first person buried in the little chapel. She had a large funeral, though I was not present. Our well-to-do neighbours wished to be civil to my father, and the poor gratefully remembered her constant kindness to them. Benzoni executed her monument. It is a high entablature, with a bas-relief below. The upper part contains a niche, with a very beautiful standing figure of the Angel of Purity holding a lily in her hand. Below, the dead girl is laid on her couch; Faith and Hope, in the usual female forms, are at her head and feet. Charity is boldly symbolized by the highest type of Divine love—the child Jesus held in his mother's arms, stretching out his hands towards the sleeping figure. The inscription merely mentions the date and place of her birth and death, and that the monument was erected by Charles Bianconi in memory of his beloved daughter, Kate Henrietta. Her full name was Catherine, but I think it was a touch of sentiment that made my father put her name Kate instead. My sister and my brother, with his little baby daughter, my husband, and my own little Elizabeth, all lie in the same vault; and my father lies alone right opposite to the altar. As yet the only bodies in the churchyard are those of Mr. and Miss O'Leary, our old nurse, Mrs. Catherine Curtain, who died here at Longfield after being with us for forty-two years, and who wished to be buried near to Kate, her foster-child, and two decent old men, John Mathews and Patrick Dunne, the steward. Poor old John Mathews had been for many years a driver, and afterwards he became a man in charge in the yard. He died at an advanced age, only four years before his old master.

"In the year 1851 Bianconi revisited Italy with his family. He stopped for some time in Milan, not very far from where he was born, and met several of his relatives, but most of those whom he remembered had been dead long since. He left Italy at a time when the French dominated in the country, and he now found it in the hands of the Austrians. He went on to Rome, and stopped there for some months. His son was appointed one of the chamberlains at the Papal Court, and the old man was everywhere well received. But I do not think he found the life and habits of the people of his native country were much to his taste. He had grown up and lived under a different system, and in the country of his adoption he had become more Irish than the Irish themselves. He had imbibed too much of the spirit of liberty. He found himself out of unison with all the surroundings, and he longed to return to what he felt had become his home. When he came back, he simply said that there were a great many things in Italy that required to be changed.

" Bianconi had bought property in the borough of Cashel, the ancient city of the kings, and at the next election that followed his purchase he became angry with his tenants because they did not vote as he wished. Towards the close of his life he got fat, but he continued to be as active and as energetic as he had ever been. He travelled about a great deal. He was constantly going from one town to another, and he used to say that he was only a lodger at home. He sat at petty sessions and at poor-law boards; he attended railway meetings, political gatherings, and charitable bazaars. He supported every desirable public object, and was very liberal in his charities. The world throve with him, and everything that he put his hand to succeeded.

"His son married a grand-daughter of Daniel O'Connell, and he had three daughters, but no son. He died in 1864 at the early age of thirty-one. The death of his son and the fact of there being no male heir to carry on the name of Bianconi was a grief and disappointment to the old man; but outwardly he showed no sign. Pity or sympathy were distasteful to his proud nature. He saw his son laid in his little mortuary chapel beside the remains of his daughter Kate, and though his death deeply afflicted him he bore the blow with all the fortitude of a Stoic.

"His second daughter, Mary Anne, married in 1865 Morgan John O'Connell, the nephew of the 'Liberator,' as Dan O'Connell was generally designated in Ireland by his friends and followers. Morgan John made an excellent husband, and he and his wife lived very happily. They passed much of their time at Longfield, where I used frequently to meet him. He was an accomplished and a most perfect gentleman, whose knowledge of men and things was almost universal. He was gifted with rare conversational powers; his anecdotes and his wit were always pleasing. He had sat for many years as member of Parliament for Kerry; he had lived much in London, and he seemed to know everybody. He had two children, one of whom only survives—a boy—and he seems destined to bear the name of Bianconi according to the old man's will. The

little fellow was very fond of his grandfather, and when
at Longfield I have often been struck with the picture
of the fair-haired child playing by the side of the aged,
grey-haired man as he sat in his arm-chair. Bianconi would listen with such evident pleasure to the
prattle of his 'little John;' and I thought of how it
has been said that fathers live over again in their
children's offspring.

" His last work was the finishing of the Glebe
House on his estate. It was well and substantially
built, and he made it over in perpetuity, together
with four or five acres of land, to the parish priest
for the time being, conditional upon a certain number
of masses being said at stated times in the mortuary
chapel.

" Morgan John O'Connell died at Longfield on the
2nd July, 1875. He was much younger than Bianconi,
and I little thought that the old man would out-
live his son-in-law. His death was a great shock to
him, for a little before he himself had had a slight
attack of paralysis—not the first—and he had lost the
use of his right hand and could no longer write. As I
saw him seated in his chair looking through the window
upon the funeral *cortége* as it passed down the avenue,
I thought he must have regarded it as a rehearsal of
what was soon to take place in his own person.

" Sooner, indeed, than I expected, in the September
following, within a few days of the anniversary of his
birth, which we had often celebrated so joyously around
his hospitable table, I followed his remains to the

mortuary chapel in Boherlahan, and saw him laid in his last resting-place with the same feelings of grief with which I saw my own dear father laid in his grave at Glassnevin. Peace be to the ashes of my oldest and dearest friend."

I quite agree with Mr. Hayes that my father rather gloried in treading on other people's corns, and I can easily understand that the whilom alien Papist, now become an Irish squire, asserted himself rather unpleasantly to many of his Tory neighbours. I know he was sometimes indignant at not being called to serve on a Grand Jury when small Cromwellian squires were summoned. However, by degrees he got to be more easy-going, and he became on intimate terms with his neighbours, from whom he received much friendliness and attention. My father was a tolerably active justice, and he was eminently a poor man's magistrate. The people had the fullest confidence in him, and he in them. Though he would talk very magniloquently about putting down drink, he seldom endeavoured to have a man severely punished for it.

During the famine time he hit upon a rather ingenious expedient. He would remit a considerable portion of rent from the tenants, and take from them their oats instead, giving them the full market value. The people knew that they were not being cheated in their bargains; and in his establishment, where there were over a thousand horses, the consumption of oats was necessarily very large.

I have a strong suspicion that my father looked upon

his property as a luxurious hobby, for in no part of the management of his estates was he so methodical or so business-like as he was in his car establishment. I have been driven to the verge of distraction over ledgers and bills of costs, trying to trace certain payments and dates of purchase, which one would naturally imagine should be indicated in the foremost place. For instance, in the ledger where his landed purchases are entered, neither the dates of purchase nor the English acreage are given. As to his farming he never had anything like a system. He bought every kind of machinery, except steam machinery, that was ever invented. Besides all the American and English machines, he adopted the local belief in grubbers, which about here are much in repute. These he generally got made by a smith on the estate. His pay-sheet used to average from £15 to £20 a week, and he used to employ the old people as long as they could continue to work. In the palmy days of the Bians he was always able to provide employment for the boys and young men on the property. He had a great fancy for what he called manufacturing his own timber; he would put fresh Irish timber into every kind of woodwork. His head carpenter lived in a perpetual state of petty warfare with him about the "Master's notions of the art." Many a time in the heat of an argument they would both be seen, their spectacles on their foreheads, fighting desperately over a sketch or an estimate.

At different times he devoted himself to long-wool sheep and Berkshire pigs. Though he paid long prices for his sheep, he never could be got to see that high-bred animals of all sorts require delicate treatment, and as he often overstocked his grass land the animals rather dwindled down under a course of low diet. The symmetrical Berkshire pigs were his last fancy, and for their accommodation he built elegant pigsties on a plan that he got from a model farm. He used to delight in having the nursing mothers and their broods let out, and seeing the little ones running round about him and grunting, as he sat in his wheeled chair. While I candidly admit the superiority of these Berkshire pigs in some points, truth compels me to say that the native long-sided Irish pig produces a longer flitch and a more streaky mixture of fat and lean than those of the more fashionable breed. Fond as my father was of improving the condition of his people, he did not encourage them to keep pigs; and I fancy the reason was that the profit arising from them after they were bought and killed was so very small.

But he made a special point of always selling picked potatoes at 4*d.* a stone, and of finding employment for those who were willing to work. He would also sell his timber at a low price,—a great boon where peat was both scarce and dear.

Until the Bian establishment was sold the place was overrun with screws of all sorts. There was a regular infirmary in some of the swampy fields where the animals, after they had been blistered or fired, &c., were turned out to graze and take care of themselves. A busy and active man as my father was, I think he enjoyed extremely the delights of squiredom. He knew that he could not have good things without paying for them, and when he wanted good things he bought them ; and he took such evident pleasure in doing what he could for himself. I have already said that his finger was in every pie within his reach ; and occasionally, if the pie was not within his reach, he would walk towards the pie. Having so many horses laid up, he must perforce constitute himself their doctor. And I am bound to say that in many cases he doctored successfully. Sometimes he would hardly leave himself a winter stocking, and many a debilitated animal would be seen limping about with my father's long grey hose filled with alum curds carefully gartered round his legs. For starts and strains, muscular weaknesses, or stiffness, to which the hind legs of coach-horses are liable, my father pinned his faith to alum curds in a knitted stocking. And he considered ploughing in tips a certain cure for all the foot disorders that come from fast work on the road.

But why, with so much horse-power at his command, he should have taken to ploughing with horned cattle, no one could ever divine. I rather think it was the recollection of what he had seen in Italy that made him take up this freak. For three or four years he kept two teams of horned cattle, and gave it up only, he said, because they were so slow that they wasted the time of the men. He had one pet bull that he called " Flying Dutchman," and I have seen my brother put this beast into a break when he was training a fine but dreadfully obstinate jibbing mare, whom not even the stoutest horse could induce to move, and the bull would resolutely put down his horns, and pull the break along, half strangling the mare in her collar as she was dragged along sorely against her will.

My father had an axiom, in which I am glad to say that so great an authority as Baron Liebig agrees: "The Manure is the Farmer," and he would lay down this dictum with all the authority of a judge. He would not content himself with ordinary manure, but he used to buy couch grass at $6d.$ a load.

The people were only too glad to get this stuff carted away from off their land. My father used to mix it with the hot stable manure, and he said it answered admirably,—his stewards were, I believe, of a different opinion; and at another time he took a fancy to covering his grass with soot from the chimneys. This did not last long, for it nearly produced a domestic rebellion. The wives of the men declared that they would not let their husbands into their homes before they had washed their clothes, and my father, to excuse himself for his freak, declared that he had to respect the good women as well as his land.

My father invested all the savings of his life in land. He used to quote the old saying, "Money melts, land holds, while grass grows, and water runs." I will now give a list of the various purchases my father made, and I will insert a few letters. But I will refrain from going into details, as they would not be appreciated or understood by an outside public :—

Date of Purchase.	Name of Property.	Cost.	Acreage (Irish).	Acreage (English).
March 23rd, 1846	Longfield	£22,000	623	..
1849	Ballygriffin	6,000	230	372
1851	Roan	3,000	162	264
1853	Glanaguile	6,000	988	1,600
1860	Cashel	11,900	220	356
	Ballinard	2,300	713	..
	Knockamora	1,620	921	..
	Liss	9,000	482	..
	Lower Pallas	4,550	248	..
	Upper Pallas	3,225	367	..
	Hill House	720	..	..
		£70,315	4,954	..

" MARETIMO, 19th September, 1846.

" MY DEAR BIANCONI,—I congratulate Ireland on the
valuable acquisition of a humane and national proprietor.
You will be just and kind to your tenants, and you will
find them grateful. I have always found it so. The
Irish have had their nature and character lowered by
ill-treatment. They may now wish for some fair play,
and they will prove worthy of it. This will be a year
of great suffering, but good will, I hope, come from it.
I shall not go near Cashel without visiting you. If
you have anything to spare from the letter of credit,
give it to the Mechanics' Institute, or any charity you
approve of, but don't put a word in the paper.

" Very faithfully, your obliged,

" CLONCURRY."

This letter is from the former owner of Longfield :—

"ROYAL HOTEL, 17th August, 1854.

" MY DEAR SIR,—I am told I will not know Longfield, it is so much improved. How fortunate I was, and how happy my former tenants have been, because of the selection I made when parting with my property in Tipperary, which part of Ireland—if I ever see again—will find me for a few days under your roof, should you be at home.

"Pray remember me to my old friends and neighbours, not forgetting the Rev. Mr. Kirwan and Mackey; and tell Denis Dwyer I am alive, though not as active as in former days.

"With sincere regards to my former tenants now in the land of the living, and best compliments to Mrs. Bianconi and family,

"My dear sir, very faithfully yours,

"RICHARD LONG.

"Charles Bianconi, Esq., Longfield, Cashel."

Here is a letter to the Lord Chancellor of Ireland :—

"LONGFIELD, 25*th August*, 1869.

"My DEAR LORD CHANCELLOR,—As you must pass
" this way on your way home, I am anxious, for many
" reasons, you should stop at Longfield for two or three
" hours, which would not prevent your reaching Dublin
" the same day.

"My want of education and my original isolated
" position has made me a child of nature through
" life.

"In 1846, I bought my present residence from
" Captain Long. Particulars: 623 Irish acres; rental,
" £1,121; cost, £22,000. I found landlord, tenants,
" and lands very seedy, but an honest and fine race
" of people, many with a grown family of six and
" eight children living in a two-roomed mud cabin,
" which I replaced with comfortable houses, the tenants
" quarrying the stones, and attending tradesmen.

"From having a spiritless, comfortless, and poor
" tenantry, I wish to show you the contrast from
" natural causes.

"I am also anxious to show you my mortuary chapel,
" which contains a memorial monument to my daughter
" by Benzoni, and though last, but not least, the glebe
" house for my P.P., and nine acres of land, con-
" veyed for ever to the Commissioners of Charitable
" Bequests.

"I am very anxious that the present Government
" should have a proper man as M.P. for this county,
" and if Morgan John O'Connell were not connected
" with me, he would be the right man in the right
" place, for he is both clever and honest. He
" should fight a Tory, but be no candidate against a
" Liberal.

"It is a pity we have no centre in the county. We
" are honest and independent, but, individually, we are
" very small to one another. We are too suspicious
" and selfish, and are still too near the effects of the
" penal code. Could you learn his Grace's views on this
" subject? I hope he will not commit himself again

" with Mr. Munster, by whom he had an infinity of
" trouble, and he a perfect stranger.

" By your leaving Killarney any day at 10.30, you
" would get here at 2.18. I would then meet you at
" the station, and that would give you time for a race
" through Longfield, and I would afterwards leave
" you at the station, so that you would be in Dublin
" by 9.30.

" Sincerely yours,
" C. Bianconi."

CHAPTER XII.

My father was not only a landlord and a farmer after his own fashion, but he was an ardent politician and a loyal follower of his Church.   He had sundry dealings with the Lord-Lieutenant of the county, and with the Archbishop of the diocese.   The Archbishop did not consecrate the mortuary chapel, nor did the Lord-Lieutenant confer on him one of the deputy-lieutenancies without a good deal of preliminary discussion. With regard to the latter I may say it was one of the very few things that my father asked for himself.   He had set his heart upon having this appointment, not from any puerile vanity, not from a desire to figure in a red coat, nor yet from a wish to be able to write D.L. after his name, but he thought it would be a formal recognition of the position he had achieved for himself, and he also thought that Catholics had a good right to a certain proportion of the deputy-lieutenancies.   I will now give a few of the letters that passed between him and Lord Lismore, the Lord-Lieutenant of the county, on the subject.

" Longfield, Cashel, 29th January, 1858.

" My dear Lord Lismore,—I am sorry to find that
" Colonel Penefather has been called away from amongst
" us. I now remind you of my claim to be named in
" his stead as deputy-lieutenant for the county of
" Tipperary, where I possess nine fee-simple estates.
" Seven of them I bought in the Encumbered Estates
" Court, and for six of which I neither pay crown nor
" quit rent. I think it right also to state that of all
" the D.L.'s for the county there are only six Roman
" Catholics, and therefore the majority of that com-
" munity are not adequately represented.

" My dear Lord, yours very sincerely,

" C. Bianconi."

" 2nd February, 1858.

" My dear Bianconi,—I have received your letter
with the account of Colonel Penefather's death, not the
first intimation that I had received. With every wish
to oblige you, I do not think it will be in my power to
nominate you to the D.L. There are a great many
names down, and some of them have been on the list
for years. Believe me, there is no person for whom I
have a greater regard than yourself, or whom I would
sooner oblige. I think the Government is shaky. The
India Bill and Clanricarde's appointment will not do
them much good.

" Yours always,

" Lismore.

" 41, Wilton Crescent, London."

" Longfield, Cashel, 5th February, 1858.

" My dear Lord,—I have to acknowledge your letter
" of 2nd inst., and to thank you for your very kind
" expressions towards me. They would, however, have
" been more gratifying by a present recognition of my
" claims.

" I understand there are at present three vacancies
" on the list of D.L. Should such be the case, you may
" probably consider it desirable that one of the three
" should be filled by a Catholic.

" I am, my dear Lord, very sincerely yours,

" C. Bianconi."

" 9th February, 1858.

" My dear Bianconi,—I am sorry that it is not in
my power to give you the D.L. There are not three
vacancies, only two.

" Always yours,

" Lismore.

" 41, Wilton Crescent, London."

" 15th June, 1863.

" Dear Mr. Bianconi,—By the death of Mr.
O'Maher a vacancy occurs in the D.L.'s. I have very
great pleasure to have it in my power to offer it to you,
and trusting that you may long be spared to prove to
your adopted countrymen what individual energy and
perseverance can accomplish,

" I beg to sign myself, ever yours most sincerely,

" Lismore.

" 34, Grosvenor Street."

" P.S.—I should esteem it a great favour if you would allow me on the occasion of your first presentation, as your fellow-countryman, to have the honour of presenting you."

"Longfield, 17th June, 1863.

" Many thanks, my dear Lord Lismore, for your
" letter of the 15th inst., offering me the vacant D.L. for
" this county, which I accept with pleasure.

" The reading of your postscript filled me with pleas-
" ing reminiscences of your venerable and patriarchal
" father for his paternity to me, when I was a compara-
" tively isolated orphan, by his standing, conjointly with
" my late friend Lord Cloncurry, as sponsor to me at my
" naturalisation, which laid the foundation stone of my
" present position ; and it is a pleasing coincidence
" that I should have his son my sponsor at my next
" presentation. I hope I may prove as worthy a child
" as I have been to my former godfather.

" I cannot describe to you my feelings of all that I
" owe to Providence.

" I am, my dear Lord, sincerely yours,
" C. Bianconi.

" Right Hon. Lord Lismore, London."

The following document relating to the mortuary chapel will explain itself:—

"Thurles, 4th Nov., 1869.

" My dear Sir,—I undertake that the parish priest of Boherlahan for the time being for whose use and

T

benefit you have built a parochial house, and attached to it a quantity of land, shall punctually celebrate, or get others to celebrate, the number of masses imposed by you, and set out in the trust deed of same holding, and on the days and place named therein. That my successor may see the fulfilment of this engagement in like manner as I promise to do, I shall have a copy of this letter preserved in the archives of the diocese.

> " PATRICK LEAHY, ✠
>
> " Archbishop of Cashel and Emlȳ.

(Seal.)

"To Charles Bianconi, Esq., Longfield, Cashel."

The endowment was vested in trustees with the sanction of the Commissioners of Charitable Bequests, but the correspondence and legal arrangements would not be of any particular interest now.

No one had ever more reason to be thankful that he was a Catholic than had Charles Bianconi when he landed in Ireland as a lad of fifteen or sixteen years of age. The boy found himself thrown among strangers whose manners, customs, and language were unknown to him. The first Sunday that he went to mass, he saw the same ceremonies and heard the same words that had been familiar to him from infancy, and he could there say his prayers as though he had been in his own church at home. There has long been a communication between the priests of Ireland and the priests of Italy, and in my father's early days that connection was very strong. All through the penal times Irishmen had sought education in the colleges and convents abroad, and when the persecution practically had ceased our priests came back to their own country. Clonmel and Waterford were then full of friars who had been educated in Rome, and among these my father found many kind and valuable companions.

He had not been many years in Ireland before he was singing the Gregorian hymns in Cahir, or before he was helping to teach Catechism to the children of Clonmel. In the eyes of the Church all men are equal, and the boy's lonely condition and his homelessness commended him the more strongly to the care of these good men. About this time Mr. Rice, a wealthy trader, was giving his life and his money to found an order for the teaching of poor boys,—the order was always known as the " Christian Brothers,"—and my father became deeply impressed with the institution. He was all his life the friend and benefactor of the Christian Brothers. He used to give them twenty suits of clothes every Christmas for their boys, and, failing direct issue, he bequeathed to them the reversion of all his property.

While my father was still a boy he came under the beneficent influence of Mrs. Tobin, a handsome, stately Ursuline nun, who, when she was the Reverend Mother at Thurles, took young Charles Bianconi under her care. I have heard my father talk of Mrs. Tobin, and

say that he did not feel afraid of God Almighty, but
that he was afraid of Mrs. Tobin. He used to dread
her penetrating glances, and her query, "Mr. Charles,
when was your last confession?" And after nearly
seventy years the man would look shamefaced when he
told us of her rebuke for a flippant answer. To her
query, "Are you a good boy?" he had replied rather
vauntingly, thinking of some mischief he had done,
"Not as good as I ought to be." And then she sternly
answered him, "If you are not a good boy, you ought
to be ashamed to tell it."

My father has told me of the good and kindness this
warm-hearted woman did him. Through her he was
brought into the society of cultivated women, and when
he was in the convent parlour he could sit down
without thinking of the nails in his brogues, or of
his parcel of prints. He was not then buying or
selling, or made uneasy as to his footing in the household.

My father was at all times a great advocate for the
education of children. He was one of the few who
supported both the Christian Brothers and the National
Schools. He always gave me £18 a-year to give away
in prizes to the children of the schools on his property ;
and at my sister's desire he endowed a small sum of
money towards the breakfast fund of the children
attending the Nuns' National School in Cashel. I rather
think he had an idea that as opposition fosters and
improves trade, it equally improves and stimulates education. I find a letter from Lord Cloncurry, and it therein

appears that the patriotic and astute politician had not quite grasped my father's opposition theory. And it was very funny to complain of the excellent old parish priest to my father, for there was a considerable amount of sly political antagonism between them. It was Father Bourke who had not inaptly styled my father " the wily Italian."

"My dear Bianconi,—When I took the liberty to constitute you my almoner for £50, my wish was that you should expend that small sum as most agreeable to your kind heart and good sense. I pray you to do so.

"The money I sent to the Very Rev. Mr. Bourke he applies to schools opposed, as I understand, to the National system. I have given him full liberty to do so, as I am much obliged to him for his very kind services to my son. But I am very sorry that a sensible gentleman should be opposed to the National system, which, with the approbation of all the Catholic bishops, I got established, after a war of twenty years against the Kildare establishment.

"It is a great pity not to let our good people profit by a means of education without any interference with the religious opinions of anybody. I fear the Repeal cause will suffer much by the divisions which have taken place amongst its friends. Young Ireland is vain and rather thoughtless. But O'Connell had no right to repudiate them, or to turn informer against the *Nation* paper, whose spirit and talent does great honour to Ireland.

"I hope both parties will see their error.

"I am, dear Bianconi, truly yours,

"CLONCURRY.

"*9th November*, 1846."

The Synod of Thurles, held in 1850, decided to found a Catholic University, as opposed to the Queen's colleges—or, as they were called, the Godless colleges, because in these institutions religious instruction formed no part of the course of education.   Dr. Newman was installed as first Rector of the University in Dublin on the 4th June 1854.

Though my father was rather fond of talking about what he called his "uneducation," he took a strong interest in, and was a warm supporter of, the University.   Writing afterwards to Sir Robert Peel, he says: "I am one of those laymen who took an active "part in the establishment of the Catholic University, "under the conviction that such an institute was indis-"pensable for the proper education of our Catholic "youth."   He was made one of the auditors, and held this appointment for two years, but he took no other part in the management of the College.

Monsignore Woodlock, who became rector after Dr. Newman resigned, tells me that my father was one of the first and best friends of the Catholic University, and that it was through him that their principal house in Dublin, No. 86, Stephen's Green, South, was purchased in trust for the University.

It was a peculiarity of my father's to do a great
deal of his almsgiving through the clergy. He was so
ready to take trouble himself, that he had no scruple in
giving trouble to others, and specially to our good old
friend, the Rev. Dr. Leahy, the late Archbishop of
Cashel. My father also had a special sympathy for poor
old maids, and for decayed gentlewomen; and I find
evident traces, in his letters and in letters that have
been addressed to him, of how he always stuck to any
one whom he had once taken up. I find some of the
saddest tales of genteel poverty among his papers. For
orphanages and the sick poor, he never could refuse a
claim made upon him; and wherever the Bians went,
he used to give to the local charities. He certainly
gave away a great deal of money in alms during his
lifetime, but after his death he left nothing to charitable institutions of any kind or description.

Irish people look upon the Castle in Dublin as a sort
of symbol of government, a combination of St. James's
Palace and Whitehall. My father's first connection with
the Castle was in the time of Mr. Drummond, when he
was the Irish Secretary; but it was not till some years
after that he was formally presented at Court. Earl
Bessborough was the first Lord-Lieutenant whose guest
my father was. My father had sent in a petition asking
that a friend of his might be appointed to a certain post
then vacant, and Lord Bessborough had replied, " I
will give you the post for your friend if you will come
and dine to-morrow." My father made some demur
about going to dine at the Castle, as he had never

attended a levée, but his objection was overruled; he was told to attend the levées in future. And he was specially enjoined that at dinner he was to tell his famous story of earning a shilling a day and living on eightpence. The story was intended, I believe, to be a moral lesson for a relative of Lord Bessborough's who had unsuccessfully tried the opposite plan. And my husband, who was at the dinner, was much pleased with the story, and rather proudly imagined that it was meant for him.

My father's special Viceroy was Lord Carlisle, and for him he had a most affectionate admiration. How that painfully popular man must have dreaded the very sight of Charles Bianconi! When my father's mind was full of any social grievance, when he thought the state of the country was worse than usual, when the Tories and the priests were aggravating the Liberal Government, he would go and lay siege to Lord Carlisle, who always received him with the most gracious affability. Before a general election he would go and ask Lord Carlisle how he should dispose of his thirty-two votes in the manner most agreeable to the Liberal Government; and then for a few days and nights he would rush about frantically, voting, as it would seem, in a dozen places at once. It was very amusing to see how thoroughly my father enjoyed being made much of at the Castle. Whenever we went to any of the festivities there the high official people always took notice of him, and presented him to the distinguished foreigner of the hour.

On one occasion, in writing to Lord Carlisle, my father allowed his feelings to get the better of him.

"Longfield, *22nd February*, 1864.

"My Lord,—I fear my anxiety for the sustentation
" of the present Government, and my sincere respect
" for your Excellency, personally and publicly, may
" carry me beyond my duty by bringing to your notice
" the strange way in which the patronage of this
" country has of late been administered. Since the 1st
" of January 1862, nine resident magistrates have been
" appointed, namely, seven Protestants and two Roman
" Catholics, and, though the Catholic population has
" greatly decreased, we are still in an immense ma-
" jority, almost as great as the inverse ratio of the above
" proportions, as adopted by the Government in our
" regard, which is a queer way of rewarding the loyalty
" and sound morality of this country.

" In my former communications I called your Ex-
" cellency's attention to the debt the British Govern-
" ment owed to the late Daniel O'Connell, who
" spent his life educating the people to an obedience
" of the laws, &c., &c., the many millions saved there-
" by in the subsequent government of this country
" as portion of the empire. Mr. ——, a connec-
" tion of the late Daniel O'Connell, than whom there
" cannot be a more desirable person to fill the office,
" is candidate for the office of resident magistrate,
" and your conferring on him the next vacancy will

" enable you not only to do an act of justice to the
" memory of the great man to whom so much is due,
" but also will add a most valuable member to that
" body. It will be very popular, give general satisfac-
" tion, and considerably remove from the friends of the
" Government the mortification they have felt by the
" recent appointments.

" I am, my Lord, very sincerely yours,

" C. BIANCONI."

" DUBLIN CASTLE, 26th February, 1864.

" DEAR MR. BIANCONI,—I have always endeavoured
to show, in my manner, the sincere deference I feel for
your career and character, but I cannot pretend to be
pleased with your last letter.

" In the first place, it would be correct to state that
three Catholic resident magistrates have been appointed
within the last two years. I will not inquire too strictly
into the amount of the support which Lord Palmerston
is now receiving from the Catholic body, but I feel conscious that I have not been wanting in my efforts to do
justice to the members of that body.

" With respect to O'Connell, I fully agree with you
as to the splendid service he rendered to his country in
the matter of Catholic Emancipation. In the agitation
for Repeal, I think he did very great mischief; he
produced a schism in the Liberal ranks of which we
still feel the evil effects. But I must utterly deny that
successive Liberal Governments have shown themselves

unmindful of the claims of his family. Three of his sons have had lucrative appointments. There is a son-in-law a resident magistrate, and I gave not long ago another resident magistracy to the son-in-law of Mrs. Fitz-Simon. I shall be very glad if the time comes for my being of service to young Mr. ———; it cannot be just yet, and I must respectfully decline to receive further rebukes on the subject.

" Always very faithfully yours,

" CARLISLE."

" MY LORD,—I beg to thank you for your candid
" letter of the 26th inst. But your Excellency labours
" under a misapprehension in supposing for a moment
" that I had presumed to express any sentiment even
" approaching a rebuke. I may have written strongly,
" as I felt, but certainly no such thought ever crossed
" my mind that your Excellency was in any way
" accountable for a policy which I, in common with
" every Irish Catholic who sustains the present Govern-
" ment, must deplore. If any word in my previous
" letter could, even by a forced construction, be sup-
" posed to attribute to your Excellency any cause
" inconsistent with all that could dignify a Chief
" Governor, and with your well-known beneficial
" administration in Ireland, all I shall say is, that so
" grave an error must be placed to the faultiness of my
" language, certainly not to any want of the highest
" respect and veneration for your Excellency, which

" would be a gross ingratitude after the several marks
" of kindness conferred upon

" Your Excellency's obliged,

" C. BIANCONI.

"To the Right Hon. The Earl Carlisle, Dublin Castle."

"DUBLIN CASTLE, 2nd March, 1864.

" MY DEAR MR. BIANCONI,—I cannot regret having
used the word rebuke, as it has brought to me such a
pleasant letter of disavowal from you.

"Very faithfully yours,

" CARLISLE."

I must not forget to mention that the justiceship of
the peace had been conferred on my father unsolicited
by himself. His neighbours paid him the great compliment of privately memorialising the Lord-Lieutenant
of the county.

There was a movement set on foot by the State, and
most heartily helped on by our Church, in which my
father took an active part. It began with the Reform-
atories, and embraced model farms, orphanages, and
industrial schools. Mr. Lentaigne's enthusiasm did
much to assist this movement. My father gave his
time and money; he bought in an old brewery in
Monaghan, and sold it without profit to the nuns who
were to work the reformatory. He exhibited at his
own cost his Raphael tapestries for another female
reformatory.

When long past eighty, when he got to be stout,

lame, and helpless, he would visit the boys' Reformatory
in the Wicklow Mountains, at Glancree, and he risked
breaking his neck on the scaffolding of the new build-
ings at Artane, near Dublin. But then this last was
an undertaking of the Christian Brothers.

The last time he spoke in public was when he endeavoured to get the grand jury to vote an additional
subsidy to the Cashel Female Industrial School.

There was hardly a convent which did not get something from him. He was the devoted friend of the Sisters
of Charity, though he would drive hard bargains about
the payment of Bian orphans in the training schools.
Every Catholic charity tried to get him on to its board,
—and was only too glad when he left it, for he was too
much used to his own way to work well with others.
When the Children's Hospital was founded in Dublin
he took the keenest interest in it, and besides pounds,
shillings, and pence, he gave them his pet musical-
box.   This was his last and favourite charity, always
excepting old maids and the Christian Brothers.

CHAPTER XIII.

I HAD filled some three or four MS. books with all the loving reminiscences of nearly thirty years before I learned that proportion was an important part in the science of book-writing. I have since cast aside a great deal of what I had written, and now I will only attempt to complete my rough sketches of my father's home life.

As I have already said, I was the third and last child of my parents, born in September, 1840, long after my brother and sister. I was my father's pet and plaything, and the darling of his old age. The tie between us was very close and tender, a sort of comradeship one does not often see between father and daughter. I was a delicate child, so I was not sent to school ; and, thank God, I never had a governess. I got my early teaching from my mother and from my lovely and gentle sister. My father was never at home for more than a week at a time, and when he was with us his business was all-pervading. Way-bills and account-books strayed into every corner of the house. His bed-room was full of them, and in spite of my mother's threats, they could not be kept out of the drawing-room. When he wrote, he wrote very fast and generally very illegibly. He was always in a hurry, except when at table. He ate his breakfast leisurely and heartily, chatting the while, and enjoying himself; but when the meal was over he would rush out and not return until dinner-time. During the day he was in a per-petual state of either mental or bodily excitement, doing at least half-a-dozen things at once. In the evening he would play long whist or backgammon, and generally go to bed by ten o'clock.

When he was at home he would ride with me, but I was made go where he wanted and at the hour he wanted. I was also sometimes under the necessity of being obliged to get into my riding habit in five minutes' time, or I was occasionally when ready kept waiting half an hour.

As I grew up I used to have to act as his private secretary whenever we were away from home; and he much preferred my reading his newspaper to him than reading it himself. He was fond of children and loved to see them playing about him. When I was a little thing I used to ride upon his back, and I was very imperious in demanding all the fourpenny fines my mother imposed upon him every time he said "By Gor!" or "By the Hoky!" As I was born in 1840 he must have been close upon sixty years of age when I first remember him; he was then a hale and hearty man with a florid complexion, his hair was turning grey, and he was in a measure losing his foreign look and gradually assuming the look of the British ratepayer. He used to talk to me about whatever was uppermost in his mind. "Dan" was the hero of my childhood, though I cannot ever recollect having seen him; and I shall never forget how my father cried when he heard of his death, and how bitterly he said, "They broke Dan's heart,"—meaning the young Irish enthusiasts. In spite of the advice of his old friend the Liberator, never to send a daughter away from her mother's side, my sister did go to school; she was sent to Sion Hill, then a small convent of Dominican nuns near Dublin. It was almost like being at home, the Prioress was a pleasant bright-hearted woman, full of common sense, and my sister was very happy there.

Kate, for that was her name, was a perfect specimen of an Irish girl. She was of middle size and had a well-proportioned figure. Her eyes were large and violet in colour, her eyebrows, eyelashes, and her hair were nearly black, and her complexion was of that peculiar clearness rarely seen except in Irish women. She had a broad and intellectual forehead, her nose was straight and more delicately cut about the nostril than is common in our country. She had my father's well-cut lips, and had the same light in the eye. She was cheerful in her temper, very firm and steadfast, yet she was very gentle from her perfect self-control. I think she was beloved by every one who knew her. I know that I loved her with that passionate idolatry which children sometimes have for beautiful women who are both tender and true. The twelve years' difference in our ages, together with her grave and earnest nature, made the love between us more like the love of parent and child than of two sisters. Fond and proud of his eldest daughter as my father was, I don't think that he quite understood her; the hundred queer little dodges and odd twists innate in him, and of which he could not divest himself, while they amused me used to irritate and annoy her. There was so much to be proud of in my father—his success, his energy, his sterling goodness, and his liberal acts—that it seemed to be a pity that he was so often thinking of some little cunning device, and that he lacked those finer qualities which, had he possessed them, would likely enough have marred his career.

No one could tell why he never brought up my brother to any profession. My brother was handsome, and very foreign-looking, but for his blue eyes. He had the peculiar aquiline cast of feature that one seldom sees except in Italy. He was foreign in his ways and notions, and he had the aptitude for easily suiting himself to the manners of strangers. He was a fine horseman and a capital whip, but in other respects he was not much like an Irishman. My father kept the quick, intelligent boy at home until he was quite spoiled; he then sent him to school, but not to the sort of school to which a boy of his parts and station ought to have gone. Though he had a taste for farming and for my father's business, my father was at no pains to instruct him in either. I have seen and heard poor Dan

I earn implore him to bring up my brother to take an interest in the establishment, but instead my father gave him horses to ride and a very irregular allowance of pocket-money. Since my father's death I have found my brother's letters to him, full of eager but somewhat absurd plans, and copies of my father's answers full of platitudes and wise-saws. What my father's ideas were in all this I am totally at a loss to conceive, and in trying to account for it I can only think that if his own boyhood had been happier he would have known better how to educate his son. I hope I am not undutiful in what I have just said, but, as I began this book with the idea of telling the truth, I must not now be turned from my purpose.

Anything approaching to authorship was so foreign to my father's ordinary avocations that ·he regarded his successful Social Science Paper, read at the British Association, with as fond a pride as any author does his first three-volume novel. He sent copies of it right and left to his friends, and amongst others to the charming and naughty Lady Blessington. He had known her as a child when she used to trip past his shop in Clonmel on her way to school, and she always showed great kindness to her old townsfolk. I will give her letter of acknowledgment. Unfortunately it bears no date.

"DEAR SIR,—Accept my best thanks for the statistical statement you have sent me. I have perused it with warm interest, and feel, as all must who have read

it, that my native land has found in you her best
benefactor. I thank you for discovering those noble
qualities in my poor countrymen which neglect and
injustice may have concealed but have not been able
to destroy. While bettering their condition you have
elevated the moral character of those you employ; you
have advanced civilisation while inculcating a practical
code of morality that must ever prove the surest path
to lead to an amelioration of Ireland. Wisdom and
humanity, which ought ever to be inseparable, shine
most luminously in the plan you have pursued, and its
results must win for you the esteem, gratitude, and
respect of all who love Ireland. The Irish are not an
ungrateful people, as they have been too often represented. My own feelings satisfy me on this point.
Six of the happiest years of my life have been spent in
your country, where I learned to appreciate the high
qualities of its natives, and consequently I am not surprised, though delighted, to find an Italian conferring
so many benefits on mine. When you next come to
England it will give me great pleasure to see you, and
to assure you in person how truly I am,

"Dear sir, your obliged,

"MARGT. BLESSINGTON.

"To Charles Bianconi, Esq."

My first actual recollection of my father was
being held up to see him on the bench when he was
Mayor of Clonmel. Then I remember going from
Silverspring, my first home, to Longfield, and getting

there on my sixth birthday. The terrible famine was then just beginning to set in, though we could not then realise all the misery that was to come. I know that it cast a fearful shadow over all my childhood. I heard of nothing and saw nothing but abject distress on every side of me. It seems to me that I can now recall to mind the horrible sickly smell in the fields of rotten potatoes, and that I can see the crows staggering from hunger. I can fancy that I still see the blank look of hopeless despair on the faces of the poor people; in many of them disease and wretchedness had engendered jaundice and dropsy.

I have already told how my father did what he could to relieve the sufferings of the poor. My dear sister also, on her side, was not less energetic. Her name is still lovingly remembered by some, and more perhaps because of her little kind acts of thoughtfulness than because of the actual money that she gave.

While the famine was slowly closing over the land disaffection was spreading. The brilliant band of young rhetoricians who wrote such noble rebellious lyrics, and came to grief in the Ballingarry cabbage-garden in 1848, were brewing their eloquent mischief. I remember how indignant my father used to be with many of his friends, the younger priests and the neighbours generally, who were carried away by this ill-directed enthusiasm.

About this time, when the famine was wearing itself away, my sister caught a severe cold which fell upon her lungs. She got well enough to go about and pursue her ordinary avocations, but the mischief had planted itself; consumption set in, from which she never recovered. I rather fancy, too, when she knew that consumption had taken hold of her, she gave herself up, as though she knew she was doomed to die an early death. My father, on the contrary, could not believe that she was dangerously ill, but when he became convinced of his daughter's state he took her to Italy. This was in October 1851, too late to do any good. Had we gone away the winter previous it is perhaps possible that the malady might have been arrested.

This going abroad was a great annoyance to my father. His car business had to be constantly attended to, he was eager about buying land, and he had to leave his house and home for an indefinitely long time, where he took such delight in seeing his tenants and watching how they prospered. For three years he lived a divided sort of life, his thoughts alternating between his daughter who was dying slowly but surely, and his business at home that could not be wholly neglected. As to poor Kate, at first he hoped and trusted when hope was no longer possible, and at length he suffered himself to be convinced of the mournful truth.

I propose now to say something shortly about our stay in Italy, and to give extracts from a few of my father's letters. They were written mostly to his private secretary, Mr. O'Leary, a kind-hearted and learned old gentleman, the only scholar and well-read man in his establishment. And these letters may be

considered as supplementary to those already given in
the chapter on the Bians. The Rev. Dr. Leahy alluded
to was, as the reader will perhaps remember, then the
President of the Thurles Clerical College, and afterwards
Archbishop of Cashel. He was a frequent correspondent of my father's, and the two men had been fellow-
workers in the founding of the Catholic University of
which I have already spoken. The prelate had also
availed himself of my father's knowledge of business in
investing certain moneys for the benefit of the nuns.

On the 4th December 1851, my father writes to Mr.
O'Leary from Rome. He briefly notices our arrival,
with a little characteristic bit about his banking account
in the middle of the letter.

"Rome, 20*th* *Nov.*, 1851.

"We arrived here on the evening of the 12th, and
" I received Mr. Hearn's letter of the 30th on the
" 13th, and yours of the same date, which followed
" me through France, I only received on the 18th, and
" yesterday I got yours of the 7th. All were very
" satisfactory and interesting letters, for which accept
" my thanks. I see Mr. Gill is still keeping my account
" open, though I requested it should be closed, and the
" balance charged to Mr. Hearn's account. Tell our
" friend the Rev. Father Kirwan, and the rest of you,
" that we get on famously, all things considered, but
" that we have, as yet, very bad weather. I am sorry
" I did not bring Miss B. here before. She bore the
" journey well, but for the last week was greatly

" fatigued. She is beginning to feel well now, and if
" the weather was once fine she would come all
" right.

" In my former reflections on the grandeur of this
" place I often conceived great ideas of its splendour,
" but all of which can bear no comparison to its reality.
" And the same may be said of its modern churches
" and collections of the fine arts, but on which I have
" not yet been able to luxuriate, having been so bewil-
" dered at its extent from every quarter, but hope soon
" to indulge in a few days' enjoyment.

" My people are as well as possible with the excep-
" tion of Miss B., who was very much fatigued after the
" journey, and is only now recovering its effects. I
" regret we did not come here sooner, as it would be
" impossible to describe the fine air when the weather
" is fine, and which is bringing her to very much. I
" trust with care and the goodness of Providence we
" shall be soon all right.

" I mentioned in my last a request that you would
" see the Rev. Dr. Leahy and send me lots of news from
" him. Is Father John dead? What about him and
" the county? Pay Jerry Lalor his bill. Tell Dr.
" Leahy we have a schoolfellow of his (Rev. Dr. Brown
" of Cork), who came here for the benefit of his health,
" and that I appointed him my honorary chaplain, by
" which I introduced'him to two of the Cardinals and
" to the Pope. He is the greatest comfort to us all,
" particularly to Charles, who is much improved since.
" My people are out driving every day. I am now

" writing in the sun, and you would think it was the
" month of April. With usual best regards,

" Yours very truly,

" C. Bianconi."

My father thus records his impressions of his Holiness to that faithful son of the Church, Mr. O'Leary :—

" Your fears about his Holiness are all unfounded.
" I saw him yesterday, and no man could look better.
" He is as fine a person as you could wish to see,
" tall and straight, and *much handsomer than me* (*sic*).
" Kate's ill-health prevented our being presented to
" him up to this, but I hope soon we shall be enabled
" to do so."

I will now give a letter from Kate to Mr. O'Leary. It will sufficiently explain itself.

" *9th January*, 1852.

" My dear Sir,—I am very much obliged to you for the kind interest you have taken in us, and for your solicitude for my recovery. I must ask you to distribute the very large sum of money that you got for my cow as follows :—Give £6 to Mr. Murphy to buy another cow, the best he can for that price ; £3 to be put to papa's account, and the rest as under. Nurse, 30*s*. ; Denis Dwyer, 5*s*. ; Jack McGrath, 5*s*. ; Mary Colgan, 5*s*. ; John Doyle, 5*s*. ; Widow Heffernan, 5*s*. ; Jem Sweetman, of Clonmel, 5*s*. ; Widow Coonane, 2*s*. 6*d*. ; Lucy Dwyer, 2*s*. 6*d*. ; Widow Curwan, 2*s*. 6*d*. ;

Tom Bourke, 2*s.* 6*d.*; William Sweetman, 2*s.* 6*d.*;
Judy Dwyer, 2*s.* 6*d.*; Ned Gibbons, 2*s.* 6*d.*; Coman
Boherlahan, 2*s.* 6*d.*

" Yesterday I had the pleasure of seeing his Holiness
quite unexpectedly. We were returning towards the city
after taking a drive up the Albano Road ; the coachman stopped and said ' here is the Pope,' so Charlie
and the servant knelt down ; we remained in the carriage, and when the Pope came close to us he gave us his
blessing. He looks older than his busts represent him,
but has a more amiable expression. He was dressed in
white with scarlet shoes and hat. He was attended by
two monsignores, who walked one at each side of him,
and one of the Noble Guard. Several servants walked
before him, then came six of the guard mounted, then
his carriage, and afterwards that of his suite. I am
sorry I cannot describe any of the wonders of the
Eternal City ; though I am pretty well, and out driving
nearly every day, I am not allowed either to go to mass
or to go sight-seeing. Remember me to Father Kirwan,
and tell him he is a very good correspondent. Tell any of
the people that ask for me that I hope they are going
on well, and that the children attend school regularly.
When papa goes back remind him of flooring the Ard-
mayle School. How is poor Father Mackey ? The
weather here, with the exception of a bad day in about
every fortnight, and occasional cold winds, is delightful.

" Please see that Tippoo is well fed, and that Minnie's
kitten gets her milk often. Denis Dwyer is to see if

her sheep has two lambs this year as she had last, and when the yearlings are sold he is to let her know.

"Wishing you many happy returns of the season,

"Your obliged,

"C. H. BIANCONI."

To me it is very touching to find the tender-hearted elder sister begging the kind old gentleman to see that my pets were attended to. Tippoo was the great watch-dog, but the kitten was mine, and for whose welfare I was often sorely troubled in mind. Far away, and knowing she would never more set foot among her poor, my sister's care for them never slackened; her memory is yet warm in their hearts.

My father in a letter to Mr. O'Leary thus speaks of the Jumpers :—

"Many thanks for the news you sent me, which con-
"tinue to do. Your last letter stating that the Jumpers
"hopped back to the old Mother Church has been in great
"request here, for I read it first to one of the cardinals.
"It subsequently, I believe, made its way to the Holy
"Father, to whom we shall be immediately presented.
"I have not had any correspondence from any of my
"colleagues of the Catholic University. Will you
"therefore run across to my friend, the Most Rev. Dr.
"Leahy, and tell him both myself and his old friend
"the Rev. Dr. Brown, one of the administrators of
"Cork, who is here with us, would be most obliged for

" all the news he can give us, and to whom remember
" us, and to all our friends.

" Be sure at your next congress, which you ought to
" have at least three times a month, that you enforce
" strict discipline, and that you apply this in all
" quarters."

I cannot find any letter describing the interview
with his Holiness, but I find some mention of my
brother's appointment as one of the Chamberlains at
the Papal Court, which was conferred in a very flattering manner.

" Charles is very busy getting his ' duds ' ready for
" office. Enclosed I hand you a copy of his every-day
" dress on duty. The state dress is most gorgeous, and
" similar to the coat worn by a colonel in the British
" army. I hope he will do honour to the great com-
" pliment paid his father in the matter. Let your
" next letter be to me, Post Office, Milan, as I have
" hopes I will be soon on my way to the old country.

" Write to Dr. Leahy and say how much I regret his
" laziness, as he will not comply with my request of
" answering my letters, and that I am very anxious to
" hear from him."

I suspect my father's excessive anxiety to hear from
Dr. Leahy arose from a desire to know how the Catholic
University was going on. He and the late Mr. Erring-
ton were auditors for a time, and my father had no

faith in the financing of the holy people. He would have liked to keep as large a lay element as possible in the working of the institution. In that, however, he hardly showed his usual sagacity, for as yet we have not a sufficiently powerful and intelligent Irish Catholic lay body to be able to work our institutions.

"It grieves me to learn the failure of the potatoes, " but I hope that the intense heat has only withered " the stalks. If the potatoes intended for the work- " men have suffered, sell them off for my account as " fast as you can at lowest market price, and stop from " each man 2s. weekly till they are paid for. Be sure " in any dealing with them that there is nothing " collateral, or that there be any cause of complaint, " but that in bargains all parties must be bound, not " for its value so much as its principle.

"Referring to mine respecting the three-acre field to " be turned up, I am most anxious to have it so, but in " addition, wish Mr. Murphy to have it drained at " 24 feet apart and 3 feet deep before it is dug up, and " this will absorb all our labour, and make those that " will not stand the screw of contract work look for em- " ployment elsewhere. Be sure that all our staff is put on " this work, and by contract, and as soon as may be. . .

"By all means give Judy Dwyer any crops that " her good mother may have in the ground, for the " old woman was a great pet with us all, and Miss " Kate has had some masses said for her repose. Pay " Miss Hearn's pension until further orders, which send

" on receipt regularly by an order on Mr. Taylor, and
" do not forget Father Mackey's dues.   Send an order
" on O'Loughlin to Father Crotty for £3. . . . .

" You say nothing of late about the tenants.   You
" ought to see that they settle on the 1st May 1851,
" in full, on the principle of the reduced rent, par-
" ticularly Wall and Tom Hennessy.   I hope you paid
" Dr. Cormack £1, having sent for him specially,
" and that poor Jack McGrath is attended to. . . . .

" Many thanks for your satisfactory letters of the
" 26th and 30th inst.   Miss Minnie complains that
" at your Christmas distribution you forgot her chil-
" dren (Jack Bourke and family).   Mrs. B. says that
" you forgot Coman, Gibbins, and Slattery the shep-
" herd, who was better entitled to your consideration
" than Paddy Morrissey, who is a respectable tradesman,
" and ought not to have taken it from you. . . . . .

" By all means in all matters of discipline represent
" me in the severest terms of punishment, and in H——'s
" case you must be of my own feelings.   You cannot
" be too severe with that dunghill. . . .

" Make Denis Dwyer go regularly among the tenants
" to see that they don't trick us, for ——, both last
" year and the year before, sold all his wheat and put
" the money into his pocket, and made us take the
" rubbish in lieu thereof.   You are aware I am taking
" 12s. in the £1.   I see no reason why they should not
" do their duty to us as we do ours to them, particularly
" Mr. ——, if he is thrashing.   He must pay 15s. per
" acre for the large field with its appurtenances next to

" the chapel, and 12s. in the £1 for the factory lot,
" and he can have the use of the factory for a barn.
" Kendrick paid you before he thrashed. McMahon
" may be able to pay us £5 for the horse. Wall and
" Hennessy not to be scheming. Myers paid me no
" rent last year. Phil Maher pays £3 annually interest
" on the money expended in draining his farm. I hope
" Mr. Murphy has arranged with Slattery for the
" watching of the crops, as it would be ridiculous to
" lose a man as heretofore about them. Write to me
" to this place. I am glad your sisters are so happy at
" the retreat. I hope the covered car has come to
" you. . . . .

　" With reference to the tenants, let Denis Dwyer go
" amongst them and see what they are doing, and see
" if they are thrashing of their own accord. Of course
" we shall expect them to give us the oats at Cashel
" prices. With regard to John Walsh's Castlefield lot,
" which he held under agreement at £2 per acre, and
" as he had the use and benefit of it, I see no reason
" why the rent may not be paid; but don't insist on it
" at present. I hope you have settled fully with Wall
" and Hennessy, and that there will be no excuse
" about their doing the needful for the past and present.
" I was sorry to find Kendrick thrashing and selling
" his corn behind our backs. What's the meaning of
" this? McMahon must do the needful this year."

We arrived in Rome early in November 1851; and
after we had been there some weeks my father endea-

voured to see his Holiness.   He had procured some very favourable introductions from the leading Irish bishops with whom he had been associated in the founding of the Catholic University, and the Holy Father was sufficiently informed about this successful and devoted son of the Church to receive him with special kindness. He was good enough to make inquiries as to the state of Ireland, and to speak in flattering terms of how our people had kept their faith all through the years of the famine.   My father solicited that his Holiness would take my brother into his service, a request which was graciously complied with, and my brother was forthwith appointed one of the gentlemen-in-waiting.

The duties consisted merely of waiting in attendance at certain times in the year.

The Italians hate the smell of all perfumes—I wish we in England and Ireland were only more like them in this respect—and one day my brother went on duty after using some very fragrant hair-oil.   His Holiness plainly showed his dislike to the nasty smell by administering a rebuke to my brother—"Che puzzo!" "What a stench!" but was otherwise good-natured, as he was about everything else.   We often used to see him walking briskly along the country roads with a few attendants, his carriage and his guards being a little way behind.   No homely priest in Ireland could have acknowledged a peasant's greeting with more simple courtesy than the Pope was in the habit of showing to those who saluted him.

My father's vanity was tickled by being made much of in high places, and being well received wherever he went. I rather expect he once disturbed the equanimity of some important personages by insisting upon bringing a few bottles of whisky to a dinner where he had been invited, and in brewing some punch after the repast. He persuaded a most amiable professor to drink a couple of stiff tumblers of his mixture, and this good-natured but unfortunate gentleman never met my father afterwards but what he said the foul fiend was in the beverage. My father always said that the Monsignori and the high clergy in Rome had a capital notion of a rubber of whist. He would often sit down with them and play rubber after rubber, all for honour and glory; they allowed themselves the use of cards, but gambling was forbidden.

Some time before we left Ireland a subscription had been set on foot in our neighbourhood for a monument over O'Connell's heart; but the people were so badly off and money dribbled in so sparingly that my father begged the subscription might be stopped and that he would erect the monument at his own cost. After we had been in Rome a few days he took me with him to St. Agatha—the church of the Irish College— where O'Connell's heart was kept in a silver urn in one of the vaults. It seemed a pity that Hogan, the eminent Irish sculptor, could not execute the monument; but instead he sent my father to Benzoni, to whom the work was entrusted. There was a great discussion about what inscription was to be on the monument.

My father, according to his custom, consulted many
people about it, and also, according to his habit, he
had his own way in the end. The inscription ran as
follows :—

This Monument contains the Heart of

O'CONNELL,

Who, dying on his way to the Eternal City, bequeathed
his Soul to God, his Body to Ireland,
and his Heart to Rome.

He is represented at the Bar of the British House of Commons,
—— 1829,

When he refused to take the anti-Catholic declaration
in these remarkable words :—

" I at once reject this declaration : part of it I believe to be untrue,
and the rest I know to be false."

He was born 6th August, 1776 ; died 15th May, 1847.

Erected by CHARLES BIANCONI, Esq., the faithful
Friend of the Immortal Liberator,
and of Ireland, the land of his adoption.

The monument consists of an entablature representing
O'Connell at the Bar of the House of Commons, and a
beautiful alto-relievo,—a weeping Erin holding in her
arms the urn with O'Connell's heart, and raising her
head to an angel pointing upwards. My father took
great pains to secure accurate likenesses of the states-
men on each side of the central figure, and he brought
over several books of prints containing portraits of
well-known political characters for this purpose. Going
frequently to Benzoni's studio gave him some pleasant
occupation, and Benzoni made for him a very fine bust

x

of my sister as a Madonna.   It was unfortunately lost
at sea.

The two winters we spent in Rome showed me a
new phase of my father's existence.   He who never
had a moment's spare time at home would take me
through the galleries and the studios; he would walk
with me, and I would have long and pleasant rides with
him through the wide Campagna, and he was very
proud of the notice my childish figure and yellow curls
attracted as I was perched up on a great big horse.
Every day drew us nearer and nearer to each other,
and from this time I date my passionate love for
pictures.   Rome at that time was full of university
men who had come over to our Church, and now for
the first time I saw my father in intimate contact with
men of thought.   He enjoyed their society very much,
though he himself used to say that " thinking was not
much in his line."   One of these English friends
accompanied him on a ride to Tivoli, and on their way
back my father stopped to examine a shepherd as to
his mode of life, and he expressed much wonder because
the peasant only put on clean linen once a-week; but
the shepherd refused point-blank to believe that my
father could be so wasteful as to want a clean shirt
every day.

My father's hopes of bringing Kate home again in
the summer were not realised.   However, she rallied
sufficiently to be able to have two pleasures upon which
she had long set her heart.   The one was to see the
Pope, and the other was to see the picture gallery

in the Vatican.   From Rome we went to La Cava, near
Naples.   My father and my brother went up Vesuvius
together, and they also went to Paestum and to Amalfi.
My brother came of age at La Cava in October, and
after this my father returned to Ireland, leaving my
brother to escort us back to Rome.

We stopped a night in the Pontine Marshes, and
there we all, except Kate, caught the fever.   It showed
itself just as we had settled down in Rome.   Kate sat
up and nursed us, and though my mother was in great
danger, Kate kept her presence of mind wonderfully.
At this time also news came to us from home that my
father was ill in Ireland.   My parents both recovered;
it was their darling girl who was so soon to be taken
from them.   When the fever left us her strength began
to fail her, and her health slowly but surely got to be
worse and worse.

That summer we wandered about for a few weeks
and then settled down for a time on the lake of Como.
We went to Venice, where we stayed for some time;
the quaint old town pleased us all very much.   It was
one evening in Venice that I saw a something in Kate's
face which even to this day occasionally haunts me.
There seemed to be a look in her eyes expressive of a
distant though blissful rest, which, though child as I
was, quite frightened me.   I had only seen this by an
accidental glance; I turned to my father, and I perceived that he also had noticed Kate's face.   I used
often to see him watching her when he thought she was
unaware of it.   It is likely enough, indeed, that the poor

girl, who knew her state, was quite conscious of her father's anxiety for her.

From Venice we went to Milan, where my father met some of his relations. There was a cousin of his, a learned old advocate who was then writing a treatise on jurisprudence; and there was also my aunt Barbara, of whom my father was very fond. She was like him, but she was handsomer, and I think she had a more frank and open look about the eyes. I became very fond of her; she used to talk to me in good Italian, but my father and she would chatter together in their uncouth Milanese patois, that I could barely understand. She had long been a widow; her husband had left her tolerably well off, she wanted nothing for herself, but she was very grateful when her rich, good-natured brother came forward to help her in the education of her widowed daughter's children.

From Milan we went to Pisa for the winter. Kate's appearance was not worse than it latterly had been, and my father still hoped, though hope was no longer possible. I think he had a feeling, though he did not avow it, that God, who had hitherto been so good to him, would not now inflict the threatened blow. Kate knew that her end was coming, she faced the slow but certain death with the most calm and perfect courage. She spoke cheerfully, and with her mind untroubled as to her future state. She wrote down on a few pieces of paper what was practically her will; and I well recollect how my father cried and how he kissed her as he took the papers from his daughter. Why should I dwell on these painful recollections? Kate lingered on for some months, and died in Pisa on the 27th May, 1854. Her body was brought home and was buried in the little mortuary chapel at Longfield.

After Kate's death we spent two more winters in Pisa, and came to be on very intimate terms with some of the leading Pisan families. My father felt and showed an unusual regard for a lovely and very gentle widowed lady, who in these times was very kind to my mother, and whose companionship afforded her much comfort. He professed this respect because she was the dowager duchess of a great Lombard house; but I think her melancholy tenderness, and the sympathy of a woman who had herself lost many who were near and dear to her, created much of his affection for her.

Nothing ever made my father so well aware of the blessings of English rule as seeing how the men suffered their lives to pass away so listlessly under the most amiable government and with the most humane of all land systems. He used to go a good deal into society, and he was an intimate friend of sundry great ladies, and he would hold forth somewhat magniloquently upon the glories and privileges of the British subject, the virtues of juries, petty sessions, workhouse boards, and such-like parts of our constitution. My father, an Italian in Italy, seemed to be twice as good an Irishman there as he was at home. It was plain that a man cannot belong to two countries and call each of them his home.

It was very melancholy for the old man to see his

daughter, his son, and his son-in-law all taken away from him during his own lifetime. My brother and my father had sometimes lived together not with that mutual trust and good understanding that there ought to be between father and son. And this, I think, was not so much owing to any innate faults of my brother as to the thoroughly bad way in which my father had brought him up. Educated for no profession, and untrained to any business, but left alone to follow pretty much his own way, it is only natural that he became idle and fond of pleasure. My father was truly glad when he married, and the more so because he married a granddaughter of his old friend Daniel O'Connell. He and his wife were constantly at Longfield, and my father was only too pleased to see them there. My father and my brother were then good friends, and we were all happy and contented. A town house was taken in Dublin, and my father's first grandchild was born there under his roof. He said he was not disappointed that it was a girl. My brother and his wife then went abroad, and while they were away a second daughter was born. Nellie, the eldest child, was sent home, and she always lived with her grandfather. After about three years, my brother, his wife, and little Lily, the second child, came back to Longfield, and there twin daughters were born. One of them has lived to bear her aunt Kate's name.

When my brother was at home this time he occupied himself with the farm ; he again took to riding, and he spent a good deal of his time in painting. All would have gone on happily but for his bad health, which was unmistakably failing him. He had to go over to England on business; his wife, who was nursing a baby at the time, went with him, and my father also sent his own servant, James Sweetman, in case of accident. My brother had long been subject to attacks of bleeding; one of these attacks seized him at Holyhead, and the poor fellow died there in the middle of his journey, from a bleeding of the head. Thank God, he had time to receive the rites of the Church. Though my brother had been ill before this, we had no reason to suspect such an early and sudden death.

Before this there had been much talk and many doubts going on at home about my own marriage. My father had long known and liked Morgan John O'Connell, and had even tried to get him a rich wife, but he was fairly taken aback when his old friend asked him for his daughter. My father then looked upon the man in an altogether different light. I was then his only child, and my lover was more than twice my age. He had let slip from him all his prospects in life, his father had been ruined in the bad times in Ireland, his own estates were so encumbered that they yielded then only a very moderate income. Such a man was not the suitor that my father wished for his daughter. He could not give a point-blank "no" to the proposal when it was made to him, though I believe he longed to do so; but instead he set to work to find all the objections that could be raked up against Morgan John O'Connell. Priests and wise men were enjoined to advise me to think no more of the matter. But I remained firm to my pledge; I had given my word, and I was not to be shaken by their unasked-for advice. My father could find nothing against the honour of the would-be son-in-law; though, indeed, it was not against the honour, but against the worldly prospects of my lover that he was trying to raise objections. We have all heard of the law that prevents the course of true love from running smooth. The law was as strong in my case as it has been in that of other people. But like other people I overcame the law; and then for ten happy years our love did run very smooth indeed. I was only surprised to find what a thoroughly domestic-minded man the once gay member for Kerry turned out to be, how reasonable and how fair-minded towards the weaknesses of others was he who had been so popular and so well-loved in every society, both in England and in Ireland. My husband had all his life in his listless way been a keen student of men and manners, and he explained to me some of the odd points in my father's character which I had never been quite able to see through. The two men soon became thoroughly fond of each other, and my father would have liked to have had us always with him at Longfield. Not only during their tumbler of punch after dinner, but while we were playing whist or backgammon in the drawing-room, my husband would poke his fun at him and quiz him in the frankest manner. Many a time when my father wanted to try a little dodge upon a friendly candidate, or to take a petty advantage of a tenant, Morgan would laugh, or would scold him out of it. " Well now, Governor, you're the divil," he would say ; or, " I declare, Governor, you're the greatest play-actor I ever met ; " and my father would raise one eyebrow and smile, and look evidently pleased at the compliment. And he was, I think, very much pleased, not so much perhaps at the words addressed to him, as in the feeling that he had in his own house a son-in-law whom he so perfectly loved and so thoroughly trusted. Had I married a man about my own age, had my father secured for me the ideal son-in-law for whom he was once evidently on the look out, I doubt whether his last years would have been so happy. My father liked a joke, and he liked even being quizzed in a gentle-manly spirit ; and I am sure that few men, Irish or English, have in them so much pleasant banter, such genial humour, so much wit and such powers of conver-sation, as had my late husband.

For a man close upon fourscore years of age, it was wonderful to see how active both in body and in mind my father was in the year 1865. He still rode Molly, his black Connemara pony, a fine frisky little animal, and able to do as much work as many a good horse. So long as the beast was kept in a trot she was as tame and orderly in her movements as a house cat, but when urged into a canter she would take two steps, put down her head, get the bit between her teeth, and dart off like any mad creature. My father was accustomed to her movements, but very frequently he lost his seat and found himself lying upon the grass. He

certainly had learnt the art of knowing how to fall,
and he had learnt another art consequent upon that.
He used always before going out to ride to put an apple
into his pocket, and when Miss Molly had dislodged
him from the saddle he would coax her back to him by
means of this bait. The cunning animal knew the
device as well as possible, and she never failed to
swallow it. It was a common saying in the stable that
"One day Molly would be the death of her master."
My father had perforce to give up riding her on account
of an accident very much worse than ever happened to
him from a tumble off his favourite pony.

My friend, and my father's old friend, Mr. Michael
Angelo Hayes, has given me an account of it, and I
cannot do better than let him relate the unhappy occurrence.

"I shall ever remember the 7th of October 1865.
On that day Mr. Bianconi met with a severe accident
which very nearly proved fatal to him, and from the
effects of which he never quite recovered. I had been
stopping at Longfield for some days, and on this morning he asked me to accompany him over the grounds,
saying that I should ride his favourite little mare,
Moll. At the hall door I rather bantered him upon
the style of his equipage. The harness was made of
old odds and ends, some of the buckles were brass and
others were plated. The outside car, too, on which he
drove was a lumbering old vehicle, and he took the
same pride in this old car that a wealthy man sometimes shows in wearing a threadbare coat. But I did

not imagine at the time of starting on our expedition that the old harness would have produced the catastrophe that followed. We had been out for some hours, we had visited the mortuary chapel—every visitor was expected to visit 'the mortuary'—and we had inspected the progress of the glebe-house he was then building for the priest of the parish, and which he intended presenting as a gift in perpetuity to all future parish priests, and we then turned back towards Longfield. I rode on expecting he would soon overtake me on the car, but I reached the house and he had not come up with me. I had just dismounted, when a messenger came running up the avenue to say that Mr. Bianconi had met with an accident. I remounted and galloped back along the road as fast as Moll could carry me, and made my way into a roadside cabin surrounded by a crowd. I found my old friend supported on a chair. The moment he saw me he said, 'Mike, I am hit.' I saw that his leg was injured, and I asked him to turn his foot if he could; he did so, but when I asked him to raise his leg he was powerless to do it. Poles were then fastened to the chair, and a kind of platform was made to support his leg, and four men carried him back to Longfield, about half a mile distant. I thought I never saw a sadder procession, as the four men, endeavouring to carry their master as gently and as carefully as they could, moved slowly along, followed by a crowd of silent people. It looked like his last progress up the demesne, for I feared that at his advanced age he could not survive the effects of such an accident. Dr. Russell, of Cashel, soon arrived, and he ascertained that the neck of the thigh-bone was broken,—a frequent accident late in life, the result of any sudden shock, as the bones become brittle with age, —but he gave no hope that it would ever reunite, or that Mr. Bianconi would ever again be able to walk.

"The old man had borne his misfortune with admirable resignation and fortitude. He was less excited than those who surrounded him, and he gave his directions while they were moving him with the greatest coolness and self-possession. Had the harness been strong the accident would in all probability not have happened. A strap had suddenly burst, which caused the shaft to rise off the back of the horse, and Mr. Bianconi was thrown violently on to the road.

" His wonderful constitution carried him through, and after some time he was able to move about in a wheeled chair, and before very long he began to drive about the estate and visit the neighbouring towns—in fact, he began to travel about as much as ever. He came frequently to Dublin, always stopping at the Imperial Hotel, where he met his old friends, and where he and I had many a hit of backgammon, a game to which he was very partial. He was at the cattle shows and at all the exhibitions—in fact, he was seen everywhere in his bath chair ; but he could not go as of yore to the Castle. Nevertheless, though he could not go to the mountain—that is, to the Lord-Lieutenant—the mountain, in the shape of Lord Carlisle, reversed the legend and came to him. That amiable, accomplished, and deservedly popular Viceroy never failed to single out Mr. Bianconi at the Royal Dublin Society's shows, or at the other places of public resort where he happened to be present in his wheeled chair, for they were great friends, and Lord Carlisle esteemed him very highly.

" Mr. Bianconi all through his life invariably made the best of everything, and he did the same as regarded this accident. He said it was the luckiest thing that ever happened to him, for it obliged him to break up and dispose of his immense establishment of cars and horses and all their belongings. The railways had not diminished his undertakings. As the extension of a railway drove him off one line of road he opened up a new line of car traffic on another, and he put new cars upon the roads in the north and north-west, and upon cross-country roads where hitherto he had not extended his conveyances. He managed to dispose successfully of his entire establishment, dividing it among many, and providing for those in his employment by advancing the purchase-money and taking time for the repayments, thus to the last benefiting others as well as himself. He never liked looking back or indulging in vain regrets, or thinking of what might have been. He always accused me of thinking too much. He said they had a proverb in Italy, ' Thinking is the business of fools.' "

At first it was hardly expected he would have lived long after his mishap, but by God's grace he remained with us for nearly another ten years.

There was no fear of immediate death from the

accident, but there was great fear of his pining away from the want of air and exercise. Happily, he had singularly sound flesh, and so escaped all dangers of bed-sores and erysipelas. I have found piles of Bian letters of that time stuffed into old pigeon-holes; some of them give an idea of the panic that spread through his establishment consequent upon his misfortune.

Good old Dan Hearn, though looking as fine and strong as ever, knew that he himself was doomed to die, for he felt unmistakably the signs of an incurable heart complaint. His fine young son at home was also dying; there was no man who was fitted to take up the large business which was to have been my poor brother's inheritance. After my brother's death my father had willed the establishment, in lieu of other provision, to Dan Hearn; but it was evident he would never live to enjoy it. He certainly shortened his life by his exertions that winter. In proportion as my father was condemned to physical inaction his mental energy seemed to increase; he would call in the steward at six o'clock in the morning, and his bed was perpetually strewn with way-bills and newspapers; his prayer-book and a volume of "Lives of the Saints" were generally to be found there also.

When my father regained some strength he began to set about getting rid of the establishment; Dan Hearn had never ceased urging him to do so. My husband had gone to see Hearn a very short time before his death, and Hearn urged him most strongly to tell my father that his dying request was that he should sell it.

Dan Hearn died on the 6th March, 1866. My father was unable to be present at the funeral of his good old friend and most faithful servant, whose whole time, thought and energies had been given up to his service.

I do not like to say for certain, as I have now no means of finding out what passed between the dead, but I rather think our old friend Dan Hearn died without the satisfaction of knowing that my father had taken his last advice. Looking through the old papers here I have found two old drafts of wills—one made when my brother was just of age, leaving to him the Bians, then a splendid heritage; another and a later will, in which, as finally fell out, I, his sole living child, was placed in the position of an eldest son as regards the landed property.

Mr. John Walsh, in his little sketch which I have given in the chapter on the Bians, relates how my father sent for him and Mr. Kennedy O'Brien in March, 1867, and sold to them off-hand the western lines.

As far as it was possible he sold the lines to his own servants, his agents, and his clerks. These men were anxious to buy up the shorter lines, which required a smaller sum to work them. My father only reserved to himself the one-horse car line between Goold's Cross and Cashel that went past his own door, and on the Clonmel and Cashel line he bargained for the right of free carriage of his parcels.

We had feared that my father would have felt the loss of his usual occupation, and that he would become weary and depressed in spirit; instead of this he soon became nearly as active as ever he had been. He found means of being carried about, he got a wheeled-chair, he was lifted into his brougham, and he even insisted on being driven upon an outside jaunting-car. He resumed his habit of rushing about everywhere, serving upon grand juries, attending petty sessions, going to the Dublin Society's meetings, and at Limerick Junction he was constantly seen being wheeled about upon the same truck as his own portmanteau. When at Dublin he always went to the Imperial Hotel. His friends used to go and see him there, and he did as much business in one day as any ordinary man would have done in two. He used to say that it was a great convenience getting people to come and see him at his hotel, for he could ask them to come when he liked, and he could send them away when he liked.

I think he was very happy in his old age. He had done the work of his life to the best of his ability, keeping an eye always to the main chance, but also striving as he prospered to help others in their troubles.

I have already said how thoroughly my father liked having all his family about him in his own house, for, like most men who can and do work hard, he could also enjoy himself when the time for enjoyment came. We used to dine punctually at six o'clock, after which he would sip his one tumbler of punch—not made as the Italian professor in Rome accused him of making it —and then he would join us in the drawing-room and play whist or backgammon, and at ten o'clock he would always go to bed. I well remember his joy when my boy was born,—I had had a little girl, but she did not live many days,—when there was a male heir come into the family. The child was, of course, according to the custom immutable in Ireland, called John, after his father's father; his second name was Charles, and the old man was evidently pleased at this little compliment paid to him. He kept announcing, however, in an almost solemn manner, that there must be another boy, that he should be called Charles Bianconi, and that he should be his heir. But no such personage ever arrived. Nothing could have exceeded the old man's affection for his little grandson, whom he would drag about with him all over his farm in the most reckless manner possible, in and out of the dangerous lanes through which only the special mercy of Providence enabled a heavy four-wheeled vehicle to be dragged. A fine old sporting squire has assured me that he never in all his life felt such fear when riding across country as he did in the two hours he was seated in my father's trap. It is true that the horses were stout and strong, the coachman was steady, and there was always a rope carried in case of an accident.

He had the happiness of having his grandchildren about him in his old age, and this I think was a source of comfort to him. My brother's two elder daughters lived then at Longfield, and the little one used to come to him frequently. My husband and I were sometimes with my father, sometimes we were in London, or at

our own little place in county Clare, where he twice came
to see us. We went about a good deal, but Longfield
was really our home.

My father, by degrees, got so used to the loss of
power in his leg that I do not think he became so
depressed in spirits as many another man would have
been. He kept four carriage horses constantly at work,
for, in spite of his broken leg, he would not, and could
not, keep still. Before his accident he was always
rushing about upon two-wheeled cars, or upon his
pony; he then used to say that a carriage was too ponderous, and that it was effeminate.

Every Saturday morning, summer and winter, he
attended the nine-o'clock mass in the mortuary, and
confessed and communicated; and he never seemed any
worse for the fasting and the fatigue of the two-mile
drive before breakfast. Every Christmas he would join
in with us in singing "Adeste Fideles," and he would
sometimes wind up with a stanza of "God save the
Queen." He was always glad to see people in his
house, and to the last his mind was quite clear and
firm.

I will now mention some few of his peculiar tastes.
Large-minded and liberal as my father was in all important matters, in trifles he was almost penurious. I
have heard him say he would walk a mile to save sixpence; and this when he was an old man. He was
anxious that his garden should be nice, and of having
vegetables, fruits, and flowers; he took care that the
place was properly kept up,—not for his own sake, for I

do not think that he cared much for these things. He saw that my mother and I liked it, and therefore he wished it to be done. Let me say, however, that in this respect, as in many others, my father's tastes were rather contradictory. Flowers generally gave him no feeling of pleasure, but he was very fond of cabbage-roses, clove-pinks, and lavender; these may have re-called some memories of his youth. And he was also specially fond of thorn blossoms, and of the singing of birds, both of which are unknown in Italy, where the people clip the thorns and eat their feathered songsters.

My father had a passion for old silver plate, and when he died he left over £1,000 worth behind him. He also spent a good deal of money on diamonds, though my mother had no special wish for them; he set a great store upon a pair of small diamond ear-rings which had belonged to his mother, and also upon an ivory statuette of Our Lady that had belonged to his uncle the Provost. These and a pair of silver-mounted pistols were the only relics that he ever cared to have from his old home, and they consequently had in his eyes a value far exceeding their intrinsic worth.

There is one other fancy of my father's that I must mention: his great interest for art. His fine pictures, busts, and tapestries were at the service of every exhi-bition. I find some interesting letters from Smith O'Brien about a bust of Father Mathew by Hogan. Our most distinguished sculptor had got the order for the bas-relief on the Wellington Monument, commemo-rating the Emancipation. He died, leaving the model unfinished. My father, Dr. Madden, and Sir W. Wilde never left Lord Carlisle in peace until the commission was given to Hogan's son, who was then studying in Rome. Benzoni superintended the work, thanks to my father. I find he tried very hard to have Thomas Drummond's likeness introduced among the Members of Parliament. This happened just before my father's accident. He was a busy member of the Dublin O'Connell Monument Committee, and was among those who desired that the work should be entrusted to Foley. Long after he was lame, he made me and my husband visit Foley in his studio, where I heard Foley express his own preference for the uncloaked model of the statue. I am perfectly certain that my husband's death alone prevented my father from attending the O'Connell Centenary, though he was then much broken down and very infirm.

About three years before his death my father got a slight paralytic stroke, which made him rather more unable to help himself, and which in some measure affected his speech, butit in no wise damped his indomitable energy. To the very end he continued to go about, and at the very time of his death he was engaged in the purchase of land.

I have now nearly come to the end of my task, but I have to record my husband's death, which took place before my father's, on the 2nd July, 1875. He had had two severe attacks before that time, from which he rallied and seemed to get almost well; but on St. John's Day he had an apoplectic fit, and from that illness he never recovered. His death was quite painless, he seemed to fall asleep, and died with a smile on his lips. My poor old father was greatly grieved, but, as at his son's death before what seemed to affect him the most was the appearance of his young widow in her weeds, so at my husband's death he cried most when his little grandchild came to him dressed in a black frock. On the day of the funeral my father wished to go to see my husband buried, but we prevailed on him to stay at home. He wheeled his chair close to the window, and watched the coffin as it was carried out and taken down the avenue, followed by a crowd of people.

I suppose there have been few, if I may be allowed to say it, who were neither rich nor great men, who were more loved than was my late husband. For thirty years past he had not owned an inch of land in Kerry, and yet in Killarney all the shops in the town were shut when the news of his death became known. Both here and in Clare we received every formal mark of sympathy and goodwill.

After my husband's death I went for a few weeks to our place in county Clare; my father seemed to fret very much as I was going, but he began to resume his usual course of life. He saw to his farm, he used to go into Cashel, and he was busy in completing the negotiations for a purchase of land. He was then gradually losing the use of his right hand. His writing had always been bad, but now his signatures were quite illegible, and he became unable even to sign his cheques. My mother used to sign the cheques for him, and he made a mark by the side of her name. He was still full of business; he used to have his farm report brought in to him every morning, and his interest about it and about the people on his property was yet keen and strong.

I had been a month or five weeks away when I got a telegram saying that my father had had a paralytic stroke. I rushed off as fast as I could, leaving my boy behind me at Limerick, and found my father very heavy and depressed, though he was suffering no pain. Later in the day, when my little boy arrived, the poor old man brightened up wonderfully, and every morning he used to have him for awhile put on the bed beside him.

He would now and then rouse himself, and for some days he could receive the sacraments, and also listen to his clerk, who came in to him daily to report on the contents of his letters. Though he could not read these letters he discovered, about a week before his death, an error of eightpence in the deduction for poor-rates out of a large rent-cheque. For the last two days, except at odd intervals, he hardly seemed to notice anything; he lay back with his eyes closed, breathing heavily. The day before he died he did not seem to heed the little child on his bed, though the boy kept crawling about and calling to the old man to speak to him. He did not even seem to notice when the little fellow's soft lips touched him. He did not bid us good-bye, and I have no last word of tenderness to recall. The day before his death my mother asked him if he would communicate, and he said, quite plainly, "With the blessing of God." Soon afterwards she asked him if he suffered pain, and he said, " No pain ;". he then dozed off, and from that torpor he never awoke. His face was calm and placid, and at last he passed away very quietly, and we just saw his head drop back on to James Sweetman's shoulder.

It seems to me to be almost needless to say with what sorrow the news of his death was received, or what respect was paid to his dead body. While he lay dead the house was thronged with people coming to pray beside him and to bid him a mournful farewell. His funeral was more than half-a-mile long; the people carried his coffin on their shoulders from the parish church to the little mortuary chapel, and I never saw shown stronger feelings of sympathy and respect. Gentle and simple, all came to his funeral—old friends of his that I hardly remembered, poor old Bian men that I did not know even by sight—all came to pay their last tribute to their good old friend, and say, " God be merciful to him ! "

THE END

PRINTED BY VIRTUE AND CO., LIMITED, CITY ROAD, LONDON.

www.ingramcontent.com/pod-product-compliance
Lightning Source LLC
Chambersburg PA
CBHW021759110726
47902CB00006B/1577